LOVE IN
HIGH GEAR

CHARLOTTE ROY

Genesis Press, Inc.

Indigo

An imprint of Genesis Press, Inc.
Publishing Company

Genesis Press, Inc.
P.O. Box 101
Columbus, MS 39703

ISBN-13: 978-1-58571-355-4
ISBN-10: 1-58571-355-4
Manufactured in the United States of America

First Edition 2006
Second Edition 2009

Visit us at www.genesis-press.com or call at 1-888-Indigo-1

DEDICATION

To my dear friend TaRessa, who sent me on this journey, and to Rena, Gail, and Angelique, who helped me make my way.

CHAPTER ONE

When the Range Rover finally sputtered to a halt on the shoulder of Interstate 75 South just one hundred miles north of Atlanta, Tallulah Quincy Pettifore—Talley for short—thanked her lucky stars that little Michael was sound asleep in the back seat. She didn't want her sensitive seven-year-old son to see her panic.

A silly rhyme from her childhood kept repeating in her head:

"When in danger, when in doubt,
Run in circles, scream and shout."

She shook her head to get rid of the beguiling ditty and took several deep breaths. The SUV was completely dead. A few miles back she'd heard a huge thud when she ran over some debris from the truck in front of her, and her oil light had come on. *That can't be good*, she thought, shivering.

Stuck on the side of the road, her first instinct was to reach for her cell phone and call for help, but she remembered just in time that Marshall's accountant would get the phone bill. It would help him to trace her. She didn't want her husband to know where they were until she'd figured out what to do.

It was late afternoon. She was tempted to crack the windows of the big comfortable vehicle, lock the doors and sleep. She'd been driving all day and she was exhausted, not thinking straight. And now this.

Before dawn this morning, careful not to wake her still sleeping household staff, Talley had packed quietly, filling suitcases and garbage bags indiscriminately. She'd tiptoed into the library and cleared the concealed safe of everything in it—jewelry, cash, a pistol and papers that she didn't take the time to sort through.

She'd carried out the heavy suitcases and bags and hefted them into the back of the black Range Rover, the one vehicle in her name alone.

Without a backward look, she and Michael had driven away from the 21-acre estate in Farmington, Michigan, just outside of Detroit. Michael's honey brown face had been pale and drawn, his eyes big as he clutched his tennis racquet under his arm. He hadn't asked any questions. He'd sat silent until they were far away from that house of horrors, heading south.

The child had seemed to sense her need for quiet. His eyes had found hers in the rearview mirror several times. She needed time. Time to get situated. A couple of peaceful months to get strong enough to fight Marshall and the combined forces of both his and her families for her freedom and her son. The strength of the Quincys and the Pettifores of Pettifore, Pettifore and Quincy, LLC, the firm owned by two of the country's most powerful African American legal, political and civic dynasties, would be intimidating. But Talley was determined.

Her son was snuggled into the nest of pillows and comforters she'd arranged for him in the back seat before strapping him in. The bruise on his tiny cheek from his father's fist was an angry red. Tears started in her eyes as she looked at him tenderly. *My little man. He tried to stop his father from hurting me,* she thought. Michael was muttering in his sleep now, twitching. She hoped he wasn't having bad dreams. "I've been a pushover all my life, but I'm fighting this time," she whispered fiercely. "I'm digging in both heels and we're not going back."

Scenes from yesterday's nightmare kept tormenting her: *Marshall in women's clothes and garish lipstick and eye shadow. Michael asking, "Is it Halloween, Daddy?" Talley laughing hysterically at that…then the violence…the unspeakable degradation in front of her son…*

She looked into the rearview mirror. Her own heart-shaped face was unmarked. Marshall preferred to beat her body. Beneath her clothing, her almond-hued arms, legs, rib cage, back and neck were a rainbow of black, blue and purple. There were older bruises too, now faded to green and yellow, and the cigarette burn on her thigh had left an ugly circular mark.

She knew she'd stained the rug by the bed in her room when she fell to the floor after Marshall finished beating her. Shame and anguish washed over her and she dropped her eyes. She was so tired.

Outside, cars whizzed by her window. This was not a safe place for her to sleep. Talley pushed the hood latch, and, suppressing a groan, eased gently out of the car, stretching her long legs. She raised the hood in the universal sign of trouble, hoping that a police car would stop.

The evening air smelled fresh and clean. She was dressed for the cool October weather up north. Her corduroy slacks, cashmere turtleneck and suede jacket were too warm here. A glance at her watch told her she'd missed rush-hour traffic and the soft breeze that touched her cheek promised a clear, starry night. She remembered it well from her days at Spelman College. She'd always loved Atlanta with its high blue skies and lush greenery that flourished nine months out of the year.

It was the first place Tallulah had thought of when she finally decided to "steal away." She liked using the historic slave term for escaping to freedom to describe her own escape. But, in an ironic twist on the tradition of slave flight, Talley was fleeing south to Georgia. She'd get a job and a divorce, she and Michael would start a new life in the green glow of this emerald city.

She eased back into the dove gray interior of the vehicle and put her head down on the steering wheel. But, when she closed her eyes, she was tormented by the image of generations of well-bred and docile

Pettifore and Quincy wives shaking their heads in horror and dismay at her. "Go away," she said to the imaginary women, her soft voice trembling with determination. "I had to leave. He hit my son!"

In the gathering darkness, she watched the passing cars before spiraling down into sleep.

~⟨⟩~

Talley woke in twilight to a persistent tapping noise in her ear. She jerked her head up from the wheel sharply. Squinting, she turned to look out her window into the most beautiful pair of blue-green eyes she'd ever seen.

As her vision cleared, she realized the tall, brown-skinned man tapping on her window was from the huge flatbed tow truck parked in front of her. He was holding his towing license up to the window for her to see.

Michael began to stir as Talley let her window down and smiled.

"I was just happenin' by and saw your hood up. Need some help?" the man asked in a deep voice.

"My hero," she said pleasantly. "My cell phone is dead. You've come to save us."

"I love to hear that," the truck driver said, smiling back at her.

"I guess you hear it a lot," she replied, unlocking her door.

"Yeah, but it feels good every time," he said. He opened the door for her.

Michael sat up in the back seat.

"I have to go to the bathroom," the boy said sleepily.

Talley gave the driver a quizzical look. He shook his head. "We're about twenty miles from the next exit. Can you hold on?" he asked Michael.

The boy looked pained and bit his bottom lip. Talley sighed.

"Tell you what, why don't you and I go over here and kick a tire?" the driver suggested to Michael, grinning. "Do you mind?" he asked Talley. She hesitated for a moment, and then, looking into those warm and direct eyes, nodded her head. The man had an aura of trustworthiness. He opened the back door and led the boy around to the side of his truck.

Talley could see his broad back tapering down to a vee of slim hips and long legs encased in jeans. "What a good-looking man," she murmured, standing beside the SUV waiting for them. She dropped her eyes in embarrassment at herself for the thought. But she couldn't help appreciating the vivid maleness of the tow truck driver.

With his back to the highway, Cassius Coleman stared up into space as the sturdy little boy took care of business in the shadow of his truck. His mind was still reeling from the impact of his encounter with the most gorgeous woman he had ever seen in his life. *Prettier than the average rich girl,* he thought.

From the moment she'd focused her amber eyes on him, he had been smitten.

He knew she was money—from the top of her luxurious golden curls to the tips of her expensive boots—everything about her screamed affluence, and as a rule he despised that type. But, her clear eyes and the genuine sweetness of her smile made him wonder if she might somehow be different from the brittle, rich African American princesses he'd seen far too much of.

Where was her husband? She was way too lovely to ever have to travel alone. And what about the dead cell phone? How long had she been on the road with the kid? He decided to do some subtle questioning during the long drive to the Land Rover dealership in Gwinnett County.

The little boy finished his task and zipped with a satisfied sigh. He murmured his thanks as the big man led him back to his grateful mother, who gave him an appreciative smile.

"So, hero, what's next?"

"You two will ride with me." He nodded toward his truck.

"By the way, my name is Cassius Coleman, ma'am," the driver told her as he handed her into the truck's cab after winching the SUV onto his flatbed. "They call me Cole."

"I'm Tallulah P-P-Parsons," she responded, stuttering nervously. "And this is Michael P-Parsons, my son."

Cole cut his eyes at her briefly. She looked away, aware she'd made him suspicious. She'd never been any good at lying.

The cab of the tow truck was worn with use, but clean and comfortable, with a fresh citrus smell, Talley noted. Sitting between her and the driver, Michael leaned against her side as they pulled out into heavy evening traffic. The child was being unusually clingy, but that was to be expected after his ordeal last night. He cuddled into the circle of her arm and closed his eyes, dropping off to sleep again.

"I'm taking you to the nearest dealership," Cole said. "It's a good little trek, but I won't charge you full price since I'm going that way anyway."

"Thank you," Talley replied in her refined voice. "How far is it?"

"Settle down. It's about ninety minutes."

"Cassius, what do you think is wrong with my car?" she asked.

"Looks like the oil pan has been hit. It's leaking. When the oil gets down to a certain level, these vehicles automatically shut down so you don't destroy the engine. It should be easy to fix.

"And please call me Cole," he added. "My mother had a Roman thing going on for a while, and I'm not crazy about it. "

There was silence in the cab for a few moments. Talley looked out of the side of her eyes at Cole's handsome profile. It had strength, with a square, dimpled chin, high cheekbones, a straight nose and a big mouth with full lips. His dark hair was short and carefully kept, gleaming on a well-shaped head.

He was a good-looking man, but it was the force of his extraordinary eyes that set him apart. In addition to being almost girlishly pretty, they were fine eyes. They looked at you peacefully, exuding quiet self-confidence.

Those eyes were glancing at her now, curiously, noting her intent survey of his profile.

"So, Ms. P-P-Parsons," he said, grinning. "Where're you from?"

"Please, call me Tallulah or better, Talley," she suggested politely, averting her eyes downward. Once again she was startled by the rare tug of attraction she felt for this stranger.

"Tallulah's a beautiful old Southern name."

"I inherited it from my great-grandmother—it's a family name. There have been many Tallulahs through the generations."

Generations? Cole frowned. *She looks and acts like old money. The quiet refinement. The unselfconscious charm.* He liked the way she had climbed easily into his old truck and settled herself and her son comfortably against the worn leather. *But she's not a spoiled brat like some of them*, he thought.

"I can't tell you how I suffered for the name growing up — though I like it myself very much," Talley went on, not noticing the frown. "It's actually a Choctaw Indian word that means 'leaping waters.'"

"Pretty," he agreed. "There's some Tallulah waterfalls in North Georgia."

"I know, Tallulah Gorge State Park."

"Ever been there?"

"Not yet."

They were silent for a few minutes as Cole gathered his courage to ask a vital question.

"You need to call your husband?" he inquired, holding out his cell phone. "I'm assuming…though I didn't see a ring."

"No. I…um…I'm separated from my husband. I plan to get a divorce," she murmured, her face flushing hot. "I took the ring off as soon as I walked out."

Her words were sweet music to his ears.

"Looks like you just left him." He nodded toward the bag-filled SUV perched on his truck's flat bed.

"Yes," she admitted, "just this morning."

"You're running away from home," he remarked matter-of-factly.

She nodded and shifted the sleeping Michael.

"Where're you from?" he drawled.

"The Detroit area."

"Cold."

"Yes, but I'm looking forward to a mild, snowless winter here. Are you from Atlanta?"

"Born and bred. My three brothers, my sister and I are all 'Grady Babies,'" he replied, referring to the historic public hospital in the center of town.

"Oh yes, Grady Hospital," she nodded. "I remember it. I went to Spelman."

"Of course you did," he said with a grimace.

"What do you mean by that?" She was defensive.

"Nothing. Just quality. That's all." *And snobbishness,* he thought. *Although this one seems pleasant enough.* "You've got the look."

She relaxed when he flashed a smile at her. "Actually I was all set to go to Vassar when I upset my parents and decided to come down here. I'd gone to white private schools all my life. I wanted the experience of a black college in the South. I'm glad I did it."

"That must have been quite an adjustment for you."

"You're right," she agreed, remembering. "I didn't understand the language or the signals. The first time a man called me a 'shortie' I was very confused since I stand five feet, nine inches in my bare feet."

Cole laughed and glanced sideways appreciatively at her long legs.

"You have friends here?" he asked. "Maybe you want to call one of them?"

"No, not now." She did know a number of people in Atlanta, one dear friend in particular, but she wasn't ready to call Alicia yet.

Alicia Henson, Talley's petite, tough-minded, Alabama-bred friend and college roommate eight years ago, was working for an ad agency in Atlanta. They had been close in college. Alicia always had been very protective of Talley.

If she closed her eyes, she could hear Alicia's husky voice and Alabama accent: "You need to stop floatin' 'round actin' like you live in a rose garden, honey. Someday somebody's gonna show you some thorns."

They'd kept in touch over the years through Christmas cards and regular emails. Alicia was one of the reasons she'd run to Atlanta. She knew she could trust Alicia.

Alicia had been a bridesmaid at Talley's lavish wedding to Marshall. Before Talley left on her wretched honeymoon, she and Alicia had hugged each other as they stood among the white trellises and hanging baskets lushly filled with pink and white peonies and trailing white clematis.

"I'm sho' hopin' you'll be happy, honey," Alicia had whispered earnestly, gripping Talley's hands tightly. "But…well, jus' remember. If you ever need to rabbit, c'mon to me. I'll *awl-ways* be your friend."

She *would* call Alicia. But not right away. The Pettifores would probably check with Alicia first thing.

"You got someplace to stay?" Cole wanted to know.

"I thought I'd find a nice Holiday Inn or something while I look for a job," Talley said.

"A place to stay and a job, huh?"

"In that order," she replied.

She had to find a job quickly. She couldn't use her gold and platinum credit cards without giving her location away. The money she'd taken from the safe was earmarked for a good attorney and for emergencies. Unfortunately, she had no knowledge about how much it cost to live day to day. *How was it possible,* she mused, *that she'd lived twenty-nine years without ever having to pay a bill or even seeing one up close?*

"The dealership will give me a loaner car, won't they?" she asked.

"Oh yeah. An expensive piece of machinery like your Range Rover comes with all the perks. Your husband must have some very long paper."

She frowned slightly at that, and looked out of the window.

Cole realized his mistake. "Real Quality Folk" never talked about or referred to their money. He knew that from his days working as an auto detailer at a Porsche dealership, where the clues for distinguishing between new and old money were very obvious. He chided himself for the slipup and was silent as he tried to recover.

"What type of work do you do?" he asked finally.

"I don't really know," she sighed.

"Huh?" He was startled.

"I've never actually had a job," she admitted sheepishly. *I'm not much good at anything,* she thought sadly.

He looked at her incredulously and then chuckled.

"I majored in art history at Spelman, but I don't imagine I'm going to see much call for art historians in the want ads," she said.

"Can you type?" he asked.

She nodded. "Yes, quite well, actually. My mother insisted that I have at least one practical skill."

"Can you read a map? Send a fax?"

"Yes and yes."

"I can't pay a lot, but I could use some help," he said slowly, looking straight ahead.

She looked over at him, embarrassed. When she'd thought of job-hunting, she hadn't seen herself working at a business as plebeian as a towing service. She'd imagined something in the gleaming halls of an art museum or a glamorous job in a high-rise building where she would wear high-style business suits and do…who knew what?

But with nothing to offer but a pretty face and an elegant manner such a job was unlikely. And, if by some happenstance she got one, it would require references and background checks. She'd have to use her real name and social security number, making her immediately traceable.

A job at a small, obscure towing company would be ideal! She could ask him to pay her in cash. She could go completely unnoticed. No one who knew her would even begin to look for her in such a setting. It would only be temporary. And this big, strong, soft-eyed man…*He makes me feel safe.*

Cole watched Talley's lovely, expressive face as the wheels turned in her brain. He wondered why she needed a job. *Maybe the money façade doesn't have cash backup. That was sometimes the case with these 'bougie' blacks,* he silently scoffed.

"Are you serious?" she asked finally.

"As a heart attack."

He had thrown out the offer casually, but his stomach was churning. To have this graceful, long-legged creature working with him in the doublewide trailer that was his office would be amazing. However, he was confident she'd never begin to consider it.

But it would be heaven to see her face every day…

"I'll take it!" Talley said abruptly.

"What?" It was Cole's turn to be confused.

"The job you're offering. I'll take it."

CHAPTER TWO

Marshall Ansley Pettifore slumped on the couch in his father's massive library, cringing at each angry word. He tended to perspire when he was nervous, and he repeatedly mopped his pallid face with its high-bridged nose with a white linen handkerchief.

"You must have done something really asinine this time to make her run off like that. She took my grandson!" Cedric Pettifore, Marshall's father, roared, his light brown complexion florid with extreme emotion. Standing near the fireplace, looking out at everyone in the room, Cedric exuded menacing power.

"Sit down before you have a heart attack," his second wife, Martine, snapped. Creole, infinitely high bred and diamond draped, Martine was not terribly worried. She was confident her pampered, indecisive daughter-in-law would soon come running home.

"She's only been gone a day," Martine continued. "She'll have to use her credit cards or her cell phone eventually, and then we'll just fetch the runaways and bring them home."

"She shouldn't have left in the first place," Cedric argued, scowling at his surly son. "Something this stupid brat did drove her off! I swear, I don't know why I let him live!"

"Leave him alone!" Martine exclaimed. She doted on the slender figure slumped on the sofa. Marshall was her only child and she'd spoiled him relentlessly all his life. "Talley is just silly and unstable. She won't last a minute on her own."

This sparked a protest from the other two people in the room. Talley's parents, Derek and Claudia Quincy, were sitting together on the other sofa in front of the roaring fireplace.

"Our daughter is not unstable. We *all* know what the problem is," Derek said, standing and glaring at his son-in-law, his black mustache bristling against his fawn-colored skin.

"Really?" Martine queried icily. "And just what is that problem?"

"Marshall…well, he doesn't treat her right," Derek said, backing off from the whole truth, unprepared to open the dark pit of murky evil he suspected. Derek, indeed the whole Quincy clan, had always deferred to the Pettifores.

Talley's mother, Claudia, sat silent. With her golden curls pulled back into a smooth chignon, she was a tawny replica of her white mother, who had courageously married an African American lawyer in the 1950s. Talley was a taller version of Claudia. It was from her mother that Talley had learned her timid, eager-to-please ways. Claudia, like Talley, was the epitome of an African American trophy wife—beautiful, "damn near white," well bred and docile.

The others in the room didn't know it, but Claudia was secretly proud of her daughter and envious of the courage it must have taken for Talley to break the silken cords of her luxurious captivity and escape with her son. Claudia had wanted to urge Talley to run since the first time, eight years ago, her beloved child had come to her with ugly bruises caused by Marshall's brutality and asked what to do.

When she'd first seen evidence of the abuse Talley suffered at the hands of her Pettifore husband, Claudia had raced to Derek, begging his support for an annulment of the marriage. Derek had turned away, unwilling to listen. He had always supported Cedric Pettifore, and Cedric wanted this marriage. Claudia knew without Derek's backing there was nothing she could do for her daughter and had advised Talley to be strong, to stay in the marriage.

Now that Talley had finally gotten the courage on her own to take this step, Claudia could help her to stay hidden. She only hoped Talley and Michael were safe and unharmed somewhere.

Claudia believed Talley was stronger than she was given credit for. She'd seen her daughter, as a child, fiercely protecting her dolls from the destructive hands of the three Pettifore girls, the offspring of Cedric's first wife, Joya. Startling everyone, little Talley had growled and snapped like a dangerous guard dog.

She remembered an evening of rare rebellion when the child had refused to eat her lima beans. Told she could not leave the table until she finished them, Talley had sat up straight-backed at the dining table practically all night. A tiny stubborn figure in the dark, vast, formal dining room, she was determined not to touch the unappetizing green things. Finally, her Burmese nurse Narye had led her sleepily away from the table to bed, the lima beans still uneaten.

It was Talley's hidden streak of ferocious protectiveness and obstinacy that the Pettifores would have to contend with if they wanted their only grandson back.

And Cedric wants him badly, Claudia thought, curling her folded fingers tighter. *He needs Michael to carry on the Pettifore and Quincy fortunes.* For a century there had always been a male Pettifore heading the famous law firm of Pettifore, Pettifore and Quincy, and Michael was the only male child.

"I want my grandson back," Cedric snarled, eerily echoing Claudia's thoughts. "I'm going to put detectives on finding them first thing tomorrow morning."

Then he walked menacingly over to his partner Derek and stood toe to toe with the shorter man.

"If I find out you or your wife had anything to do with this, anything at all, I'll destroy you," he said, his eyes blazing fire.

"Just back away," Derek said gruffly, his eyes dropping to his shoes. "Talley did this on her own."

—⟂—

Talley unpacked their things at a Red Roof Inn on the outskirts of Atlanta. Michael was wide awake now, bouncing a tennis ball listlessly on the brightly lit sidewalk just outside the door to their room.

"C'mon, sweetie, help me carry some of these things into the room," Talley said. "You've been sleeping all day, but I'm tired. I want to take a bath and then sleep."

"What will I do?" Michael asked, picking up and dragging a garbage bag full of clothes.

"You'll take a shower and put on your jammies. You'll eat your Happy Meal. Then you can sit quietly and watch TV until you go back to sleep," she said, stroking his hair. "Please."

"How long are we going to stay here?"

"Until we find a place of our own."

"Do you think Daddy will find us here?" he asked. His long-lashed amber eyes, so like his mother's, were suddenly fearful.

"I don't think so."

"Daddy won't come to live with us here, will he?" His upturned face pleaded for confirmation.

"Definitely not." Talley shut her eyes in pain at the entreaty in his voice and face. *Oh Michael, what did I do to you by staying in that situation for so long?* she asked silently.

"Then, can I get a dog?" he asked with a sigh of relief. Marshall didn't like dogs and wouldn't have one in his house.

"We'll see," Talley replied wearily, locking the steel door to the motel room and drawing the curtains shut.

"Maybe Papa Pettifore will come visit us. That would be nice," Michael said. He adored his grandfather, Cedric Pettifore.

After Michael showered and changed into his pajamas, Talley sat him at the desk in the room and opened his meal for him, laying napkins under it and filching a few French fries. She was too tired to eat a full meal.

Talley wanted to sink down and soak her aching body in a nice warm bath. She searched among the luggage until she found her foaming Vitabath gel. But when she took a good long look at the stained bathtub, she thought better of a bath. She took a shower instead, leaning her forehead on the cool ceramic tiles and letting the water beat down on her sore back. She would miss her huge whirlpool bathtub at home.

There would probably be a lot of things at home she'd miss, she admitted to herself, sighing. But she wouldn't miss the state of constant fear and anxiety she'd been living in for eight years. Tonight, huddled together in this tawdry little motel room, she and her son could feel completely safe for the first time.

Though this was the first time Marshall had hit Michael, the child had sensed his mother's tension and despair all of his life. He'd never bonded with his father, so Talley was fairly sure he would not miss Marshall.

As she came out of the bathroom dressed in a nightgown from one of the plastic bags, she noted with relief that Michael was already asleep on one of the two double beds in the room. She covered him and stroked his face gently, then stretched out on the other bed.

Talley was so exhausted that sleep eluded her. Her mind raced with questions about their future. On the twelve-hour drive here she'd tried to think things through, but her mind had been numb, overwhelmed with worry about what she was doing.

She'd need to rent an apartment. Could she do that with a fake name? She'd have to get Michael into school. Would they want transcripts from his old private school? How could she arrange that without tipping off the family to her whereabouts? Maybe this Cassius Coleman could help her with some of these things. He'd been so considerate already.

Cole had stayed with her at the dealership, overseeing the description of the damage to the vehicle, helping her arrange for a loaner car, transferring everything into the loaner. Talley was glad of his support since Michael had been a handful. The boy was understandably nervous and antsy.

Cole was apparently well known and liked at the dealership. She figured it was his easygoing self-confidence that attracted people to him. Salesmen had hailed him, slapped his hands and his shoulders. Behind her back, he'd endured raised eyebrows, manly winks and teasing punches from the repairmen in the shop. She'd seen it all reflected in the dealership windows. Unaffected by the overt admiration, Talley had just smiled and shook her head.

Cole had led her to this modest motel and seen to it she was properly checked in. She believed he would have stayed longer and helped her unpack if she hadn't insisted he go on his way. He'd left her a card with all his phone numbers on it and instructed her to call him if she needed anything. Anything at all.

It was kind of him to be so nice, she thought. *But people will usually be nice if you let them.*

⁓

"Marcus! David! Winston! Come to the family room!"

Cole's voice set off a veritable stampede through the neat red brick house in southwest Atlanta. The sounds of his younger brothers' heavy feet came from odd corners and made him smile—they might be damn near grown, but these big-footed males still acted like kids. They were men, though, and they shared the rambling five-bedroom home they'd inherited when their parents died in an auto accident ten years earlier.

David, first in the room, lifted a long skinny leg and vaulted over the back of the couch. He smirked in triumph when he managed to snare the television remote from beneath Winston's fingers, then frowned when his brother lifted a bag of potato chips above his head.

"Uh uh," Winston gloated, settling on the couch beside David. "You want 'em, you gotta give up the remote."

David thumbed the remote, and the volume rose on a rap video on the screen. He waited for the telltale shift of his brother's eyes and renewed his attack on the snacks.

"Y'all are worse than puppies," Cole muttered, watching them wrangle on the couch.

"Get your feet off that coffee table," Marcus yelled from the kitchen doorway. "If our sister, Lucy, still lived here, she'd break your legs."

"My legs ain't hurting the table, you neat freak," Winston grumbled.

"Yeah, Betty Crocker," David teased, pushing his wire-rimmed glasses up on his nose. "Why don't you get back in the kitchen and rattle those pots and pans."

"I'm in there trying to make a healthy meal and you're in here eating snacks and tearing the house apart," Marcus fussed, smacking at their legs with his long-handled spoon.

"Get out of the way, Marcus," Winston grouched. "You're blocking my view of the hotties on TV."

"You're preoccupied with hotties," David said. "What does your baby's mama say about your obsession?"

"She don't say nothin', that's what." Eyes still on the sultry singers on the screen, Winston took an idle swing at his brother. "Least I got someone. You sleepin' with your medical books."

"Worse than puppies," Cole muttered again. "All y'all hush up and turn down the TV. Pay attention!"

The brothers grew quiet. Cole's word was rarely challenged.

"I've hired a new person for the office," Cole announced, looking from one to the other of his handsome siblings. His brothers all drove trucks for him in the business—Marcus, the oldest, worked full time, Winston and David, the youngest, drove in between classes at the Atlanta University Center.

"Okay," Marcus shrugged. "If you think we can afford it." He started back into the kitchen. David and Winston looked bored.

"Wait," Cole demanded. "I want to invite her and her son over for dinner tomorrow."

"You want to invite the new office girl over to dinner?" asked David, puzzled.

"Okayyy," Marcus drawled. "And we're doin' this because…?

"She's new in town and she doesn't know anybody. I just thought it'd be nice…" Cole said defensively.

"Where'd you meet this girl?" Winston wanted to know, a knowing grin starting on his face. Winston, with his quick wit and smooth ways, was the family ladies' man.

"Her car was broken down on I-75," Cole answered.

"You're hiring someone you met tonight by the side of the road in a broke down hoopty?" Marcus asked, incredulous.

"It was a luxury car," Cole noted. "Oil pan was hit, that's all."

"She's a star, huh?" Winston smirked. "A dime piece."

"Yeah," Cole said with a sheepish grin. "She's nice."

"Hey! What about Rozilla?" David inquired, referring to Cole's on-again, off-again girlfriend, Roberta McAfee.

"Don't call her that," Cole snapped. "You know Ro and I broke up. But this isn't like that. I just thought I'd have Talley and her little boy over since they're new in town, staying in a motel."

"Oooh, Talley," Winston cooed, punching David on the couch.

"Alright," Marcus nodded, "I'll roast some chicken."

"Can you do that lobster thing you do?" Cole wanted to know.

"That's for special, man," Marcus grumbled. "I ain't gonna have time."

"Oooh, lobstah!" Winston teased.

"Never mind. I was just hoping…" Cole muttered going toward the stairs.

"Damn, man," Marcus said, heading back into the kitchen.

CHAPTER THREE

Talley felt warm breath on her cheek and she opened her eyes. Michael was hovering over her, staring directly into her eyes.

"I was looking to see if you were awake yet," he whispered.

"I am now, sweetie," she said, pulling him to her for a hug.

"I've been awake for hours," he said, cuddling close. The TV was on, the volume low. "I'm hungry now."

Talley lay on her back for a minute staring at the water-stained ceiling. A wave of anxiety rushed through her, causing her to close her eyes and hug Michael tighter. She'd never in her life done anything as aggressive or courageous as this. Overnight she'd become a different person—one who could make an important life-altering decision without dithering around. She'd been sneaky, ruthless and resourceful.

"God, what have I done?" she whispered, wavering between pride, astonishment and fear.

She didn't have time to wonder. Michael was full of questions, wanting to know what, where and when they were going to eat.

"Do you think Narye misses us?"

Talley looked at her son and realized how much she missed the loyal Burmese nurse who had cared for her as a child.

"Maybe Narye can take a vacation while we're away," Michael grinned. Talley grinned back.

If they were at home, Narye would be helping Michael dress in his school uniform and get on his way to his private school in the Rolls, driven by Bennie, the family chauffeur.

"Anyway," Michael insisted. "I'm all dressed and not in any uniform." He glanced at his mother, checking her reaction. Today, Michael had dressed himself in his favorite jeans and striped knit shirt.

"Well, I suppose it's up to me to locate similar attire."

The little boy nodded happily.

Talley washed and dressed quickly. She helped Michael tie his Nikes and they headed out to scout for breakfast. The morning was bright and shimmery, the cool fresh air redolent with southern breakfast aromas coming from the Waffle House next door—hash browns, sausages, grits and eggs. Talley felt her spirits rise. She grabbed Michael's hand and they ran, giggling, to the restaurant.

Sitting in the Waffle House watching Michael make short work of blueberry waffles, Talley enjoyed her fruit, toast and eggs. She made a mental list of the things she had to do in a hurry.

"Mom?" Michael pushed his heavy-laden fork through a puddle of syrup. "That nice man from yesterday? Are we going to see him again? What was his name?"

"Mr. Coleman," Talley answered, watching the waffles disappear.

First on the list was contacting Cassius Coleman to make sure she really had a job. Perhaps he'd also help her to get an apartment. Once she had an established residence, she could enroll Michael in a school. Then she needed to find the best divorce attorney in the world—a pit bull with no fear of the famous firm of Pettifore, Pettifore and Quincy.

She had a man in mind, Robert Edwards. He headed the small Atlanta firm of Edwards and Worth. She'd met him and his pretty salt and pepper-haired wife at a National Bar Association Convention three years ago and had immediately clicked with the older couple.

The annual event for the African American counterpart to the American Bar Association had been held in Detroit in 2000, and Talley had been on the committee of lawyers' wives helping to organize the convention's centerpiece fundraising dinner. Edwards, a distinguished-looking white-haired man in his midfifties, was president of the association that year and had sat at the head table with Talley's family. She'd liked the way Mr. Edwards treated the Pettifores with just the right balance of deference and equanimity.

She would call and make an appointment with him for this evening.

She also had to call her mother and tell her she and Michael were all right. Talley knew that was risky, but it had to be done. Otherwise, soft and gentle Claudia was capable of fretting herself into an illness. While she could trust her mother not to reveal her whereabouts, her father was another story. Long ago Talley had come to realize that Derek Quincy was a hopeless coward when it came to his overbearing partner, Cedric Pettifore. She loved her father, but she had lost all respect for him. He would not protect her.

Looking around the restaurant, she spotted pay phones near her table. She could call and watch Michael at the same time. She spoke to Cole first.

"I just want to make sure you meant it when you said I could have a job," she said.

Cole was happy to hear her voice. The deep amber pools that were her eyes had haunted his dreams and he'd awakened full of doubts that she'd actually call him back. It had been all he could do to keep from calling her at the motel.

"Yeah, I meant it," he said. "Where are you?"

"I'm at the Waffle House near the motel," she said.

"I'm at a dealership right now, loading a car to take up to Roswell, but my brother Winston is in your area," Cole said. "How about if I have him meet you at the Waffle House in twenty minutes so that you can follow him over to the office at our impound yard."

"I have Michael with me," she noted.

"I figured you would. He'll be fine at the yard."

"We didn't talk about salary or anything," Talley mentioned timidly.

"I can pay you ten dollars an hour."

"That sounds wonderful!"

"Hey! Hey! Don't be so happy. Makes me think I could have gotten away with eight dollars an hour," he chuckled.

"Thank you so much, Cole."

Actually, Talley didn't have a clue what she should be paid. She'd heard somewhere that minimum wage was around five dollars an hour, so twice that amount must surely be significant. In any case, she just needed enough to pay for minimal living expenses. An apartment. Groceries.

She called her mother on her private line at their Grosse Pointe house.

"Mama, is it safe?" Talley asked.

"Yes, there's no one here but me," Claudia whispered. "Are you okay? Is Michael okay?"

"We're fine."

"What happened? Why did you run away?"

"Marshall hit Michael." She paused as she heard her mother's gasp. "And…and…there was some other stuff. I can't tell you now."

"I'm so *proud* of you, sweetie," her mother said, her voice wavering with emotion. "Do you need anything? Anything at all?"

"I need Narye," Talley said. "I've got a job and I need help with Michael."

"Why didn't you take her with you when you left?" Claudia asked.

"I couldn't risk going to her quarters and waking the household staff," Talley explained.

"Well, you know Narye will come to you in a heartbeat," Claudia said. "Do you want me to arrange to fly her to you? Where are you?"

"As soon as I get settled, I'll tell you. She *must* slip away without anyone knowing," Talley insisted.

"Listen, sweetie, your father-in-law is livid. He's hiring a private detective to find you and make you bring Michael back."

"I expected that. But I'm not coming back and they can't make me give up Michael. I've got some leverage. I just need time to hire an attorney and get situated here. A month or two should do it. I have to go now."

"I love you," Claudia whispered anxiously.

"I love you, too, Mama. Please don't tell anyone I called. Not even Daddy. Don't say *anything*."

"I won't. I won't."

Talley then placed a call to Edwards and Worth and made an appointment for Ms. Talley Parsons. Leaving a message under her real name might draw attention.

Michael was busy with his Game Boy, silent except for the occasional beep beep of the toy when she returned to the table.

"Your Gramma Quincy sends her love," she said to him. He nodded without looking up.

⟿

Winston was on his cell phone talking to Cole when he walked into the Waffle House. "C'mon, man, can't you break me off a fifty? My baby's mama is bugging me, y'know what I'm sayin', and I need…Oh. My. God." His first glimpse of Talley rendered him speechless.

She was luminous. Her golden curls tumbling to her shoulders were backlit by the morning sun. Her heart-shaped face rested on the palm of her fine-boned hand as she leaned forward talking to Michael. David, the family intellectual, had forced Winston to see *The Lord of the Rings* with him. To Winston, Talley looked like one of the enchanted elven people of Middle Earth, a gossamer lady of light and magic, out of place in this mundane setting.

"What's wrong?" Cole demanded at the other end of the phone.

Winston flipped the phone shut and stuck it in his pocket, ignoring his startled brother's query. He sauntered over to the table, putting on his Romeo face. Winston was wearing the current uniform for twenty year olds: far-too-big slouch jeans, and a red and black baseball cap turned sideways. He had on a shirt with the word "Hey!" all over it in red and black.

"Hello there," he intoned in a deep, manly voice.

"Hey!" Talley said, reading his shirt and smiling. Michael giggled and said "Hey! Hey! Hey!" Talley looked at her son in delight. It was the first happy sound she'd heard from him in two days.

"You Miz Parsons?" Winston asked. "Gotta be, you the only angel in here, y'know what I'm sayin'?"

"You must be Cole's brother Winston," she replied with a gentle smile. "I'm ready to follow you."

"Yeah, I wish you was," he leered.

Talley raised an amused eyebrow at him and began gathering her things.

⎯⎯ ⟋⟍ ⎯⎯

Cedric Pettifore sat behind the huge bronze and mahogany desk in his office, eyeballing the sharp-looking private investigator standing stiffly in front of him, arms clasped behind him, military fashion. The man was of average height, but looked taller because of his bearing. His face was strong, but made youthful by the crease of his deep dimples.

"You're too young," the older man said. "I thought I was getting a seasoned detective."

"My father, Paul Griffin, runs the agency, sir," the P.I. replied. "I'm Joe Griffin. I do the legwork. I've been working with my dad for nine years, since I got out of the marines. I'm thirty-two years old, sir."

"Well, you don't look it," Cedric growled.

"Helps sometimes to look young, sir. Fools people," Joe said crisply.

"Your father has been very helpful to us in the past," Cedric noted. "With divorce cases."

"Yes sir, we've worked for your firm for a long time," Joe said, his nut-brown face curiously blank.

"You think you can find my grandson?"

"I think so, sir. I may need to hire a team of men to assist with the…"

"I don't care, whatever it takes." Cedric waved a hand dismissively. "I don't need the details. I just want you to bring Michael back here. You can leave that fool daughter-in-law of mine wherever you find her."

"We don't want to have to kidnap the boy," Joe said with a frown.

"Do as you're told. Bring the boy here to his father. We'll make it worth your while."

Marshall, who had just come into the office, spoke up.

"I want you to bring my wife home, too," he demanded.

Joe looked him up and down with steely, black eyes. Marshall was leaning against the closed door to the office, his long spider-like legs and arms crossed, a discontented frown on his thin face.

"Grab her by her yellow curls and drag her back here," he muttered.

"Why did she leave?" Joe wanted to know.

"That's none of your business, dick," Marshall said putting a sneer on the last word.

"I need some idea about why she left in order to begin hunting for her," Joe said, unperturbed. "For example, did she go to another man?"

"Absolutely not," Marshall and his father said almost in unison.

"It was just an argument that went too far," Cedric said briskly.

"Hey, listen," said Marshall, his face distorted. "You don't need to know anything but that she has run away with my son. You find them and you get them back. We don't care how you do it."

Joe narrowed his eyes at Marshall for a minute, then looked away.

"You probably will want to go over to my son's home and look through Talley's things," Cedric said with a moue of distaste. "Her staff has been alerted. Here's a picture of her and Michael and a list of her friends here in Detroit you should talk to. My secretary has called them to let them know you'll contact them," he continued, offering a white envelope from the center of his immaculate desk. "Talley's father has the office across the hall. You might want to start with him."

Cedric glared across the office at his son and sneered as Marshall quickly ducked out without meeting his father's eyes. His son was the biggest disappointment of Cedric's life. His first wife, Joya, had given him nothing but girls—three fat, lazy girls who'd grown up to be indolent women. Martine had been his mistress for years and when she got pregnant, Cedric had been elated to discover that the child was a boy. He had quickly discarded Joya and married Martine, triumphant that at last he had produced a male Pettifore to take over when he was ready to retire.

But as the years went by and Marshall grew into a sly, effeminate creature with a sadistic streak, Cedric got to the point where he couldn't stand the sight of his son. With hope for the next generation, he'd planned the pairing of Marshall with Tallulah. Although Talley had been a shy and retiring little girl, she had brains and charm and Cedric had spotted a core of strength in her. He was rewarded when she produced Michael.

Michael was the love of Cedric's life, his golden boy. Spirited, smart, brave and sturdy, the boy was everything that Cedric had wanted in his son. There was no way he'd let Talley keep Michael from him for long.

Cedric didn't like that Joe Griffin had raised objections to kidnapping Michael. *I need to speak to his father and remind him of his obligations to me. Paul Griffin needs to whip his son into line. I want Michael back, no matter what it takes.*

Outside in the hall, Joe opened the envelope and pulled out the list of Talley's friends. It only had three names on it. His heavy dark eyebrows came together in an incredulous frown as he looked back at the office door he had just left. Then he shrugged and entered Derek Quincy's domain.

The office Mr. Quincy's secretary led him into was almost identical to his partner's, but it somehow seemed smaller. It had too much furniture in it, for one thing. Messy files were piled up on the small conference table. The light-skinned, mustached man behind the desk lacked the commanding air Cedric Pettifore had.

"I don't know where my daughter is," he said immediately upon being introduced to the detective. "I can't be of any help to you."

"Would you help me if you could, sir?" Joe asked.

"Of course not," Derek said, flashing Joe a surprisingly shrewd look.

"I understand. I met your son-in-law in there," Joe responded.

"Marshall doesn't make a good first impression on everyone," Derek said with a wry chuckle. "You should see him with clients, though. He's all oily charm."

"Hmmm," Joe said noncommittally. "I have a very short list of your daughter's friends from Mr. Pettifore. I guess she wasn't very popular." *That should get a rise out of him,* Joe thought. *Maybe if I stir things up a bit, I'll get more information.*

"You won't nettle me young man, so don't try," Derek said shortly. "If the list is not long it's simply because it's not easy being a Pettifore in this town. Nor a Quincy. And my daughter was both. And beautiful to boot. Besides, Talley's shyness sometimes comes off as snobbery. Let me see the list."

Derek ran his eyes down the list quickly, nodding, while Joe glanced at Talley's picture in the envelope for the first time. She took his breath away.

Joe had seen pictures of Tallulah Quincy Pettifore before. Anyone living in Detroit and reading the local newspapers and magazines would have seen photos of her opening the Pettifore Room of the African

American History Center or on the Hostess Committee of the Delta Sigma Theta Debutante Ball.

Tall and willowy with long legs and narrow hips, Talley was not his type. He preferred his women brown and round, with ample bosoms and high, soft butts. But, Talley was definitely a beauty and her adoration for the handsome little boy beside her gave her a glow that clutched his heart.

He looked up to see Derek watching him and noting his obvious admiration.

"She's lovely, isn't she?" her father asked proudly. "Takes after her mother."

"Are she and her mother close?" Joe wanted to know.

"Very close."

"Then I'd like to talk to Mrs. Quincy and get a feel for your daughter's habits," Joe said. He wrote something in the notebook he pulled from his suit pocket.

"Claudia is very upset, I'd rather you…"

"I insist," Joe said with an implacable smile.

"I'll call her," Derek sighed, resigned.

"I'll swing by Mrs. Pettifore's house first, then head to your home in Gross Pointe," Joe said. "Please tell Mrs. Quincy I'll be by this afternoon if that's okay."

⟶

Joe didn't much like the firm of Pettifore, Pettifore and Quincy. He felt his dad was too dependent on their business for the survival of the detective firm

they shared. Griffin Investigations, Inc., or GI, as they
called it, with its yellow and black griffin-on-a-shield
logo, had been founded by his father twenty-five years
earlier. Paul Griffin had retired early from the police
force and opened the doors of his business with the
Pettifore firm as his first and only client.

Joe knew there was something odd in the history
of the relationship between the two firms, but he
could not get his father to speak of it. All he knew was
the law firm had thrown so much business their way
over the years that GI had grown and prospered. His
father had always handled the Pettifore law firm with
kid gloves.

Griffin Investigations, Inc. now had six operatives
and handled cases for a number of law firms and
insurance companies.

A vigorous sixty-five years old, Paul had recently
made his son a partner in the business. Joe was a
former M.P. with a sharp eye, a confident manner and
a good feel for investigations.

Though Joe was not normally squeamish about
even the most sordid assignments, this particular piece
of work was leaving a bad taste in his mouth. But his
father would have a conniption if he tried to turn it
down. Either he or his son managed the Pettifore
investigations, no one else.

Driving out to Farmington, Joe reviewed what he
knew about Tallulah Quincy Pettifore. Before he left
the firm's offices, he had been given her official bio
prepared by a public relations agency. It listed the

charities she was involved with, the clubs she was a member of and the schools she had attended.

She apparently liked charitable organizations benefiting African American girls and contributed generously to a number of them. She was on the board of the Pettifore Foundation and of the YWCA Interim House, a shelter for victims of domestic violence. She belonged to an equestrian club, a gardening club, an African American arts organization and her sorority, Delta Sigma Theta. She'd gone to Spelman in Atlanta, and done postgraduate work in art history at the Sorbonne in Paris. There was no work history at all.

At age twenty-one she'd married Marshall Pettifore, had one son, Michael, aged seven, and had turned twenty-nine on her last birthday. It was the resume of a cosseted and pampered lady of leisure with a high level of public service consciousness, and it was printed on damned fine, heavy linen paper. But it told him nothing about a woman who would run from a gilded cage and take a young child with her. Joe reached for his cell phone.

"Hey Pop, anything shaking?" he asked when his father answered.

"Nothing but the leaves on the trees," Paul Griffin responded. "She's only been gone a couple of days and she cleaned out the safe before she left, I understand. I didn't really expect to see any activity on her credit cards this soon. And, like I figured, she's been smart enough not to use her cell phone."

"Yeah. They say there was about eighteen to twenty thousand dollars in the safe. That should keep her going for a while," Joe said. "Anything at the airport?"

"Naw. The way she packed, carelessly, with garbage bags, she probably planned to drive where she was going."

"I'm at her house now," Joe said. "I'll call you back."

Passing through wrought-iron gates, Joe approached a huge stately brick home with white columns and arched Palladian windows. A small middle-aged, Asian woman in a neat black suit answered the doorbell.

"Mr. Griffin?" she asked. Joe nodded.

"I am Narye, Mrs. Pettifore's housekeeper," she said with a slight accent that evoked images of pagodas and rice paddies. "Mr. Pettifore asked me to assist you."

"I need to look through her things," Joe said. "I want to see what she took, what she left. Perhaps I can get some idea of where she went."

"What if she does not want to be found? Does that not matter?" Narye asked, inscrutable mask intact.

"Well, my client hired me to find her," Joe responded. "That's my job."

"And you do not care what her wishes are," she said quietly.

"Nope," Joe declared. They had climbed a huge marble staircase from the foyer and were walking down a wide hallway with tall windows looking out onto a vast expanse of emerald silk lawn studded with mature oak trees. He could see tennis courts and a white gazebo in the distance. Beyond that were horse stables. Closer to the house was a serene, shaded infinity pool that flowed into a glassed indoor pool area at the back of the house.

"What will you do if you find her?" Narye asked suddenly.

"My job is to bring her and her son back here."

"And if they don't want to come back?" she inquired. Her tiny head turned sideways toward him.

"Not my business."

Narye opened the door to Talley's suite of rooms and Joe gave a soft whistle. The rooms were decorated in creamy almond white and soft peach with touches of deep green. A huge gold-flecked antique Italian bed canopied with wispy peach hangings dominated the bedroom.

"Why would she want to run away from this luxury?" Joe asked the Burmese lady beside him. Narye said nothing. She led him to a large mirrored dressing room with a system of closets and drawers. He noticed a windowed area housing an antique gold inlaid desk.

The rooms were immaculate. Joe rummaged through scented drawers of neatly folded lingerie. He sifted through multi-hued dresses and neatly stored shoes.

"You've straightened things up in here, haven't you?" he looked at Narye with an arched eyebrow.

"Yes." She shrugged.

"Doesn't look like she took any fur coats," Joe mused, opening the door of a closet full of them. Narye said nothing, but Joe noticed that her eyes shifted slightly.

Joe wandered over to her desk alcove and began leafing through the small pile of papers there: invitations to fundraisers, weddings, soirees, thank-you notes for gifts and donations, Neiman Marcus catalog.

In a niche in the desk he found a photo of an attractive brown-skinned woman with warm brown eyes smiling out at him confidently. *She* was definitely his type, he noted. He kept the photo to be identified by Talley's mother later.

He opened the doors of the gold-leafed armoire across from the bed. There was an enormous television inside and above it, a video camera. The camera was situated to aim through a small hole. A finger passed over the hole showed that it had recently been drilled through the door of the armoire so that camera could tape the bedroom while concealed. *Hmm, kinky stuff,* he guessed. He looked at Narye and she looked away from him.

He walked over to the bed. There had clearly been a scuffle beside the bed. One of the hangings very recently had been torn and mended. There was a rubbed and cleaned area on the carpet.

"What happened here?" he asked.

Narye looked away. "Juice spilled," she said.

"Human juice?" he asked. She said nothing. He could bring equipment back and confirm that blood had stained that spot, but he didn't feel he needed to. He thought he knew what had happened here. *I bet that asshole Marshall Pettifore hit his wife hard enough to make her bleed, and she bolted with her son*. He also bet that Talley had videotaped the whole incident. The existence of that tape with the evidence it provided had made her brave enough to run with her child, he surmised.

Now, where would they go? Someplace as far away from the Pettifore influence as possible. Someplace she could drive to. Though she was well traveled internationally and she'd taken her passport, he didn't think she'd taken the boy out of the country. She probably headed for the one other place she'd lived besides Detroit—Atlanta. That's where he'd start.

CHAPTER FOUR

Talley sat in Attorney Robert Edward's office clutching a videotape and staring at the floor. She dreaded showing the degrading tape to him.

When she'd walked into the offices to meet with a junior associate, she'd bumped into Robert Edwards as he was leaving for the evening. He'd opened the door for her, and then stopped when she smiled at him tremulously.

"Mrs. Pettifore, isn't it?" he'd asked, peering at her calmly through his wire-rimmed glasses.

"Yes," she'd whispered with a warning finger up to her lips. "I have an appointment under a fake name with one of your associates, but I planned to tell him that I actually wanted to see you."

"Of course!" he replied. "I'll take care of that."

Then he had bundled her into his office and left to speak to the associate. When he came back into the office, he was carrying two glasses of white wine.

"Here, have this," Robert said, handing her a glass. She sipped the wine while he took a seat next to her on a couch across from his massive chrome and glass desk.

From out of nowhere, tears started pouring down Talley's face. Robert handed her a tissue and sat silently beside her while she tried to gain control of herself. Embarrassed, Talley blotted uselessly as the big tears kept rolling down her cheeks. "I'm so sorry," she gasped. "They just won't stop. I think it's eight years worth."

Robert nodded sympathetically and Talley smiled ruefully at him through the tears.

"You've been married to Marshall Pettifore eight years?" Robert asked.

"Exactly," Talley replied, gulping and wiping her chin.

"Never much liked the guy, myself. Why'd you marry him?" Robert asked.

"It was ordained by Pope Cedric Pettifore," Talley explained. She gave a tired sigh.

"Yeah, but this isn't Afghanistan. Couldn't you just say no?"

"Marshall and I grew up together and we both accepted the inevitable. It seemed like the thing to do at the time."

Robert studied the stunning woman. She was perched like a timid butterfly on his office couch with her long-lashed eyes downcast. Only a very sheltered life could have created the kind of fresh, soft innocence that belied her age.

Now, looking at her trembling beside him, he realized that it was actually surprising she had found the courage to run away. He knew firsthand how intimidating Cedric Pettifore could be. Most of the country's African American legal community knew and had a healthy respect for the ruthlessly powerful old man.

Robert had once watched Cedric destroy a promising young attorney's career simply by lifting a disdainful eyebrow when someone at a gathering of business and political opinion leaders mentioned the young man's name.

"So, why'd you decide finally to leave Marshall?"

"He beat me and he punched my son," Talley said stiffly, shivering with mortification.

"What the…?" Robert exclaimed. "Is he crazy?" *What kind of maniac would mistreat this gentle creature,* he wondered. *And his own son!*

"He has a cocaine problem. And he likes to put on women's clothes and makeup."

"He's gay?" Robert asked incredulously. His eyes searched her face.

"Not precisely." With forced calm she explained, "He's a cross dresser. He likes to have sex that way. Let me show you." She handed him the videotape.

"Did Michael see his father dressed up?" Robert asked as he opened the doors of a black lacquered media center and inserted the tape.

Talley nodded sadly.

"Where's Michael now?"

"He's with some friends," Talley said.

"We may need to get him to talk to a psychiatrist."

"I know."

A bedroom scene with Talley and Michael came up on the huge TV screen. Robert realized that Talley was urging Michael to leave the room.

"*Get out of here, now, sweetie,*" *she gasped desperately to Michael.*

"*Why, Mommy, aren't you going to finish reading to me?*"

"*No, honey, not now. I hear Daddy in the other room and I think you should go to your room now.*"

"*Oh. Daddy,*" *the boy complained grumpily, hopping off the bed.*

At that moment, Marshall slammed into the room from a side door. He didn't see Michael at first. In heavy makeup, he wore a short, high-necked satin dress and was tottering on high heels.

Michael's eyes widened. Wiggling from his mother's grasp he ran to his father, tugged at the hem of his dress and asked, "Is it Halloween, Daddy?"

Talley laughed wildly and nervously.

Marshall, his eyes glazed, shoved the boy aside, heading straight for Talley.

"*What you laughing about, you ugly white-looking bitch?*" *he asked.*

"*Michael, leave here now,*" *Talley said urgently.*

Michael just stood, staring at his father.

Marshall stood in front of his wife, blocking her from the camera.

She was whispering now.

"*Marshall, your son is in here. Please. Don't. Can't you see? Michael is right there.*"

"Take off that robe," Marshall demanded, his voice blurry.

"I'll do what you want. Just let me get Michael to leave the room."

Abruptly, in a fury of violence, Marshall began tearing at his wife's negligee, knocking her, half-naked, to the floor.

Michael screamed "Mommy!" and ran to try to stop his father.

Marshall shrugged the boy off as though he were a pesky insect, and continued struggling with Talley. The boy ran at him again, his arms flailing. Marshall, as though noticing the child for the first time, turned and punched him in the face, hard.

Michael fell to the floor, dazed, and his mother tried to crawl to him. Marshall stopped her with a vicious kick to her side and pulled her up again. The little boy, recovering consciousness, crawled across the floor and bit his father on the leg.

Talley saw him and pleaded. "Michael, stop. Run away."

Marshall kicked the boy off his leg and dropped Talley like a rag doll. She sat on the floor gathering her son to her, trying to cover her nakedness with the shreds of her robe. They huddled together, weeping. Marshall stood looking at them. And then, as though coming out of a trance, he gasped and staggered back. He crossed his arms in front of himself, bent over and ran from the room.

Mother and son sat huddled on the floor by the bed.

Robert clicked off the TV. A muscle quivered in his jaw as he punched the buttons to rewind the tape. *Dear God! That was hard to watch.* He swallowed hard.

"Is this your only copy?" he asked, pulling the tape out of the machine. When she nodded, he put the tape into a wall safe behind his desk.

"I should take it with me," she protested.

"No. It will be safer here. No one has this combination but me," he said, twirling the knob on the safe.

"Please don't let anyone else see it," she begged.

"A judge and Marshall's attorney may have to see it," Robert explained.

"His father will represent him, I'm sure. Isn't it enough to tell them we have it?" she asked.

"We'll see. Trust me," he insisted.

Talley looked at him closely, taking in his wide smile. As she studied him, his eyes wavered slightly, sending an uneasy feeling skittering through her. "Okay," she said slowly. Her body drooped tiredly.

"We'll need to get some things started," Robert noted briskly. Then, looking at the pale, exhausted face in front of him, he added, "But not tonight. Give me your address."

"I'm staying at a motel north of town," she replied, "but I'm looking for an apartment." *Maybe I should just keep my address to myself for now.*

"Who are these friends Michael is with now?" he asked.

"Just some nice people I know."

"All righty then," he said, noticing the newly stubborn set to her mouth. He shrugged impatiently. "Why don't you come by the office tomorrow morning…"

"I have a job," Talley said hesitantly. "I'm not sure I'll be able to get away."

"What! A job?" Robert gave a short barking laugh. *What kind of job could she have found here so fast?* "You don't need a job. If you need money, I'll be glad…"

"No, I want to work," she interrupted him. "I'll come by on my lunch hour. How about noon?"

"Okay," he said, still chuckling. "I'll see you tomorrow. We'll get things signed and my representation of you will be official."

Robert took her to the elevator and waved as the doors closed, then returned to his office and dialed his phone.

"You were right," he said when the line was picked up. "She came straight here."

He listened for a minute and then said, "She knows nothing about our relationship, Cedric. She trusts me completely. And yes, she does have a videotape.

"It was pretty damning," Robert went on, "but I have the only copy in my safe. No. I think you need to look at it, Cedric. Suffice it to say, your son is one sick bastard." He paused to listen again.

"Okay, I'll seal it up and give it to your man Joe Griffin when he gets here tomorrow. No, I didn't get her address, but she'll be back tomorrow at noon. She has a job. Yes, a job."

The sound of laughter was audible through the phone.

———————ও

"You as nervous as a rabbit in a foxhole," Marcus said to Cole, who was fidgeting with the floral arrangement on the dining room table. "I ain't never seen you like this before. Why don't you sit down somewhere?"

"I just hope she didn't get lost," Cole muttered. He peered out of the drapes in the front room.

"You gave her directions five or six times. I heard you. She has your cell phone number. She'll be here."

"These drapes are dusty. When was the last time you had them cleaned?" Cole asked.

"A little dust ain't gonna hurt Miz High Pockets," Marcus groused.

"I'm just sayin'…"

"Sure, sure…"

When Talley had walked into the trailer that morning, Marcus had done a double take. He was the self-appointed family worrier and Tallulah Parsons had worried him right away for a number of reasons. First, she looked familiar. He was pretty sure he had seen her stunning face in a magazine or on TV, maybe the news somewhere, and he suspected that meant trouble.

Second, his normally stoic brother Cole was almost visibly drooling over the girl and he didn't like that. He'd never seen the big man so taken with a woman.

And third, she didn't look like she'd ever lifted a finger to do anything but summon a butler. *Why would she want to work in a doublewide office trailer in Georgia?* he wondered.

Even her little boy was strange, with his big haunted eyes. His English was too precise and he was much too quiet and mannerly for a child. He had ridden in the trucks with Marcus or Winston all day long and done exactly what he was told, politely and deftly. It was unnatural.

But Marcus had been impressed when Talley listened intently and took copious notes as Cole explained how TowMasters, Inc., worked. It appeared she grasped quickly what Cole and their cousin Vickie said about dispatching and responding to calls.

And when Talley took over the phones, her well-bred voice gave a classy tone to the business. Marcus and Cole had grinned and nodded at each other the first time she answered the phone with a crisp, "TowMasters. How may I help you?"

Vickie, who dispatched for them part time, was ordinarily wary and reserved with strangers. She was even more so with this alien creature. But at the end of the day, she'd glanced sideways at Talley and had given Marcus and Cole a curt little nod and the "O.K." sign with her fingers.

"Is that a car turning into the driveway?" Marcus asked his antsy brother. Cole jumped back from the windows.

"You and Winston are going to be out on call tonight and David is going to keep Michael busy, so I can have dinner with her alone, right?" Cole asked.

"That's the plan," Marcus agreed as Cole strode to the front door.

Cole opened the door before Talley could ring the doorbell and stood looking down at her with a wide, warm grin. The porch light glinting on her gold hair looked like a halo. Talley had changed into a slim brown suit for her meeting with Edwards, and her long shapely legs caught Cole's admiring eyes as she stepped over the threshold. *You only see legs like that in fashion magazines,* he thought. *They go on forever.*

"Welcome to our humble home," he said, ushering her into the formal living room, his hand on her arm. His fingers on the soft, creamy skin of her elbow felt tingly, as if jolts of electricity were coming through them.

Talley smiled up at him, turning his knees to jelly. "Thank you so much for this. Thank you for keeping Michael. How has he been?"

"He's a good kid. He ate earlier and he and David are in the family room with a video game."

She sighed and sank down onto the living room couch, her mind busy reviewing her meeting with Robert Edwards.

"You know how, when someone says 'trust me' you immediately begin not to?" she asked.

"I know exactly what you mean," Cole nodded, standing in front of her with his hands in his pockets.

"Well, this attorney…he…I thought I could, but now I don't know." Talley heaved a huge sigh.

"Let's talk about it while we eat," Cole suggested, taking her hands and lifting her to her feet. He kept her hand in his as he walked her into the dining room.

The formal dining room was softly lit with candles and soft jazz played in the background. The table was set carefully with his mother's good china set, one of few nice things that his hardworking parents had accumulated while struggling to raise a large, loving family. Cole could still hear his sister's voice insisting that he keep it. "My husband and I are starting our own set," Lucy had said when she moved out of the family home after her wedding to her big policeman. "You might need it for a special guest." Right now, Cole could think of no one more special than Talley.

Dinner was ready in covered dishes. Roasted chicken, mashed potatoes with gravy, buttermilk rolls, green beans, sweet tea.

"This is delightful! The table is beautiful." Talley flashed a warm look at him. Cole smiled widely. *I'm grinning like the village idiot,* he thought. He tried to calm his delight at her reaction.

While Talley ate her fill, Cole was too busy watching her tiny delicate bites and her obvious enjoyment of the comfort food to eat much himself.

She even eats gracefully, he thought, dazzled. *I wonder who she really is. I wonder why she won't trust me with her real name.*

"I'm so full," she said, polishing off the last dab of mashed potato and dabbing her lips with a napkin. "I haven't eaten like this in days. I needed it."

"Would you like some Kahlua?" he asked, going to the teak breakfront beside the table. He poured drinks for both of them at her nod. "Now tell me about this attorney."

Talley's face turned solemn. A frown furrowed her brow.

"Hey, I didn't mean to make your face look like that!" Cole exclaimed.

"I'm sorry, I just don't feel the way I thought I would about Robert Edwards," Talley explained. "When I met him three years ago in Detroit, I liked the way he handled himself. But tonight…The more I think about it…Something was wrong. He was too eager. He didn't seem surprised enough to see me. Almost like he was expecting me."

"That *is* strange," Cole nodded.

"Do you know a good divorce attorney?" she asked suddenly.

"Matter of fact, I do," Cole said. "Name's Jerome Richmond. He's an old friend. He's my age, went to night school at Emory. Real smart. He helped Winston work things out with his baby's mother."

"I'd like to see him tomorrow."

"You gonna tell him your real name?" Cole asked.

"Yes," Talley said sheepishly.

"Will you tell me?"

She was quiet for a moment.

"I'm afraid," she sighed.

"Afraid of what? I'm not going to tell anybody."

"Tallulah Quincy Pettifore," she said quietly.

"Pettifore," he repeated slowly. "Like the famous law firm. The assistant attorney general. The Supreme Court Justice. Those Pettifores. And Quincy, like the U.S. senator and the famous civil rights leader. Those Quincys."

"Yes. All my relatives."

"Damn."

"Please don't tell your brothers. Please don't let it change anything." Her eyes pleaded with him.

Talley had seen it happen far too often. New friends becoming suddenly distant, wary or overly solicitous once they found out about her family. She had been enjoying the easy camaraderie she had with the Colemans and Vickie. She wanted it to continue. More than anything she wanted to keep the friendship and warmth she had been feeling all evening from this wonderful man.

Cole got up from the table and began pacing.

"Pettifore, Quincy," he muttered. "I had no idea."

Talley was silent, looking down at her brandy snifter.

"You really don't need to work, do you?" he asked, his voice tight with anger. "You don't need my little pitiful job."

"Yes. Yes, I do. I left without enough money and I can't use any of my credit cards or they'll find me."

"Find you and do what? Increase your allowance? Raise the limit on your platinum cards? Oh, 'scuse me, do those even have limits?"

"Cole, it's not like that. You can't understand…"

"Why? How much does understanding cost?"

"I…We…I had to go."

"You're just a little spoiled runaway," he spat, unreasonably mad and getting madder. "What happened? Your husband wouldn't let you buy another yacht?"

"Why are you so angry with me?" she cried, standing up and putting her hand on his arm.

"It's just that I thought…I hoped…" He looked into her beseeching eyes until he could stand it no more. Cole knew exactly why he was mad. For the briefest time over their cozy dinner, he'd allowed himself to dream of a relationship with Talley. It was as if he had lit a small candle and let the promise of light creep into his life. The candle had quickly been doused when he realized just how far beyond him Talley's background, family history and money placed her.

He had always felt a contempt as potent as acid for those phony materialistic African Americans he called "bougie"—including those with inherited or easy wealth. And he believed the hatred went both ways. He couldn't imagine why Talley was here with him.

Her soft pleading voice caught his attention. "Please don't be different with me. That's why I didn't tell you. Please. I need you."

Cole turned again and looked down at her. There were tears in her huge amber eyes. And those last three words were killers.

Weakening, he pulled her to him abruptly and buried his face in her hair. It smelled of apricots. She was a perfect fit for his arms and she clung to him, melting into him, her softness molding into his barrel chest. It took iron control for him not to plunge his hand into her thick silken hair, to take her mouth and unleash the passion that he was suddenly feeling. The restraint caused him to shudder.

Talley felt him tremble and for the first time in her life was sexually excited by a man. She savored the unfamiliar feeling and pressed against him harder, seeking more. Resting her head on his chest and feeling safe in the circle of his big arms, she sighed.

Cole dropped his arms and backed away from her, trying to regain his composure. She looked up at him, puzzled and surprised.

"I'm sorry," he said, taking a deep breath. "I shouldn't have grabbed you like that. Just forget it happened. I gotta admit, I don't know how to act around you now."

"Can't you just act like you did before?' she begged. "People are always uncomfortable around me. It was nice when you and your brothers weren't." *It was nice in your arms,* she thought.

"Yeah, I guess. I hadn't thought about that," he said slowly.

Cole picked up their drinks and led her back into the formal living room. They both perched gingerly on the brocade couch.

"Why did you leave your husband?" he asked.

"He hit my child."

Cole sucked in an angry breath and asked, "That bruise on Michael's face?"

"Yes."

"Son of a bitch! That had to be done with a fist!" Cole exploded. "Did he hit you?"

"Yes. Frequently."

"Hitting women and children? What kind of man is he? "

"He was my husband," she said softly.

"Makes my blood boil," Cole hissed, his lips curled in anger. "Why'd you wait so long to leave him?"

"I didn't have anyplace to go," she admitted.

"What about your parents?"

"They wouldn't…couldn't help me." At his startled look, she put her hand up and shook her head. That subject was off limits.

"Okay, what about friends?"

"I don't have any that I'm close enough to."

"Aw c'mon, there must have been someplace you could have gone…a church, a shelter…" He stopped abruptly. *There was no way this glowing creature would have been able to fit in—or trust—a shelter,* he realized.

"I'm on the board of a battered women's shelter. I used to listen to stories about the women there, trying to find the courage to do what they did. But I couldn't see a life for myself and for Michael other than the one I had. I wasn't very strong."

"But you found the courage this time," he soothed.

"He hit my son," Talley said again stiffly, looking into the dark brown liquid of her brandy.

"I still can't understand why you have to run and hide from your family. Can't you just put him out your house and get a divorce?"

"Put Marshall out?" She shook her head sadly. "You don't know the Pettifores. One hundred years of wealth and influence makes its mark. They're so powerful. My father-in-law would never let me divorce Marshall and I'm not sure what Marshall would do to me if I tried."

"I don't get it."

"It's really Michael that Cedric wants. I was just a tool in the making of the heir."

"But they want you too. Right?"

"Because Michael still needs a mommy. And my husband still needs the respectability."

"What about the law, the police?"

"The Pettifores *are* the law in that community," she sighed. "Their influence reaches all kinds of people. Even people who would do illegal things for the Pettifore money. My mother says Cedric Pettifore has sent a private investigator to find us and make us come back." She shivered at the thought.

"I have to hide from them until I can get the divorce proceedings started," she continued. "I had to wait until I had a secret weapon…some leverage to keep them at bay. I have it now, at last."

Cole was silent, taking this in. "What kind of leverage?" he asked.

"I have a video tape of Marshall hurting us," she sighed. "I left it with Robert Edwards."

"Don't worry. If you go see Jerome, he'll get it back," Cole soothed.

"Oh, I made a copy," she said, her soft voice suddenly steely with purpose. "I stopped on the way down here."

David came wandering into the living room.

"Michael is asleep on the couch in the family room," he said. "One moment we were playing and laughing and the next he just keeled over. Scared me! I had to check his pulse!"

"He does that sometimes." Talley said, grinning. "He plays until he absolutely can play no more."

She stood up.

"We'd better get going," she said. "Do I still have a job?"

"Yeah," he said shortly. "I still need the help."

Cole led Talley into the family room where Michael was sprawled on the couch, sleeping soundly. As Talley watched, Cole tenderly lifted the boy in strong arms and carried him out to their loaner car.

"Your Range Rover should be ready tomorrow," he said gruffly as he settled the sleeping child in the back seat and gently stroked his little head. "You should pick it up before you come in."

"Thank you, Cole," she said.

"Why's she worried about her job?" David demanded after they left. "I thought you and Marcus liked her. Hell, I just like lookin' at her," he gushed. "If she doesn't kiss the mirror every morning, she sure should!"

"I know, it's like that," Cole sighed. "I like her a lot."

Then he added with a shrug of his heavy shoulders, "But don't get too used to her. She ain't gonna be around for long. Once she gets her divorce settled she'll be gone."

~⌒~

"Marshall, what the hell is on that tape?" Cedric Pettifore asked his son. As soon as he'd hung up from Edwards, Cedric had called Marshall and insisted he come over right away.

"What tape, Dad?"

"Apparently your wife had a video camera in her bedroom. She taped a fight you and she had the night before she left."

Marshall was silent for a few minutes, his brow furrowed as he tried to remember that night. He had been very high and it was all a blur. Then he began to tremble. He felt a rush of hot, then cold, as flashes came to him.

"Daddy, is it Halloween?"

"Marshall, your son is here. Don't you see him?"

"Michael! Stop! Run away!"

"Nobody can see that tape," he gasped. "I gotta get that tape."

"Relax," his father said, staring coldly at his frantic son. "Edwards has the only copy. I knew she'd go straight to him. I could tell she liked him when they met three years ago. But we've been shoring up his raggedy firm for years, so he had to call us."

"Did you tell him to destroy it?" Marshall asked nervously.

"He thinks I should see it," Cedric said.

"I don't want you to. I'd really prefer if you didn't." Marshall was sweating again. His small mouth was wet.

"You make me sick, you perverted slime," his father spat at him. "The only thing you've ever done worthwhile is marry that girl and donate enough sperm to create Michael."

"I've tried to be a good son," Marshall pleaded. "I went to law school and I've worked in the firm."

"We bought your way out of law school. We carry you at the firm."

"That's not true," Marshall protested. "Clients like me."

"The sick ones. The ones that want to join you in debauchery. I don't know what you do at night with them. I don't want to turn over that rock. And don't worry. I won't look at that tape. You already disgust me enough."

"Where is it now?" Marshall asked, wiping his mouth with the back of his hand.

"I'm sending Joe Griffin down to Atlanta to pick it up from Edwards and overnight it back to me. He's going to stay there until he finds Tallulah and Michael."

CHAPTER FIVE

Joe got off the plane in Atlanta and immediately took off the heavy topcoat he'd automatically put on before leaving the plane.

"Is it always this hot in October here?" he asked the Hertz car rental agent.

"We usually stay pretty warm through October," she said. She had a little flirt in her smile. It was hard for her to ignore the handsome, well set-up male. "It'll cool down some next month."

She was still smiling as she handed Joe the keys and paperwork for the reserved Impala. She wasn't his type, but the rich Southern lilt of her voice stayed with him.

"Welcome to Atlanta," he echoed as he moved on to the highway.

Joe drove to the Ritz Carlton in downtown Atlanta and called Edwards and Worth as soon as he got settled in his room.

"I'm in town, sir. I'd like to come over about 11 A.M. to pick up the tape and wait for Mrs. Pettifore to get to your office."

"Fine. Where are you staying?"

"I'm at the downtown Ritz," he said.

"Good, you can walk to us. We're at 100 Peachtree Street, a couple of blocks down on the right. Tenth floor."

At eleven precisely Joe presented himself to the receptionist and was ushered into Robert Edward's office. There was no offer of coffee or tea, no pleasant questions about his trip and barely the offer of a seat. *Man is treating me like a bad rash,* Joe mused, *wants to get this business over fast.*

Joe tightened his game face and went to work. They discussed Talley's visit the night before. As Joe consciously watched the other man's face and body language, he realized Robert Edwards' confidence was a façade. Edwards wasn't going to be much help. He was just a minor player in Atlanta…a Pettifore puppet.

"Do you know what's on this tape?" Robert asked him, opening the safe in his office.

"No, but I'm the one that warned Mr. Pettifore it might exist. I saw the camera setup in her bedroom." Joe waited, curious.

"It's pretty lurid," Robert said. "But I'm not supposed to say more. Cedric told me to wrap and seal it. You're to send it back right away."

"Is this the only copy?"

"That's what Mrs. Pettifore said," he replied, smugly.

"I don't believe her," Joe said.

"Why not?" Robert responded in surprise. "She had no reason to lie to me. I could tell she trusted me."

"If what you say is true, this tape is dynamite. If it got out, it could embarrass the entire Pettifore clan. I can't believe she'd only have one copy."

"She is not a devious woman. She is naïve, trusting," Robert said, shaking his head.

"I'm sure she made a backup," Joe insisted.

"You'd have to know the type." Robert smiled with a shade of condescension. "The rich are not like you and me and this one is richer than most."

"Still…"

"Well, I don't think so," Robert sighed. "But we'll ask her when she gets here."

"*If* she comes back," Joe said complacently.

It was two P.M. before Robert Edwards conceded Talley was not coming back to his office.

"You don't know where she is or how to get in touch with her, do you?" Joe said to Robert with a tight smile.

"No. I wasn't concerned. I was sure she would…"

"Did she say who these friends were that Michael was with?"

"No."

"What about her job?"

"Nothing," Robert snapped.

"Hah!" Joe said. "I bet she knew you'd contact us right away. She came here and left a copy of this 'lurid' tape as a warning. Telling us to back off or else. Very subtle. And you said she's not devious."

"That girl does not have a sly bone in her body," Robert insisted. "I would have known if she was attempting some coy subterfuge."

"Uh huh," Joe grunted skeptically. "I'll need to use an office here until I can get a team hired to scour the city for them. I'll move to my own space as quick as possible. "

"I don't know if I want to be put in the position..."

"My understanding was that I would have your full cooperation. Was Mr. Pettifore wrong?"

Robert's lips thinned as he buzzed the intercom. "Give us ten minutes."

Joe sat behind the desk in the empty office he was assigned and pulled the photo he'd found in Talley's bedroom out of his inner pocket. He set it squarely on the blotter in front of him and admired the pretty girl's sassy smile.

Talley's mother had identified her as Alicia Hansen, Talley's college roommate. Joe's father had traced her to an advertising agency in Atlanta.

"Okay, Miss Alicia Henson," he muttered, "you sweet little Hershey kiss. What are you going to tell me?"

He reached for the phone.

～✑

The "sweet little Hershey," wrapped in a stylish beige and black knit suit, was clicking across the marble tile floors of offices of The Boyd Group advertising and public relations firm. A petite dynamo, Alicia Hanson, Director of New Business Development, was on her way to the president's office.

Christina Boyd, the agency owner, an attractive fortyish African American woman was in her office and spotting Alicia through the glass panes of her French doors, waved her in enthusiastically.

"I've talked to Marva over at the Atlanta Business League," Alicia told Christina, her enthusiasm heightening her soft Southern accent. "They're launchin' this year's Minority Business Marketing Makeover raffle by offerin' raffle tickets to their membership."

Christina's smile reflected the pleasure she took from the other woman's magnolia-drenched accent. Slow, sweet and comforting, Alicia's voice always harkened back to the Old South's genteel ways. She sounded like "homefolk" to Christina. It took a moment to redirect her focus as Alicia continued.

For the past ten years, The Boyd Group had been working with the ABL, the city's premier African American business association, to annually raffle off free marketing advice to an up-and-coming small business. The business was selected by a drawing held at the ABL's black-tie Christmas dinner. Money raised by the raffle went toward the ABL's scholarship fund. "A wonderful cause," Alicia offered.

"Oh yes," Christina sighed. "Pro bono work."

"It's excellent public service and it gets us visibility and kudos every year," Alicia said as she left, repeating Christina's own mantra to creative staff reluctant to participate.

Back in her office, Alicia was sending an e-mail to the ABL when the phone rang. Clearing her throat, she answered in her best voice.

"This is Alicia Hanson."

"Good afternoon, Ms. Hanson. My name is Joe Griffin."

Nice voice, Alicia thought, giving the caller and his clipped Northern accent her complete attention. "Yes?"

"…I'd like very much to meet with you. Would this afternoon be convenient?"

"What would you like to discuss, Mr. Griffin?" Alicia knew her tone was polite, but maybe a bit more formal than this confident and attractive-sounding man deserved.

"I need some advice," he responded, wondering how she wrapped her tongue around the word "mister" and made it come out "mistah."

"I'm assumin' you're lookin' for marketin' advice. What business are you in?"

On his end of the line, Joe smiled. This sassy sister was a charmer without even trying. She said 'business' and it sounded like "bidness." No, truth be told, it sounded like poetry. He had to haul himself up short to keep his mind focused.

"I'd prefer to talk to you face to face. It's easier to describe what I need." Intrigued by Alicia's husky Southern drawl, with its cultured undertones, Joe knew that anything less than face-to-face would be out of the question. He felt his body harden in response to her next words.

"I can do that. Would you like to come to the office?" she asked.

"Can we meet more informally? Perhaps an after-work drink?" he suggested.

"That's a bit unusual, Mr. Griffin."

"The information I need is unusual, Ms. Hanson, but I'm hoping that won't stop you from meeting me." *Damn, she's got me flirting!*

Alicia paused for a moment, clearly surprised. "What is this in reference to?"

Joe put a smile into his voice, hoping she wasn't figuring him for an ax murderer or something. "Again, Ms. Hanson, I really think it will be easier to explain what I need…"

"In person," she finished for him. When she spoke it again it was in a breathy rush. "Well, okay…Meet me at Dailey's at five-thirty. It's on International Boulevard right 'cross the street from our offices in Peachtree Center."

"That sounds good," Joe said.

"I'm wearing a beige and black suit…" she started.

"I'll know you," he interrupted.

Joe hung up with a grin and stretched his legs out to try to cool his body's reaction to her. The picture in front of him seemed to wink knowingly.

⚊◠

Instead of returning to Robert Edwards' office, Talley met with Cole's attorney friend, Jerome Richmond, a short, stocky man with a shock of reddish-brown hair and brown freckles on beige skin.

Far from being intimidated, he relished the idea of going up against the famous Pettifores in a divorce case, even rubbing his hands together in eager anticipation.

"This will be a challenge," he said gleefully. "Those folks at PPQ hate to lose."

Talley told Jerome of her meeting with Robert Edwards and of the circumstances under which she'd fled from her house in Farmington just two days ago.

"Marshall has been hitting me off and on throughout our marriage," she confessed. "But it's worse than it has ever been this year. I'm afraid that he'll kill me."

"Have you ever reported the abuse to the police?"

"No," she said in despair. "I couldn't. It would have been all over the front pages the next day."

"That's unfortunate. He can deny that he ever abused you."

"Except...I have a video tape of the most recent incident." Talley pulled a tape out of her purse. "My housekeeper Narye helped me set up a camera in my room…She thought…"

"Very shrewd. Very smart," Jerome grinned. He reached for the tape and patted it happily.

"I left a copy with Robert Edwards," Talley said, twisting her hands in her lap.

"I'm glad you did that." Jerome's smile widened. "Edwards has been in your father-in-law's pocket for years. He'll probably call and tell him about it right away."

"Oh my God! I sensed there was something wrong when I left his office."

"By now I'm sure Edwards has called your husband to let him know where you are. Did you give him an address?"

"No, thank God. I had an instinct…" Talley felt a shiver of fear down her spine. "I told him that tape was my only copy."

Jerome was cheerful. "I'll go ahead and disabuse him of that notion and then serve divorce papers."

"But…Jerome, I don't really want to release that tape," Talley said. "The media would have a field day. It would be destructive to the whole family, not just Marshall. Michael would have that picture of his father forever."

"Don't worry. We can bluff. We're in the catbird's seat."

～♋～

Joe was sitting on a stool at the center bar in Dailey's facing the door when Alicia walked in and surveyed the room. For a moment the red brick archway into the room framed her and Joe felt his heart take a tiny leap. At about five feet tall, Alicia was smaller than he expected. But every inch of her was perfectly proportioned for him—her heavy bosom, her tiny waist, her rounded hips and shapely legs. The photo he had taken from Talley's room was of a pretty young college girl, but, unquestionably, time had passed since it was taken. This vision in the archway was a WOMAN.

Joe was a cynical guy. He liked to call himself "down to earth," "pragmatic and realistic." But when Alicia turned her small head with its cap of shiny hair and moved with a glowing smile toward him, he was lost in a fantasy, transported to an Arabian tent and alone with this beautiful dusky woman with her deep eyes. He could swear he caught the scent of incense in his nostrils, felt a warm wind rustling silken hangings and heard the sound of exotic music tinkling.

He was brought back to reality when she reached him and, putting out her hand, said flirtatiously, "I sho' do hope you're Joe."

"I sure am glad I am," he said, standing up and taking her hand in both of his big ones.

⟿

Talley felt like an old hand at her job. With two weeks of experience under her belt, she laid claim to veteran dispatcher status. She was settling into her job and taking pride in her ability to do the work well.

Unbeknownst to her, Marcus and Vickie had been testing her every day, throwing extra work and even some demeaning jobs her way. Even Cole was taxing her mettle by treating her coldly and distantly.

Cole was in his own personal hell. On the one hand, he was convinced that Talley was there temporarily and he should not pin any hopes on her. On the other his heart soared every time he walked into the small trailer and found her there.

The combination of tough work and inaccessibility to her boss might have defeated a lesser woman, but Talley was made of stern stuff. Generations of hardworking Quincy stock had been bred into her. She took to the work easily and gracefully, responding to Cole's abruptness with charm and a soft manner and cheerfully completing the extra duties.

Before long she impressed Vickie and Marcus with her quick grasp of the business.

"Nobody likes to do the record keeping and filing," Vickie said to Talley with a grudging smile. "But you do a nice job."

"It's easy. I'm ready to take on something harder," Talley smiled. "Like making this place look better."

She stood in the center of the trailer and surveyed the bland setup. Cole's office, the part-time accountant's office and the filing room were at one end. A reception area, the bathroom and kitchenette and a small conference room were in the middle. At the other end was the dispatcher's office, which was also where people came to claim their impounded cars.

"We have to keep the dispatch area locked up tight," Vickie said, pointing to the bulletproof glass with a small pass-through counter. "We get some crazy folk in here coming to get their cars. Lot of times they'll be drunk and mad."

The trailer squatted on ten acres of undeveloped, wooded land that Talley learned Cole had inherited from his grandfather. Cole had borrowed against the valuable piece of real estate, Vickie told her, in order to start his business. Then he and his brothers had worked like slaves to clear space for the trailer and parking lot.

Out on the yard, just beyond the parking lot, was a small garage that Talley had not inspected, though she had observed young men going in and out of it.

"What's in there?" she asked Vickie one day when she noticed Cole carrying boxes into the garage.

"Cole's working with some teenagers from the Boys' Club," Vickie said. "He's helping them to rebuild a van for the club."

"Really?" Talley said, smiling. She was pleased to learn that the big man shared her commitment to helping others.

"Yeah. He does that community service thing. Cole doesn't like to brag about it, but he's always doing something for other people."

"I imagine he's a good role model for the teenagers."

"He's real good with the kids. He knows how to keep them in line," Vickie said.

"He's real good with people in general, isn't he?" Talley responded wistfully. "I wish he liked me more."

Cole's treatment of Talley had been the subject of some discussion among the brothers. They didn't understand it. "Why you think he's acting like that?" David wondered.

"She's got his nose wide open and he don't want to admit it," Winston said, nodding shrewdly.

"Why you so snappish with Talley?" Marcus finally asked Cole. "She may come from a wealthy family, but she's shown us all that she ain't too uppity to work hard. She keeps the place neat and she's always nice to everyone."

"Yeah," Cole muttered. "I can't complain."

"Then why do you sweat her? She seems real eager to please you," Marcus pressed. "She does extra stuff, then smiles all over herself when you notice it."

"I haven't seen anything like that," Cole responded.

Marcus rolled his eyes. "Tell that to somebody who'll believe it."

"I don't know what you mean."

"Okay, man, how about what she did with the office?"

Talley had been decorating. There were plants everywhere now. She'd rummaged around in the storage area and found a colorful poster series of red, white and blue classic cars Cole had had for years.

She'd mounted them in Plexiglas frames for the reception area. Thanks to her Internet auction search, there was even a bright red and gray and blue Oriental rug in the entranceway.

The old stained and scuffed brown office chairs that once graced the waiting room, facing a battered TV, were replaced by stainless steel seating with gray and red leather. Marcus said Talley had found them cheap at an office furniture warehouse sale she'd seen announced in the newspaper. Flourishing green plants topped the TV now, masking its age and blending it with the cleanly eclectic rooms.

"It looks nice in here," Cole said to Talley one day, sparking an ear-to-ear grin from her. "You got a real nice touch."

"I just added a few things that I got at a sale," she told him. "I'm glad you're pleased."

"Yeah, it looks, uh…real good." Cole basked in the glow of her smile for a moment, then forced himself to turn away. Thinking back on his conversation with Marcus, he thought his brother might have a point. But Cole was determined that he wasn't giving it up. Talley Quincy Pettifore was first, last and always a rich girl. Despite evidence to the contrary, it wasn't likely that Talley could ever return his growing affection. She was not for him. *The rich are different,* he believed. *And Talley bleeds blue.*

⁓〇

The bulk of TowMaster's business was emergency rescue work for Triple A and ferrying cars around the metropolitan area for various automobile dealerships.

"Eventually I'd like to have a fleet of big Peterbilt trucks transporting classic and luxury vehicles in enclosed trailers from coast to coast," Cole told Talley. "I have the name 'TranportMasters' registered for that purpose. Thing is, trucks cost as much as a house, and I need to have the business confirmed before I spend $100,000 or more."

"I'd like to help with that," Talley said. "I can work on developing new business for you."

Talley was ready to take on that challenge. If there was one thing she knew, it was rich people and the love they had for their expensive cars.

While going through the mail, Talley noticed an announcement of the sale of raffle tickets to win a free "Marketing Makeover" from the Atlanta Business League, courtesy of The Boyd Group. She decided to persuade Cole to buy a handful of tickets for TransportMasters. If they won, she'd get help introducing and marketing the new division.

When Cole told Talley he'd like to take her to meet his major client, Greg Carver, at the Porsche dealership, Talley dressed for the occasion in a sleek black business suit with a slim skirt and peplum jacket. Walking into the showroom with her, Cole noticed heads swiveling. The understated elegance of her well-tailored designer outfit was like a clarion. It was as though he were invisible as salesmen stumbled over one another to try to reach her first and sell her a car.

When Cole took Talley's arm and began introducing her as his new office manager, jaws dropped. While Cole took care of some details with the accounting department, Talley sat and chatted comfortably with Greg about cars, the transport business and "the care and special handling of the upper-class customer."

Greg slapped Cole on the back as they left and said, "Give me a call later, I might have some good news for you."

"You made quite an impact in there," Cole said on their way home. Talley didn't notice his tight, ironic smile. "Those salesmen can smell money a mile coming. They were all over you."

"I suppose it's their job," she suggested.

"With some people, it's a religion," he sneered.

Talley stared at his profile. "You're mad at the salesmen for wanting to try to sell me a car?"

"No…not that…it's just…hell, they were just *too* impressed."

"But…I thought that was why you took me there," she said. "To impress them. To show me off. That's why I dressed up."

Cole's jaws tightened. "You know, I've been working for them for years now. I've been dependable and honorable. I've taken the heat for them when they made mistakes with the cars. Now, just because he's seen you, Greg is going to have some 'good news' for me. It's all so damn phony. The grinnin' and skinnin'…just because someone has a little money."

"So you're saying that you don't like money. You don't want anything to do with it," she teased.

Cole refused to lighten up. The subject was too sore with him. "I just don't like the way it makes people act. Those with it think they run the world, and can do and say anything they want to. And people around them suck up and let them walk all over them. It makes me sick to my stomach."

Talley was silent, listening to his diatribe. There was a lot of pain and hatred in it and she wondered where it came from.

"Not all rich people are like that," she said in a small voice.

Cole looked at her, startled, and stopped abruptly. "Hey, I'm not talking about you and Michael. You're different. You've got class."

"So do you," she said.

Cole's lips twitched. "Now that's crazy."

Talley could have argued with him further. She had been taught by her lovely democratic mother that "class" had nothing to do with money and social status and everything to do with kindness, generosity, honor and "good home training," all of which Cole had in abundance.

⟿

In the past weeks Talley had accomplished a number of personal tasks. She'd found a little townhouse near Cole's office in College Park, a southern suburb of Atlanta with a large middle-class African American population, and had enrolled Michael "Parsons" in a small African American private school in Southwest Atlanta. It had taken a good chunk of her money and a long conversation with the principal, but they had allowed the discrepancy in the names on Michael's birth certificate and health records.

She'd sorted through her loot from Marshall's safe at the house and sent back most of it through Jerome. She kept the cash and the small twenty-two caliber pistol. *A woman alone needs some protection,* Talley rationalized as she hid the gun in a shoebox in her closet.

Cole did not reveal Talley's secret to his family. His brothers continued to tease and accept her and Michael as though they were just plain "folks" and that was fine with Talley. She met "Lanky Lucy"—as the boys called their older sister, and the two very different young women clicked immediately. They bonded over shopping, with Lucy leading Talley on an eye-opening tour of wholesale furniture stores and warehouse clubs to furnish and stock her new town-house.

"Mind boggling," Talley breathed as she pushed a shopping cart piled high through Sam's Club. Lucy giggled at Talley's wide-eyed wonder, amazed that the lovely woman had never bought her own groceries before.

"Talley, you crack me up. Please don't buy a ten-pound can of black olives. I don't care how much you love them," Lucy warned.

It was from Lucy that Talley learned the sacrifice that Cole had made for his family and the root cause of his anger at wealthy black people.

"Mom and Dad were killed by a drunk teenager in a fancy car—a black kid from a 'famous' Black Enterprise 100 family," Lucy told her over Starbucks coffee after one of their shopping forays. "The boy's parents hired an expensive attorney who got him off with just the proverbial 'slap on the wrist.' We were all angry and so frustrated with helplessness. But Cole was the worst. He hasn't been able to let it go."

Talley thoughtfully stirred sugar into her latte. "How long ago?"

"Eleven years. Cole was nineteen and in his freshman year at Morehouse. I'd finished school and was teaching sixth grade. The boys were still in elementary and junior high school."

Talley had a vision of the family in dark clothing huddled together at a double gravesite and gave a shiver. "That's so tragic. I'm so sorry."

"It's worse than that," Lucy sighed, leaning forward to touch Talley's hand. "Cole had to quit school and take a job so we could keep the family together and make ends meet. I know he was devastated. But he never showed it. Not to the boys, anyway."

"Oh!" It was as though Talley felt the sharp pain of it herself.

"Yeah," Lucy said sadly, reading the sympathy in Talley's expression. "Grandma used to say to him, 'There will be stars in your crown in heaven'."

"Where did he work?"

"He knows and loves cars, so he took a job as an auto detailer at a Porsche dealership. They loved him there, 'cause he's a smart and dependable hard worker but I knew he didn't like it. Then, three years ago, when Grandpa, we called him Big Daddy, made our aunts and Uncle Winfrey mad by leaving Cole the ten acres of land, he fulfilled a dream by starting his own business."

"I can tell that Cole loves his business," Talley smiled.

"You betcha!" His sister grinned back.

～⌒⌐

Marshall was in his mother's bedroom lounging in her floral lilac slipper chair, paying a good bit of attention to what Martine was putting on that evening to go to a reception at Mayor Archer's residence.

Martine loved having her son advising her on her toilette. She was proud he had such a good eye for a flattering style or an enhancing color. She gave herself credit for his fully developed taste in clothes. Growing up, she'd encouraged him to shop with her, to feel the fabrics, to know what was acceptable and what was not.

"You should wear the pearls, Mama," he said now. "They will glow against that brocade fabric."

"Are you sure you won't go with us?" she asked him.

He made a face. "I hate being around those stiff folk."

Martine gave him a disapproving look.

Marshall sighed and unfolded his long legs, sauntering over to his mother to plant a kiss. "Besides, I've got something else to do," he said.

"Wait," she said, catching his arm, "Don't go yet. Tell me what's going on with Tallulah. Your father is up to something."

"I don't know much. I know she's somewhere in Atlanta and I know I want her back here," Marshall said.

"You love her, don't you?" his mother asked.

"Let's just say she's the only one who knows me," Marshall said sardonically.

"What about me?" his mother said jealously.

"You think you know me," Marshall said, twisting his thin mouth, "but I believe I could still surprise you."

"I think you would be the one surprised," Martine said, her gaze burning. "You hit that girl, didn't you?"

"I will admit to losing my temper with her," he said.

"It had to be more than that," Martine insisted. "We all know what a mild and submissive girl Talley is. She wouldn't have just up and left because you lost your temper."

"She's not as easy to get along with as you think," Marshall whined.

"I overheard your father speaking to Robert Edwards in Atlanta. Apparently Talley has proof on videotape of you hitting her."

"That tape will never see daylight. Edwards has the only copy."

"The detective thinks Tallulah made another copy."

"I...I hadn't heard that," Marshall said nervously. "That doesn't sound like Talley."

"Perhaps Tallulah *is* a lot shrewder than we've given her credit for. She was conniving enough to make the tape. She probably did make copies," Martine frowned.

"You know, I think I might just go down to Atlanta," Marshall said suddenly. "I know a lot of people there. And I might be able to be helpful to that detective."

"I wouldn't do that if I were you," Martine said. "Leave it to the professionals."

Marshall didn't look convinced.

CHAPTER SIX

Alicia was on the phone to her married sister in Montgomery talking about Joe.

"I've met someone, Boo," she said, trying to calm the exhilaration in her voice. "He's a darlin'!"

"He must be," Barbara said. "I've never heard you this excited."

"I'm tryin' to contain myself, but it ain't easy. He makes my heart go pitty-pat."

"Good Lord, chile! Do Mom an' I need to come down there?"

"Not yet. I jus' met 'im. I got to hook 'im and reel 'im in first." Alicia laughed gaily.

"Seriously, Ali, where's he from? What's he do? Who's his family? Is he a Morehouse man?"

"His name is Joe Griffin. He's from Detroit. He's a private investigator, a partner with his father in a firm called Griffin Investigations. His father was a policeman. Joe's an ex-marine."

"Oooh, sexy," Barbara breathed.

"He's rugged-lookin' and muscular. Got a voice that almost made my clothes fall off. All male," Alicia said. "But he has the sweetest smile. Big dimples in his cheeks. Makes him look like a big kid."

"How'd you meet him?"

"Well, that's the problem."

"Oh Jesus, I knew there was gonna be a problem."

"It's bad, but not too bad. He's in town looking for my girl Talley. You remember, Tallulah Quincy Pettifore."

"Your college roommate? The rich one?" Alicia's parents were both surgeons and could lay claim to considerable wealth, but Talley had still been "the rich one" all through her years at Spelman.

"That's the one. She took her son and ran off from her husband. Her family hired Joe to look for them. She's here in Atlanta and he thinks she either has or is gonna contact me."

"Has she?"

"Not yet."

"So what're you gonna do?"

"If Talley's left her husband—and, you know, I never liked him anyway—it's for a good reason. I told Joe I wouldn't be the one to give her away."

"What'd he say?"

"He said he'd just have to stick close to me in case she does contact me." Alicia said with a giggle. "I told him he could stick as close as he wanted to. The closer the better."

"Oh no, you didn't."

"I sure did."

"You heifer," her sister squealed.

"If you saw him, you'd understand. He brings out the bad girl in me."

"Stop! Listen at you!"

—cᴏ

With Claudia's assistance, Narye slipped out of the Farmington house with a small bag and was hugging Talley tightly at the Atlanta airport before anyone noticed she was gone.

On the ride home from the airport, Michael snuggled up to Narye and whispered something in her ear. She laughed and said, "Of course, *mon petit*, as soon as we get home."

"What's he asking you?" Talley wanted to know.

"He wants me to fix him something good to eat," she said.

"You ungrateful wretch," Talley growled, poking at her son playfully. "I slave over a hot stove for you and this is the thanks I get."

"Mom, everything you cook gets all black around the edges," Michael said with a pained look.

"That's okay," Talley said, faking hurt feelings. "I'll never, ever cook for you again."

"Oh good." He sighed in relief.

Narye made a chiding noise. "Don't be rude, little one. Manners make the man, you know." Then she turned to Talley. "You've been cooking?"

"You bet," Talley preened. "But I haven't yet got the hang of that stove."

"What kind is it?"

"The kind with round burners on top."

"Oh yes, Miss Tallulah," Narye replied solemnly. "Those can be difficult."

———⌒⌒———

That night after Michael was fed, washed and put to bed, Talley sat at the counter of the tiny kitchenette watching Narye deftly wipe and put away their few dishes.

"I've missed you more than anything," Talley said. "I know Michael has too."

"Thank you, *ma petite.*"

"I don't think I can pay you what you were getting…"

"Hush. Don't speak of it. I am quite comfortable after all these years. Besides, you and Michael are my only family. We will make our way together."

"I did the right thing in leaving," Talley said.

"I agree."

"I'm never going back."

"I think it best. But we must be very careful not to be found. Mr. Marshall is very angry. And Mr. Cedric would stop at nothing to get his grandson back."

"I've already cautioned Michael. Over and over, Narye, I've drilled him on our new names and all the little details. I hope no one will think to look for us in these circumstances."

"This new life will be a difficult adjustment."

"It's not hard at all," Talley argued. "I'm loving it. I have a job. I'm making friends—wait until you meet the Colemans. Especially Cole."

Narye turned and looked at Talley sharply. She heard a caress in Talley's voice when she said Cole's name.

"You like this Mr. Cole?"

"Yes I do," Talley said, not noticing the shrewd look Narye gave her. "He's the nicest man. He's been incredibly helpful to us. And I'm learning new things from him about business every day!"

Smiling, Narye shook her head. "You're like a child. Excited by an adventure. But hopefully you won't have to stay hidden in this tiny place for long. You would soon begin to miss your old life."

"I know. Alicia used to say, 'Poverty sucks. Absolute poverty sucks absolutely.'"

"This is not poverty, Miz Tallulah," Narye said with a frown. "I hope you never feel the hopelessness and despair of absolute poverty."

"I know," Talley said, chastened.

"Your mother sent money. All the cash she could get her hands on. It's only about $6,000, but she didn't want to raise suspicions by going to the bank for more."

"Good! Tonight you sleep on my new couch. But tomorrow we go to *Rooms to Go* and buy you a whole bedroom suite for under $1,000! Can you imagine?"

"Go to bed," Narye smiled, shaking her head.

～৫১

For their first few weeks in Atlanta, Talley and Michael stuck close to home or to the office, using surface roads and feeling fearful every time they had to take the Michigan-tagged Range Rover out on the highway. But as time went on without discovery, the runaways began to relax in their new setting and take chances.

One Saturday, Talley, Narye and Michael were blithely on their way up the center lane on Interstate 85 North, a main thoroughfare through the city, headed for Home Depot's big Expo store, when Michael said "Mommy, there's some men waving at us."

Narye looked out of her window on the passenger side into the face of a tough-looking man motioning them to pull over in front of him. The long, black luxury sedan had the driver and a second man in it.

"I don't believe they are policemen," Narye said, puzzled.

"Oh no, oh no," Talley breathed as she pressed down hard on the gas. "It must be some of Cedric's detectives."

Talley fumbled frantically in her purse for her new cell phone and tossed it to Narye while she sped through traffic, weaving in and out of cars dangerously. "Push one two," she shouted at Narye. "It's Cole's programmed number." Talley was not an accomplished driver, but with her adrenalin pumping, she was determined to lose these men.

"They're still behind us, Mommy," Michael cried. "They're honking at us."

The cars raced against one another, hindered by traffic on the crowded freeway. Michael caught the fear in his mother's face and started to cry in the back seat.

"Mommy, make them go away. Don't let them catch us."

"I'm trying, baby." Talley's brows were knit, her lips tightly pressed together as she bent over the wheel, focused on wending her way through cars as fast as she could. Images of Marshall backhanding her, knocking her across the room, raced through her mind. She heard Michael's high-pitched voice asking, *"Daddy, is it Halloween?"*

They're not going to get us, she said to herself over and over again. *We're not going back there.*

Narye was breathing deeply, trying to maintain her composure as cars sped by them, when Cole came on the phone line.

"What's up, Talley?" he asked cheerfully.

"Mr. Cole, we are headed north on I-85, and we are being chased by some men," Narye screamed into the phone. "We believe they are detectives hired by Talley's father-in-law. What to do?"

"How far are you from 'Spaghetti Junction'?" Cole wanted to know, recognizing Narye's voice and grasping the situation immediately. "I mean, from I-285?"

Narye looked out the window as they zoomed by a direction sign, "Two miles from I-285."

"What kind of car are they driving?"

"It is a large black car. Very long, very shiny," she said, clutching the phone with white knuckles.

"Talley knows my truck. I'm coming up I-285 east near I-85," Cole said. "Tell her to just keep ahead of them. I'm going to merge onto 85 between you if I can. As soon as I get in front of them, y'all need to go like the wind."

"Exactly, sir."

Knowing what needed to be done, Cole gripped his steering wheel tighter, and dropped a heavy boot to the gas. Responsive as a well-trained stallion, the big rig jumped to do his bidding. Cole spotted the big black car as soon as he got on the access road. His timing could not have been better. Quickly and surely, with the practice of having driven his big vehicle in Atlanta for years, he downshifted, easing into traffic and moving into the center lane in front of the black sedan. Then he slowed to a snail's pace, while Talley whizzed ahead, getting lost in the crowded five-lane highway.

Trapped behind Cole's truck, the men in the sedan slammed on brakes and leaned on their horn, but they never saw Talley turn off the interstate onto a surface road and disappear.

"Thank you, Cole. Thank you," Talley wept into the phone Narye held for her.

"No problem," he said calmly. "We were lucky this time. You need to trade the Rover in. It's too noticeable."

"I will. I'll do it today!"

⎯⎯◌⎯⎯

Marshall stood in his father's office staring blindly at the portrait of his great-great-grandfather Pettifore, the founder of the firm, hanging behind his father's desk.

This first Michael Pettifore had been born in Detroit in 1850. The son of a free houseman in the home of a white attorney, young Michael had been fascinated by the sartorial splendor of his father's employer whenever the attorney was going to appear in court.

"I want to be a lawyer so I can dress like that," he told his father. This, repeated to the employer, tickled the man so much he financed Michael's education through law school.

Michael Pettifore graduated from Howard University Law School in Washington, D.C., in 1872. In 1884, after practicing in Washington, D.C. for twelve years, he returned to Detroit and worked in his mentor's law firm for ten years before meeting Malcolm Quincy, the son of a barber, who had received his law degree from the University of Michigan in 1888.

The two joined forces in 1894 to win freedom for a young black man unjustly accused of murder. The defendant's church held pew rallies to raise money to pay the two lawyers for his defense.

When Michael's son, Christian, finished law school in 1902, the firm of Pettifore, Pettifore and Quincy was established.

Over the years as blacks flooded into Detroit, attracted by the high wages of the auto industry, the firm grew rich handling civil rights cases, representing labor unions, and continuing their criminal work.

The firm drew the attention of the white power structure in Detroit in the 1940s when they won their lawsuit against Ford Motor Company for a black worker injured on the job. They were then hired by Ford to assist with union negotiations.

By the time Marshall stood quaking in front of his father's desk waiting for Cedric to come out of his private bathroom, PPQ had more than three hundred employees of both races and billed more than one hundred and eighty million dollars annually.

Cedric walked in, wiping his hands on a small towel.

"I understand from Paul Griffin that Talley's Asian housekeeper has disappeared from your household," he said.

"What?" Marshall was stunned.

"You didn't notice," his father said with disgust.

"Dad, we have a lot people working at the house. Talley handled everything. How am I supposed to keep track of one little chink maid?" Marshall whined.

"So, you know nothing about how the woman left or where she went," Cedric said tiredly.

Petulant, Marshall shrugged. "She was Talley's servant. I guess she went to Talley. I don't know how it happened. How am I supposed to know?"

"You're hopeless," his father ranted. "I'm surrounded by incompetence. Joe Griffin tells me that his detectives in Atlanta spotted the Range Rover, then lost it somehow. Now you…The next thing I know, Talley's entire household staff will be in Atlanta and you probably won't even notice. Get out of my sight!"

⁓

Roberta McAfee stood in front of the mirror and pulled her faux satin negligee tight across her hips. The soft mound of her stomach and deep belly button molded against the fabric. She held her breath, sucking in the stomach. Roberta was a tall, shapely woman, with sable-colored skin and gleaming black hair, which she wore pulled back from her strong-boned face.

Earlier in the evening she'd phoned Cole and persuaded him to drop by. Though it hadn't been easy to talk him into coming, she was eagerly anticipating his arrival. Their last fight had been harsh and they hadn't spoken in nearly a month. She'd finally convinced him he needed to come pick up a box of belongings he'd left in her apartment. Once he got there, though, she knew she could seduce him into staying. They had fought many times before and made up. And the makeup sex was always intensely gratifying.

Roberta and Cole had been dating off and on since college. Both Atlanta natives, they'd known each other as children. Roberta had been with Cole when he found out his parents were dead. She'd ached for him when he had to quit school in his sophomore year at Morehouse. They had come close to getting married after Big Daddy, Cole's grandfather, left Cole the land and it looked like the Colemans' financial troubles would be over.

But the relationship had gone rocky when Cole wouldn't sell the land and return to school. Instead he'd mortgaged the land to buy trucks. His decision to start a towing business instead had thrown her. *Who and what does he think he is? TowMasters. More like "Po'Masters,"* she thought. Miss Roberta McAfee had no interest in marrying a struggling truck driver. Roberta's father was a university professor and her mother a high school principal. Roberta had gotten a master of business administration degree in finance from Boston University. She worked for an elite brokerage firm in upscale Buckhead and was surrounded by men who wore suits and ties every day.

She and Cole fought about her constant correction of his English, his intense dislike of the people he called her "phony" friends, and his parking his tow truck in front of her building.

The first time Roberta had seriously broken up with Cole, it had been in order to date a promising stockbroker at her office. But he'd been transferred to the New York office, and the relationship didn't survive the distance. Set adrift, Roberta had called Cole and begged him to come back.

The second breakup fight had been about his objection to Roberta's insistence on introducing him to her friends as an "entrepreneur in the transportation industry." The invective had been bitter, but the makeup sex had been sweet.

This last time, she'd wanted to buy him a tuxedo to attend a fundraiser for the One Hundred Black Men of Atlanta.

"I don't care about those one hundred fat cats," Cole had said.

"As long as you stay black in this city, you need to care about them," she'd insisted. "They can make or break our social life."

"You know what, Ro, we're never going to agree about how to live our lives, are we?" he'd sighed. "Why don't we just call it a day," he said.

"Why don't we?" she'd agreed.

Roberta had gone to that gala event with a lawyer she knew. But when she'd brought him back to her place and let him spend the night, it had been a very disappointing experience. There was no one in the world that could thrill her to her core like Cole. She loved him. She was sure he loved her. He just needed to learn to appreciate and accept the lifestyle she wanted for them.

The doorbell rang.

"Alright," Cole said briskly when she answered the door. "Where's my stuff?"

"Oh come on in, Cole," she urged softly. "I haven't seen you in weeks."

He stood at the doorway, fidgeting with his cap, trying not to look at her seductive body. The negligee was backlit, and the outline of her lush curves was clearly visible. He was having flashbacks of the many nights of passionate sex they had enjoyed together.

When he stepped inside the apartment, she turned away from him to close the door, a smug smile lighting her face. *I knew it,* she thought triumphantly.

Roberta acted quickly, pressing the advantage of surprise. Her eager fingers snagged Cole's cotton work shirt and held tight. Pulling him close, she slipped one hand under the shirt, tracing his chest to the tight flatness of his nipples. Her thumb and forefinger teased a knotting bud as she looked deep into the blue-green swirl of his gaze.

"You could take that old box of yours, or…" Her tongue deliberately swept the fullness of her lips. "…or I could give you something we both know you'd like."

Cole blew out a quick breath. "We've done this dance before…"

"And we can again," Roberta purred, tugging Cole closer. She lifted his shirt and pressed her lips to his skin, felt the flush of victory when he moaned.

Cole's fingers were hot and urgent, as they slipped the negligee from her shoulders. She shrugged free of it, wiggling with purpose and desire. Naked, she worked at the buttons of Cole's trousers while he clasped her in strong arms.

"Come with me," she whispered roughly, dragging him by the front of his pants. He followed.

In her bed, Cole's grip on her body was rough and demanding, leading her where she wanted to go. When she stretched her legs wide for his plunge into her welcoming core, he threw his head back and blindly delved deep, seeking release.

She tightened her legs around his lean hips and ground into him, desperate not to lose him. As their breath quickened together, she met him thrust for heated thrust.

Later, Roberta and Cole lay together in the dark, spent and relaxed. Roberta slowly rubbed her hand across Cole's big chest and his concave stomach.

"Whatever we have problems with, we never lose this, do we?" she murmured. "It's always good."

"Mmm," he responded noncommittally.

"You hungry? You want me to get you something to eat?"

"Naw, I gotta get home," Cole said, sitting on the side of the bed and reaching for his underwear.

"You're not going to spend the night?"

"I gotta get up early in the morning."

"That's never stopped you from staying the night in the past. You always like your morning quickie," she whispered seductively, rubbing against his back.

He shrugged away from her and stood.

"What is this?" she asked angrily. "You're just going to use my body for a flash and leave?"

Sliding his work pants over his legs, he looked at the lush body she displayed so wantonly, then shook his head. "Ro, you wanted this as much as me. You're the one come to the door half naked."

"This is my home. I *came* to the door in my negligee because it was late and I was ready to go to bed."

"There you go, correcting my English again."

"I'm sorry," she said, quickly coming to her knees on the bed. "Please stay. Please? I want us to talk some more. After all, we still love each other. We proved that tonight."

"We proved we enjoy each other's body," Cole corrected. "But that's got to stop, because it isn't enough."

"Are you saying you don't love me anymore?" Roberta asked, her eyes wide and incredulous.

"I'm not saying that, Ro. I'll always love you in some way. I'm just saying we aren't going to make it together. We don't want or need the same things."

"Things like what, Cole?"

"I need someone who's in my corner helping me with my business."

Roberta stood, clutching a pillow in front of her. "We've had this conversation so many times before. You know I'm in your corner. I just wish you'd give up this truck-driving thing and go back to school. I can support both of us while you finish college," she said.

"We shouldn't have done this tonight," he sighed, rubbing his forehead.

"Yes, we should have," she insisted. "We both needed to reaffirm our love. We've been apart for a whole month!"

"You're not listening to me, Ro. I don't think we should see each other anymore. We just torture each other." Cole was dressed now, heading for the door. The pillow was forgotten as Roberta clung to his hand, dragging herself along with him.

"Let me go." He lifted her hand away.

"Aw, Cole, don't do this," she whined, her need as naked as her body. "We belong together. Why do you think we keep coming back to each other?"

"This is it. I'm not coming back anymore." He pushed the restraining hand from his arm.

"You say that now. Now that you got your rocks off," she hissed, suddenly angry. "But wait 'til your nature rises again. You'll be back." She slammed the door behind him.

Cole climbed into his truck and sat for a few minutes, the muscle along the square line of his jaw working. He hated scenes with Roberta. He'd loved her deeply once. It caused him great pain each time they broke up. This past breakup really had been final for him, and he'd hoped she'd understand. If only he hadn't weakened tonight. But she'd looked so good in that sheer black nightgown.

He leaned forward and put his head down on the steering wheel. *The worse thing is…the whole time I was with Ro, I wasn't with her at all. I put my hand on her skin, and I felt the softness that I know would be*

Talley. Roberta's breast was full and heavy in my mouth and I looked for the sweetness that I know would be Talley. Then, when I hit it, when I should have been giving Ro all I had...all I could see was Talley. Everything was Talley.

He stopped and looked out at the night beyond his truck window. *What the hell am I thinking? Talley isn't for me.* If Roberta, who had grown up with him in the same neighborhood, rejected his lifestyle and looked down on him, how on earth could he ever aspire to someone like Talley? He wondered if she even noticed he was a man. Generally around people like her he was the "invisible man." *People like her don't really think of truck drivers or bus boys or car washers as human.*

Talley knew Cole was a man, all right. Cole would have been surprised and very encouraged if he'd known what was going on in her honey-gold head.

Whenever he walked into the trailer, shaking the whole structure with heavy black boots, his six feet, three inches of height and his broad shoulders, Talley felt her heart speed up, her stomach clutch. She couldn't help comparing Cole's robust masculinity to Marshall's attenuated, overbred elegance.

Talley took great joy in Cole's approval. She insisted he teach her to drive a flatbed truck and basked in his pride when she mastered complicated turns in the parking lot in front of the office trailer.

She loved the way Cole smelled—like leather and gasoline mixed with a subtle, husky man scent. She found ways to touch his arm and his hand accidentally on purpose. Once she'd laid her hand on his upper arm and when he clenched it reflexively, the muscle bulged under her fingertips. She'd felt a fluttering in her abdomen and realized that his animal virility both attracted and frightened her.

She knew he was a man, alright. And the new feelings he awakened in her were crying out to be explored.

⌒

Towing was a 24/7 business, Talley soon learned, and someone had to be in the office all the time. Talley and Vickie, who had become fast friends, worked days and weekends, and a couple of college students worked nights. Vickie's new boyfriend, Jamal Foreman, started using his own tow truck to pull for Cole. With the added income to the business Cole began talking about putting up a permanent structure on the land.

Isolated as they were at Cole's impound yard, word still spread about the 'foxy new assistant' Cole Coleman had working for him. Other truck drivers dropped in to get a look at her and wink at Cole. One Saturday brought Uncle Winfrey to the yard to satisfy the family curiosity.

When Uncle Winfrey pulled up, Michael and Cole were washing Talley's new BMW SUV while Narye waited in the office.

"That's a pretty fancy ride you got there," he said to Cole with a tight smile. "When'd you get it?" Jealous resentment flashed in his eyes as he recalled how Big Daddy had cut him and his two sisters out of the will, leaving Cole the land he was standing on.

"It's not mine," Cole said quickly. "It belongs to this young man and his mother, my new assistant." He indicated Michael.

"The office gal?" Winfrey asked incredulously.

Cole nodded and went back to scrubbing a tire.

"You payin' your help mighty rich, ain't cha?"

"I guess so." Cole winked at Michael, who giggled and winked back.

Winston and Marcus came out of the office and spoke to their uncle. They leaned against the side of the trailer and hid smiles as they watched Cole wielding his wet rag on the car.

"What're *you* doin' washin' it?" Uncle Winfrey wanted to know.

"It needed cleaning," Cole said. The brothers began to snicker.

"Uh oh," Uncle Winfrey said, looking at Cole's brothers with a chuckle. "We all know what that means, don't we?" Cole's tendency to wash the cars of women that he fancied had always been a subject for ribbing.

They started to laugh out loud.

"Didn't he used to be washin' on Roberta McAfee's car all the time?" his uncle asked. "And I seem to recall in high school him scrubbin' on li'l Linda's car…"

"What do they mean, Mr. Cole?" Michael asked quietly. "Why are they laughing?"

"They're just crazy. Pay them no attention," Cole said.

Just then Talley walked out of the office to see what the commotion was. Even in relaxed jeans and a bulky sweater, her beauty and elegance were apparent. She smiled expectantly at the newcomer.

Uncle Winfrey stopped laughing immediately and stood silent, goggling at her. Winston and Marcus watched him with big satisfied grins.

"Talley, come meet my Uncle Winfrey," Cole said.

Talley held out her hand gracefully and approached Winfrey. He wiped his hand on his shirt before taking hers. Then he bowed and kissed the air over her hand.

"Pleased to meet you."

"I'm delighted. What were you all laughing so hard about?"

"Just some foolishness."

"Cole, when you get a chance, would you come take a look at these dispatch forms I've ordered?" Talley asked.

"Yeah, I'll be in in a few," Cole mumbled.

She walked back into the trailer and Uncle Winfrey let his breath out with a loud puff.

"Nephew. She gon' take your heart, squeeze all the juice out of it and then hand it back to you shriveled up like a nut," he said quietly.

"Nothing's going on there," Cole insisted.

"You tryin' to tell me you ain't in love with that gal?"

"That's right. We're just working together."

"You got that right," Uncle Winfrey agreed. "And don't you forget it."

Uncle Winfrey's advice went unheeded.

~⌒~

Cole could not help being seduced by Talley's interest in the business to which he was devoted. She shared in his excitement as new clients were signed, her eyes sparkling as she handed him crisp paperwork or created a new file for the additional business.

Cole noticed that she was reading towing and trucking magazines in an effort to get up to speed in the industry. The sight of her intently studying *Towing Times*, twirling a shining curl with a slender finger, took his heart.

Slowly, he relaxed his cool manner with her and began spending more and more time with her. They worked quietly together reviewing paperwork or discussing new ways to promote the business.

"We need to develop a mailing list of collision repair shops," Talley suggested. "Send them a good-looking flier."

"That's a good idea," Cole nodded. "Can you make that happen?"

"I believe I can if that's what you want. We could send it to gas stations too." She nodded, her curls bobbing around her face. "And…we should create a compelling web site!"

"You like this, don't you?" Cole grinned.

"I guess I've got business in my blood. I'm loving it."

"Well, I've got something I want to run by you."

"Okay." Talley looked up eagerly, her amber eyes bright with intelligence and something Cole couldn't name focused clearly on him.

"The city requires the approval of the Neighborhood Planning Unit before we can build another structure on this land. I gotta make a presentation."

"I'd love to work with you on it," Talley said. "I've had to give presentations almost all my life for the charities and civic groups I've worked with. I'm an old hand."

"Good, because I hate speaking to crowds."

"You'll be fine, once we practice. Your natural honesty will come out, if you let it."

She walked across and stood in front of him, taking his hands. "For example, when you talk, make open gestures with your hands. It will make people feel invited to listen to you."

Cole tingled at her touch and forced his eyes away from the swell of her neat bosom. *Lord, what have I got myself into?*

At the podium of the Neighborhood Center later that week, Cole took a deep breath, and Talley felt as though it surged through her own breast. They had grown so close in the last few days as they prepared for this speech that she felt they were sharing the same emotions. His presentation was compelling and articulate. She couldn't help feeling pride and elation when the vote was in his favor.

"Well done!" Talley applauded.

"It helped to see you smiling at me," Cole grinned. "I just talked directly to you."

"You sounded great."

"My English is always better around you," he said. "You don't make me nervous correcting my mistakes."

"I don't care about your minor mistakes. You always mean the right things."

Cole carried a natural air of authority, a gentle dignity that encouraged respect. In truth Talley liked everything about him—the kind and temperate way he treated his brothers and the way he taught Michael manly self-confidence by example. Cole was shy and courtly around strange women and gentle and respectful with the elderly. And when the drunk and angry people whose cars he had towed and impounded acted up, he soothed their hostility with a polite and restrained manner.

"Sometimes those rude people make me so mad," Talley told Lucy. "I don't know how Cole keeps from punching them."

"Cole has a terrible temper that he has to keep under tight control," Lucy responded. "When he was a teenager he was arrested for beating up some ole white guy who called him the 'N' word. He beat him to a pulp. The case was dropped once the police found out the man and a group of his friends had challenged Cole to 'step outside' and then had thrown the first punch."

"Really?" Talley was amazed.

"And he can be overly sensitive, too," Lucy warned her. "He'll get his feelings hurt at the drop of a hat by one small thing or another. Then he broods."

Lucy saw her concern and chuckled. "You don't have to worry, he'll never get mad at you. And as long as he keeps washing your car for you, you'll know you're still his friend."

Talley never saw evidence of Cole's temper and her respect for him continued to grow by leaps and bounds. The more she learned from Lucy of the sacrifices he had made for his family, the more she admired him.

His strength and independence in starting this business alone and from scratch impressed her. She saw in him the same pioneering courage and spirit that she believed had driven her great-great-grandfather and his partner when they founded Pettifore, Pettifore and Quincy, LLC 100 years earlier.

One evening, Talley came upon Cole in his office poring over projections his accountant had sent him.

"Oh," she said. "I didn't know you were still here. The night dispatcher just came in. I was going to turn out the light."

"I'm just trying to make sense out of these numbers. I want to find a way to pay all the expenses, taxes, salaries, truck maintenance, insurances and still have enough left over to get a bigger truck." He sighed. "I borrowed against the land to buy the first two trucks. I don't want to have to keep doing that."

"I wish I could be more helpful to you," she said. "I took art courses when I should have been taking business or accounting courses."

"You probably never thought you'd need to read a spreadsheet," Cole said. "All I ever dreamed about was going in to business for myself. I'd hoped to get a business degree and bank some money and experience at a larger corporation before I took the plunge. But I didn't have the time."

Watching him bend his head over the figures in front of him, Talley thought about how carelessly she used to spend thousands of dollars on shoes or clothes in one shopping spree and shivered with the shame of it. That money could have paid salaries for months for Cole.

After working together on the speech, Talley and Cole's relationship took on a new depth. They fell into the habit of having lunch together whenever he was free and near the office. Talley was surprised to discover how much she coveted the few private moments the lunches gave them. She'd never before looked forward to spending private time with any man. Their lunchtime conversations were personal and intimate, ranging all over the place

"Did you love your husband?" Cole asked her once.

"No...yes...In a way. Once. Like a brother. We grew up together. We were both lonely as children, but we had each other. I still care about him, I guess. But Marshall...he's under a lot of pressure from the family. He's sick. He needs help."

"He needs an ass kickin'," Cole said grimly.

"Yes, that might help some." She grimaced.

"If he got help, would you go back to him?"

"Of course not. I want a different kind of life. I've been like a thistle blown here and there by the wind. I've never taken control of anything. I want...I need...I don't know...to build something...to be a part of something...like what you're doing."

"Just trying to survive," Cole muttered.

"Oh no, don't you see? It's so much more than that. You're trying to create a legacy, a heritage that will last...to be passed on for generations."

"Hah!" Cole laughed, shyly basking in her admiring smile. "You're right. But I wouldn't have said it so flowery."

"How would you have said it?"

"Just...wanting to make my mark. Something to show I've been here. And...if I have a son..."

Talley's eyes grew misty as she listened to his deep, earnest voice.

"So this is what they sing all those songs about," she murmured.

"Beg pardon?"

Cole jarred her out of her reverie and she grabbed her burger. Hoping to mask her embarrassment, she took a massive bite. Cole chuckled and reached across with his finger to wipe ketchup off her cheek. Talley's heart lurched when he licked the sauce from his finger.

"What were you saying? About songs?"

"Just dreaming," she said, her eyes avoiding his mouth, his lips and his tongue. "What about your dreams?"

"Well, I'd like to go to Europe one day," Cole told her, "see where Porsches are made. See the places you see in James Bond movies and such."

"It would be fun to go back with someone who was seeing it with new eyes," Talley mused.

"I suppose you've been everywhere, haven't you?"" he asked.

"Well, not everywhere," she smiled.

"So if I was to invite you to go with me to Paris, say, it wouldn't be me taking you to someplace new and exciting. It would be old hat to you."

"What difference does it make if we were to go and have fun together?" she wanted to know.

"A man wants to take a woman someplace special," Cole asserted gruffly. "There's nothing I can do for you."

"I've never been to Six Flags," she said.

"What?" Cole was astounded.

"Never."

"Yeah, but you've been skiing in the Alps and skin diving in the Caribbean, haven't you?

"Yes," she admitted.

"See what I mean? You'd be bored going to Six Flags."

I would never be bored going anywhere with you, Talley thought.

⁓

It was not long after Uncle Winfrey's visit to the yard that Aunt Jessie and Aunt Maizie made their way out to inspect the new 'high-falutin'' office girl.

They scoffed at Uncle Winfrey's description of her as "classy," wondering why such a woman would deign to work for a towing company. After spending less than twenty minutes with Talley, they were charmed but still mystified. They, too, were anxious for Cole's heart, which they predicted would soon be stomped on.

"She's nice," Aunt Jessie said later to Lucy. "She's got pretty ways. But Cole needs to look out for hisself. She ain't gon' be interested in him no time soon."

Narye quietly observed that Talley and Cole's friendship was growing. She could find nothing to dislike about Cole. Indeed, as time went on, she found she liked him very much. Though she could tell that Talley was beginning to have feelings beyond friendship for Cole, it would have been impossible for her to object. Cole was completely respectful and courtly with Talley. Narye never saw him put his hands on her in any way she could disapprove of.

This latter fact was a subject of mixed emotions with Talley. Try as she might, she could not help thinking of how safe and warm she'd felt in Cole's arms that first evening at his home and of the frisson of sexual excitement she'd felt when he shuddered against her.

On the other hand, her experiences with Marshall had left her hesitant to explore the physical side of love. From the first night on her honeymoon when Marshall had revealed his twisted need to inflict pain in order to achieve climax and his penchant for women's clothing and cocaine, Talley had tried to suppress her sexuality for fear that if she aroused Marshall, he'd abuse her.

Over the years Talley had begun to see patterns in Marshall's behavior. He'd go for months without coming near her. Sometimes he'd come to her bed and he would just lie there holding her like a child. Then something would trigger his bizarre behavior. A stressful case at work. An argument with his father. Whatever, he would turn into a vicious, doped-up, cross-dressing monster, determined to beat her and rape her viciously.

I would like Cole to hold me again, she admitted to herself shyly. *But he doesn't seem inclined to.* And though she thought about him far too often for comfort, there was no chance of a romantic relationship between them until she got her personal issues resolved.

When Cole remembered his violent reaction to holding her that first time, he tried to shove it into the back of his mind. *Just a natural male response to a pretty woman,* he argued with himself. And, just because he looked forward to their lunches all morning long and spent hours thinking of things to say that would make her eyes dance with laughter, just because he pressed his TowMaster's shirt and the crease in his jeans every morning with special care in case she noticed, well, it didn't necessarily mean anything.

CHAPTER SEVEN

After being in Atlanta for weeks, Joe was no closer to putting his hands on Talley than when he first came down. Other than that one close call when his men had spotted her, then lost her on the freeway, they had not seen hide or hair of Talley and Michael Pettifore.

Joe and his team of investigators spent days visiting the museums, art galleries, and antique shops where Joe thought Talley might have sought employment, and they'd done surveillance at a number of public and private elementary schools in upscale North Atlanta where she might have enrolled Michael.

He had taken one short trip back home to confer with his father when Marshall Pettifore was presented with divorce papers. Then Cedric had had Joe in his office to complain vociferously about his frustrations.

"She is refusing to reveal her whereabouts and the judge has allowed it," Cedric fumed. "My hands are tied because of that damn tape! I need…want the boy here with me," he said.

As Cedric's tongue slipped, Joe caught a glimpse of the pain that the older man was feeling. He felt an involuntary stab of pity.

Cedric lowered his eyes and shuffled papers on his desk.

"There's not a law enforcement officer in the country who would force his way through my gates to take my grandson away once he's here," he continued. "You get him back here by any means necessary."

Joe and his father understood what those "means" might involve. Joe knew he was expected to go around the law, if necessary. Though he was not a thug, nor a brutal man, Joe could do what had to be done with grimly efficient dispatch. The Pettifores had asked for and received those extreme services in the past.

Once Joe had left his office, Cedric cursed himself for the weakness he had revealed to the detective. He thought he had seen pity in the young man's eyes and this infuriated him further. Yet he had to admit where Michael was concerned, he was fragile. His love for the child sometimes overwhelmed him.

When Michael had started school, Cedric had begun to spend as much time as he could manage with the boy, fascinated by Michael's inquisitive mind and youthful athletic aptitude. Watching Michael slam a tennis ball with all of his seven-year-old strength gave Cedric great joy. "He's a budding alpha male," he'd brag to his cronies at his tennis club.

The fact that the boy had also inherited his mother's trusting nature and sweetness of spirit did not concern Cedric. He believed in time he could breed those "flaws" out of the boy. "But not if she keeps me from him," he said aloud.

He was convinced that he had learned from his failures with Marshall. "I should never have left raising him in your hands," he had accused Martine. "I should have started with him earlier. By the time I got to him, he was tainted, ruined."

Martine had never responded to these accusations. She knew it was a waste of time to try to point out that Cedric had always been visibly and vocally repelled by Marshall's effeminate ways.

The more Cedric had bullied Marshall, the deeper the youth—and then the man—had pulled into a shell around his father. He had never shown Cedric the intelligence and sensitivity that she saw.

Except that she was tired of her husband's grousing and complaining, she didn't care if they found Talley and Michael or not. She was only worried that Cedric would heap more blame on Marshall if Joe Griffin didn't find the pair soon.

~ひ~

Joe was eager to get back to Atlanta, but finding Michael was only one of his reasons. He had fallen in love with the city and discussed with his father the possibility of opening a branch office there. "There's a lot of business to be had in Atlanta, particularly for African Americans. It's in a growth mode," he argued.

His real motivation, though, was a bit of brown sugar he'd acquired a strong taste for. He and Alicia had played back and forth mating games for the past few weeks. Though they talked endlessly on the phone and saw each other often, all their dates had been in public places: dinners at restaurants both elegant and casual; biking in Piedmont Park; shopping at Lenox Square; playing bid whist at the homes of Alicia's friends.

Their first deep and serious kiss had been as delicious as his first taste of strawberries dipped in chocolate. At her car in a parking lot, he had leaned her against her door, stretched her arms out to the sides and pressed his full length against her. He'd not stopped kissing her until little purring noises came from her throat.

Joe didn't mind the games, but he was enjoying the play far too much. For reasons related to his hunt for Talley, he needed to get into Alicia's house as soon as possible.

Joe didn't think Alicia had heard from Talley yet, but he was pretty sure she would any day now. He was equally sure her loyalty would prevent her from telling him she'd been contacted. So when the call came, he wanted to have a bug on Alicia's phone line. For that, he needed a few minutes alone in her basement. The rest of the time in her house, however, would be devoted to pure pleasure.

For her part Alicia was just as determined to keep him out of her house until she was sure the relationship had legs. She liked Joe a lot but, at twenty-eight, she'd been hurt more than once. And, much as she enjoyed sex with an attractive partner, she wasn't interested in purely recreational sex. Alicia was looking for a husband.

"You're right, in my work I've seen a lot of marriages fall apart," he said when Alicia broached the subject impersonally over dinner at Veni, Vidi, Vici. "I've taken some ugly pictures," he added.

"I imagine you've got a bad taste in your mouth for marriage," she sighed.

"Nah. It doesn't affect me. I'm not like any of those guys running around on their wives," he said.

"And the women?"

"My wife will be too satisfied to even think of another man," he bragged.

"Oh, please." Alicia gave him a teasing sideways glance from beneath her long, curly lashes.

"No, seriously. I'm an honorable man and loyal. I'm hardworking, neat and easy to get along with. I'm also a good cook."

"You're all that?"

"I'd be a great husband to the right woman. And I'm sure that I'd be a good father."

"Well, that's encouragin', " Alicia said, nodding happily. "But how are you gonna know who's the right woman?"

Joe smiled enigmatically. "Aah, that's the question…"

"She could be right under your nose," Alicia said, touching his nose with a polished fingertip. "You could be lettin' her slip right past you." She slid her finger down over his lips and flipped his chin with her thumb.

Joe grabbed her hand and kissed the fingertips. "I'm not gonna let nothing slide."

"Nothin'?" Alicia asked, wide-eyed. "That's too bad."

"You need to stop teasing me, girl," Joe warned. "Why don't you let me cook dinner for you at your house tomorrow?"

"Would you be wantin' me to take care of the dessert?" she queried seductively.

"If you'd like," he said. "It would be your call. Anyway you want to play it. But I'm gonna cook something good enough to make you want to go home and smack your mama."

"That good?" she giggled. "I should warn you, my mama's a formidable cook."

"Take pity on me," Joe continued, "I've been living in a hotel eating restaurant food for nearly a month. I need a home-cooked meal. Even if I have to cook it myself!"

"Aw right, honey, you've made your case. Why don't you come on over Saturday night?" Alicia suggested.

"I'll get the groceries. You just provide the place and an appetite," Joe said contentedly.

⁓

That Saturday night, between mouthfuls of delicious beef stroganoff, yeast rolls and Caesar salad,

Alicia said, "Good gracious, Joe. Someone better warn my mama to take covah!"

"What did I tell you?" Joe smirked.

Alicia had provided a lace tablecloth, fragrant roses from her backyard garden, Jon Lucien background music and candle-lit ambiance in her neat house in one of the many tree-lined neighborhoods of south-west Atlanta.

She had on alluring black satin hip huggers with a colorful silk halter top. Just above her belly button, she'd pasted a small diamond that winked at him in the softly lit room.

Over dinner they talked about Talley.

"Tell me about her," Joe said.

"I don't want to give you any clues, 'cause I'm just not gonna help you find her."

"Just tell me about her personality. What's she's like?"

"She's just the sweetest girl. People say that about just about anybody without meaning it, But, with Talley it's real, down-deep sweetness of the soul. But not sticky saccharine sweet. She can be funny and a hoot to be around.

"In college she was easygoing and liked to make people happy," Alicia went on. "She'd loan money like it was nothing. She'd let people borrow her clothes, her books, her CDs...I had to watch to make sure the sisters at Spelman didn't take advantage of her."

"They took her kindness for weakness, huh?" Joe asked.

"Yeah. And she'd been so protected all her life, she thought everyone was good and wished her well. Half those heifers were jealous of her or just wanted to use her. There were even some who resented her just for livin'. Bless her heart, she got hurt a lot, but she stayed sweet and softhearted. She always saw the good in people."

Alicia's face was shining with tender emotion as she recalled her friend.

"She's very dear to you," Joe said.

"I do love her a bushel."

"Listening to you talking about her, I get a different picture from the one I had," Joe admitted.

· "What did you think?"

"That she was a typical spoiled, stuck-up, social butterfly."

"Far from it."

"What about boyfriends? Did she date in college?"

"No. She was true to her Marshall. He was in Boston getting his law degree, and he'd come down to visit her here, making everybody mad with his supercilious ways. I knew when she married Marshall there was somethin' wrong with him. I tried to warn her. Well, maybe not strongly enough. All that money and power *is* intimidatin'."

"So, you think she's done the right thing running and hiding from her family?"

"Abso-posi-lutely," Alicia said emphatically. "And I wish you'd leave her alone."

"I wish I could," Joe sighed.

"Why can't you?"

"I gotta do my job."

"You got some military sense of duty? Like you gotta follow orders, no matter what?"

"I suppose there's some of that. But my father has an obligation to the Pettifores that predates my coming into the firm. I have to help him honor it."

"Well, I won't help you find her."

"You shouldn't. I don't expect you to."

"And Joe, you got to solemnly promise me that you won't use me to try to find her. Okay?"

"Sure thing," Joe said, digging into his salad.

"No, look at me," Alicia said earnestly, reaching for his hand.

Joe looked up into those big brown eyes and lied. "I promise."

Earlier, with relative ease, Joe had attached a recording device onto the phone line in the basement of Alicia's house. He'd sent her to the grocery store for romaine lettuce, then dashed down there while she was gone. He'd also found her spare house key under one of the vine-filled urns outside her front door. It would be a simple matter to come back during the day and check the recorder.

Alicia was his best chance for finding Tallulah, and it was his job to find her. Though he felt a little uncomfortable about his "solemn promise," he let it go and continued to enjoy the evening with her. He could tell by the way he was feeling, and by the way she was looking at him, that they would probably end up in her bedroom.

He thought he'd regret it later, but he ignored the tiny pricks of conscience and kept smiling at her, admiring every inch of her tiny being. She smiled back at him.

They drank after-dinner brandies on the down-pillowed couch in her cozy living room.

"You keep looking at my little diamond ornament," she said, "Do you like it?"

"You need to stop playing games with me, girl," Joe said.

"Since you insist I'm playing games, let's play a real one," she responded. "Truth or dare?"

Joe laughed. He had an idea what was coming.

"Okay, truth."

"Have you ever been in love?"

"Yep, once that I'm sure of."

"What happened?"

"That's two questions. It's my turn. Truth or dare?"

"Truth."

"How many men have spent the night in this house?"

"Ouch! Can I change to dare?"

"Nope."

"Okay, countin' my father and my brother, four."

"I'm not counting your relatives. Two, huh? How long have you lived here?"

"Uh uh, too many questions, my turn. Truth or dare?"

"Truth."

"What happened to your love relationship?"

"Her parents moved and she had to go to a different elementary school."

"Not fair!"

"It was your question. My turn. Truth or dare?"

"Dare."

"Lose that halter top."

Alicia slowly untied the strings and undid the clasp that had been tenuously holding the silky fabric on her. The nipples on her perfect, round, copper-toned breasts were dark brown and taut with anticipation. Joe's eyes appreciated her.

"My turn," she said in a husky voice.

"Dare," he said.

"Take off your sweatah."

He stood and pulled the V-necked burgundy cashmere sweater over his head, then, while she admired his hard muscular chest, said, "Truth or dare?"

"Dare," she whispered.

"Those pants have got to go."

She stood and shrugged the pants off her hips, revealing tiny G-string underpants. The fabric disappeared into the cleft of her full, dimpled brown bottom as she bent over, purposely, to pick up her pants. Joe sucked in his breath and reached for her.

They came into each other's arms easily.

He enfolded her petite form and lifted her against him, his lips working against hers as he carried her to her bedroom. When his tongue sought the tender crevices inside her mouth, she opened her mouth wider.

He laid her on her bed and finished shedding the last of his and her clothing; then he stood before her completely nude, a bronze statue with his manhood standing straight up in front of him. She reached for it with her small hand and pulled it to her hungry mouth as he leaned over her, one hand against the headboard of the ironwork bed. He grunted with pleasure as she licked the moisture off the tip of the rigid member, then ran her tongue down the underpart.

From the drawer beside the bed, Alicia pulled a condom and quickly sheathed him.

Joe rolled onto the bed beside her and pulled her to his side, nuzzling her breast. He took the taut nipple into his mouth and flicked it with his tongue, alternating licks with gentle sucking motions. She felt wetness in her nether regions, and her legs opened involuntarily. He put his hand between her legs, his fingers seeking and then massaging the sensitive nub in her mound.

With a swift motion, she sat on top of him, easing his turgid shaft into her moist opening, and with a sigh, pushed him deeper into her. He was a big man. She felt as if she were riding a strong, dark, untamed horse.

She sat still for a moment, feeling him fill her insides, his heat warming her. Then she placed both her hands on his concave stomach and lifted herself up until he was almost out of her and sat back down on him. She did it again.

He chuckled. "Playing games again, huh?"

She giggled.

He pulled her down to him, holding her captive against his chest as he moved his hips slowly, controlling the rhythms of their love. She wiggled loose and sat up again, grinding herself against him, her breath coming in little gasps. He held both her breasts in his palms and rubbed his thumbs across the nipples. Her movements became swifter. She bucked and ground herself against him wildly until, with a cry, she threw her head back and arched backwards. Her hot sheath pulsed against him, exciting him further.

He pulled out of her quickly. Then, turning her over onto her back, he knelt between her legs and plunged into her with a gasping groan. She arched to meet him, wrapping her legs around his back.

He moved swiftly, thrusting eagerly into her wetness while she guided him with her heels against his buttock. She rubbed her hands up and down the sides of his big arms, fondling the curves of his tight muscles. Suddenly, with a groan, he fell forward onto her, and she felt the throb as he released his seed.

They lay there like that for a while until she squirmed. Then he asked, "Am I too heavy for you?"

"Jes' a tad," she said, her voice muffled under him.

"I'm sorry, baby," he said, moving off her onto his back. He pulled her close to his side and said, "My Lord."

She giggled. "My sentiments eg'zactly."

—⁀ᴐ

Marshall sat on the tile floor by the toilet in the tiny private bathroom next to his office. He had just watched the videotape. And then he'd lost his lunch.

When the tape came from Joe Griffin in a FedEx package, he'd retrieved it from his father's in-box and locked it in his desk drawer. Afraid to look at it, he'd let it sit in the drawer.

But, after the divorce papers were served and Talley's attorney threatened release of the video, Marshall thought it time he looked at it. He had locked his office door and inserted the tape in his player.

Marshall's memory of the night was spotty. He had been very high. Though he'd known it was going to be bad, he was not prepared for the sheer horror of it. His glazed eyes; his bizarre outfit; Talley's frantic and desperate pleas; his son's look of shock and confusion.

One saving grace—his father had not looked at it and didn't know that Michael had been in the room. *If Daddy knew I hit Michael, he'd kill me*, Marshall thought.

Marshall didn't understand what compelled him to do those vicious things. As a boy growing up with Talley, they had played together and clung to one another as friends. It wasn't until he was asked to see her as a sexual being that he had begun to want to hurt her.

Depression and self-pity would lead him to crave the escape of cocaine and cross-dressing. Then his bizarre behavior while high and his violence toward Talley would lead him to self-disgust and more depression.

Though he knew he should seek help, he didn't want to openly confirm his father's opinion that he was weak and pathetic.

Unfortunately, he was under constant pressure from both his father and his mother to live up to an impossible standard of behavior. The only person who had even understood and sympathized with him had been Talley, and yet he had always despised her for being so soft and foolish as to care about him. She was both his torment and his salvation.

He had to go to Atlanta and find her. He had to talk to her and beg her to destroy that tape and come back to him. *It's my only chance,* he thought. *Talley won't let me down.*

Marshall pulled himself up from the bathroom floor and going to the sink, washed his mouth out. He looked at his face in the mirror. Tiny red capillaries in his cheeks had burst from the strain of vomiting. His eyes were red and watery.

"I hate you," he jeered at his image; "you perverted bastard. Why do I let you live?"

~ ᘓ ~

Cole was helping Talley out of his truck, lifting her down from the high running board with his hands on her tiny waist, when Roberta drove into the impound yard. She gasped and accidentally bit her tongue when she saw them. As she watched, Talley and Cole stood close together, face to face, for just a moment too long before turning away.

Roberta's face felt hot with anger and her tongue hurt. The pair, unaware of her and her reaction, began laughing hilariously at something Cole had said. Walking together to the office, Cole said something else that made the golden girl laugh, then turned back to his truck.

In all the years of Roberta and Cole's on-again, off-again romance, she had never seen him with another woman. In the past when she and Cole had broken up, she'd been the one who quickly began dating new men. He'd usually just thrown himself deeper into his work and his business. Handsome and appealing as he was, Cole was not a ladies' man. In fact, he'd always been very shy around women. Buried in his work and raising his brothers, Cole had had few chances to play the dating game. Roberta had always been the aggressor in their relationship.

The sight of him laughing and flirting with a woman who appeared to be *white* was chilling. She was stunned into inaction.

When he spotted Roberta's car, Cole stopped for a second, blinked, then walked toward her. Roberta got out of the car, straightened the short slim skirt of her black and cream suit and stood trembling with tamped-down rage.

"Hey, Ro," he said nonchalantly. "What's up?"

"Who was that?" she asked with a tight smile.

"You mean Talley? She's my new office help," Cole said.

"Where'd you find her?"

"She and her son were driving to Atlanta and broke down on I-75," he said. "She needed a job."

"You mean to say you picked up some white penny ho' off the highway?" Roberta asked, her voice getting shrill.

"Hey! Why's she gotta be all that?" Cole asked heatedly. "She's *not* white and…and…What's it got to do with you anyway?"

Roberta staggered backward, as though she'd been struck. Then with visible effort, she took a deep breath and calmed herself down. "You know I take an interest in everything you do."

"You've never taken an interest in this business," Cole said with a short laugh. "As a matter of fact, isn't this the first time you've been out here?"

"Of course not, silly, I came out here with you when Big Daddy first left you the land, remember? Remember what we did in those trees over there?" she said with a sly grin.

"Yeah, that's right," he muttered, flushing with embarrassment.

"Well, I just came to see if you wanted to go have some lunch with me," she purred.

"Can't. I've got to take a car to Macon. Besides, I thought we agreed we weren't going see each other anymore."

"Not even as friends?" she asked.

Cole sighed. "We can't be just friends, Roberta."

"Sure we can. We've known each other all our lives. We've got a lot of history between us. We should be friends!" she insisted.

"Maybe later. A lot later. But not now," Cole said.

Roberta shrugged and put her hand on his arm. "Okay, then, we'll try later." Cole shrugged her hand off his arm and backed away.

Pretending not to notice the insult, Roberta got back into her car and waving goodbye, drove off the yard. Cole climbed in his truck and followed her until she turned off into a strip mall right before the freeway. He nodded stiffly as he passed her.

Roberta was determined to go back to Cole's office and get a closer look at Talley. She suspected that the light-skinned girl was the reason for Cole's new determination to end their relationship.

She was equally determined that the romance she and Cole had shared for years wouldn't end until *she* was ready to end it. After all, there was still a chance that, with her continued urging, Cole might change his mind and give up his truck driving for a more respectable profession. There was also the wildly remote chance, but only when she'd exhausted all other possibilities, that she might be willing to settle for a sexy truck driver husband with a gentle way about him.

Cole is my property, and I'm not turning him over to some golden-haired hussy, she thought.

Roberta turned her car around and headed back to the yard.

Breezing into the office, Roberta felt a clutch of savage fear and bitter hatred when she saw how pretty Talley was, even in her casual uniform of blue jeans and gray shirt with the TowMaster's logo on the pocket. It didn't help that her tongue still ached.

Close up, the evidence of Talley's African American heritage was apparent in the fullness of her lips and the almond tint to her coloring, but the radiant honey-blonde hair in soft curls had been hued by God, not Clairol. Talley's long-lashed amber eyes were clear and honest and her rosy lips wore a ready smile. *She looks familiar,* Roberta thought. *Where could I have seen her before?*

Vickie's eyes had widened when she saw the fashionably dressed and coiffed woman enter the trailer. She knew Roberta was Cole's off and on girlfriend. Vickie had also, over the past weeks, watched the growing friendship between Cole and Talley. Like all of Cole's family, she knew he was hopelessly smitten.

Vickie sat rooted to her desk chair surveying the reception area. Dynamite could not have blasted her from her vantage point.

Talley and Roberta were like opposite ends of a spectrum. Both were beautiful and the same height, but there the similarities ended.

Roberta was all cool, polished sable with sleek, confined hair, long bright fingertips, and a statuesque body with generous curves. She oozed sexuality from every pore.

Talley was a willowy pillar of liquid gold with riotous curls, an easy charm, and touchable warmth.

"Well, hello," Roberta said in her most stilted voice. "You must be Talley, the new help. I'm Roberta, Cole's fiancée."

"Hello," Talley responded, puzzled. "I didn't know Cole was engaged. I'm glad to meet you."

"Oh, Cole didn't tell you about me? He's told me all about *you*. How he met you and your son on the side of the road. He's always picking up strays. It's his nature."

"He's certainly in the right business, then, isn't he?" Talley asked slowly. Her female antennae were all atwitter. *This is not good,* she thought.

"He once picked up a stray dog and wanted to keep her," Roberta said with a little sniff. "I made him get rid of the bitch. She had fleas."

"Oh, I see," Talley said faintly. *Trouble.*

"I don't expect he'll be in this business for long, now that his brothers are all grown, so I wouldn't be quick to entrench myself if I were you. Cole's probably is going to shut this down and go back to school when we get married. I plan to support him through college."

Talley frowned at that. "I don't think he'd shut TowMasters down. He loves this business. He has all sorts of expansion plans for it. We talk about it all the time."

"Don't count on it," Roberta responded swiftly. "Where are you from?"

"Michigan," Talley said.

"Is that where your son's father is?"

"Yes."

"So you're divorced?"

"In the process."

"What does your husband do?"

"He works in his father's business."

"Doing what?"

Talley decided at that point it was time to call a halt to the inquisition. She squared her shoulders and, with the easy politeness that is achieved from three generations of wealth and breeding, said, "You know, Roberta, it's been a real pleasure chatting with you. But I really must get all these papers filed before Vickie leaves me with the phones. I am so happy to have met you."

Talley escaped to the back of the trailer, slipped into her office and closed the door.

For the first time, Roberta noticed Vickie behind the bulletproof glass wall in the dispatch office.

"Oh, hello, Vickie," she said sourly.

"Ro, you know y'all broke the engagement a year ago," Vickie said, looking pointedly at Roberta's ringless finger. "I know 'cause Cole told the family that he put his mother's ring back in the safe at the bank."

"We had a little fight, that's all," Roberta replied. "We're tight again in every sense of the word and that's all you need to know."

Vickie lifted a skeptical eyebrow. "Oh, really?"

"Yes, *really*," Roberta said as she stalked out of the trailer.

⌁

Talley sat at her desk staring blindly at the gravel parking lot that was visible from her office window. Though she had not revealed it to Roberta, Talley had been shaken to the core by the news that Cole was engaged.

In the past two months she and Cole had fallen into an easy camaraderie, sharing many of their hopes and dreams for the future. She felt betrayed that he had not told her he was planning to be married.

Why didn't he ever tell me? she fumed silently, getting up and pacing around the tiny office. *I thought we were close friends!*

She finally had to admit that despite her determination not to let her attraction to the big sexy truck driver get out of hand, she was ferociously, despairingly jealous.

CHAPTER EIGHT

Joe lay across the bed in his hotel room listening to the flattering conversation recorded from the tap on Alicia's phone. He savored every word. To his credit he did feel guilty, but the guilt was mixed with pride and pleasure.

He was listening to a call from Alicia to her sister on Sunday morning, apparently shortly after he'd left her bed.

"Boo, I need to talk to you," Alicia said when her sister answered. "I'm lyin' here on my bed, barely able to move!"

"What's wrong?" Barbara was concerned.

Alicia giggled wildly. "I jus' been thoroughly loved, gal!"

"No! You vulgar hussy!"

"It's true, I feel like I been rode hard and put up wet."

"This guy Joe you've been talking about?"

"Umm, Joe. His new nickname is 'the big thang'!"

"Was he big, sister?"

"He was big and hot and juicy!"

More screams.

"Really, Boo," Alicia said, her voice earnest, "he was so sweet and felt so good to me. He doesn't know it yet, but I'm gonna keep him."

"Ali, don't start. You barely know him. Give it some mo' time."

"You get to a certain point in your life when you know when it's right," Alicia responded thoughtfully. "This feels right to me."

"Honey, jus' give it some time. Jus' don't say anythin' to him yet."

"Oh no! I won't say a word to him! I'm gonna try and stay cool, calm and collected!"

Joe just shook his head. He knew how unfair this intrusion was and he wasn't going to take advantage of the information. In truth, when he had finally torn himself away from Alicia, he'd felt sated and a little giddy. *This little girl is a keeper,* he thought.

But first he had to find the elusive Talley. The phone calls on the tap this week had revealed nothing about her. But sooner or later, he was sure, Tallulah would call her friend.

―৽

"Mommy, it's cold as a witch's tit out here," Michael said, getting into the car with Talley and Narye.

"What did you just say?" Talley asked, startled. She and Narye exchanged bemused glances.

"It's real cold?" the child said, looking puzzled.

"Where did you hear the expression you just used?"

Michael giggled. "Marcus. He says that all the time."

"Well, we'd prefer if you didn't say it. It's not very nice," Talley chided.

"Okay. It's cold as a brass monkey's balls!" he said cheerily.

"Oh, Lord," Talley sighed. "Truck drivers!"

However, Talley was not too annoyed. Michael's newly colorful language was a small price to pay for the wonderful role models he'd begun emulating. Cole and his brothers were good men. They were hardworking and aspiring. They were manly without being belligerent, self-confident without being cocky, and completely genuine.

Michael adored Cole, who continued to treat the boy with an affectionate equanimity Talley liked. Whenever the big man was around, Michael stuck to him like glue, copying his movements, his gestures. The boy didn't seem to miss his father at all. He never asked about Marshall or about that horrendous night. It seemed to Talley as though he wanted to wipe his mind of the man and the madness surrounding him.

She would have been startled indeed to learn what sort of conversations Michael had with Cole when they were alone in the truck, conversation that revealed the little boy had been more affected by that last experience with his father than she realized. As Michael had grown closer to Cole, he'd felt comfortable asking him things he couldn't ask his mother for fear he'd see the sad, shuttered expression that came over her face every time he mentioned his father.

"Why would a man dress like a lady when it's not Halloween?" Michael asked Cole one day.

"Maybe he's in a play or a funny show," Cole said, looking at the little boy oddly.

"No, I don't think so. Daddy was at home," Michael replied with a frown.

"Your daddy dressed like a lady?" Cole asked.

"Yes," the boy whispered. "Why would he do it?"

"Some men like the look and feel of women's clothing. It's real different, but I guess it's okay for them to dress strange if they're not hurting anybody," Cole said calmly.

Michael was quiet for a moment then, "He hurt Mommy."

Cole blinked and swallowed, his mind reeling at these revelations. He wanted to gather the boy and his mother into his strong arms and protect them.

"He hit her and tore her nightie," the boy went on. "She screamed and cried."

"You saw this?" Cole asked, his eyes turning dark and ominous.

"Mommy told me not to look, but I bit Daddy." the boy said defiantly.

"I'm glad you did that."

"He hit me real hard."

Cole shook his head, his jaw clenched tightly. His insides writhed with anger as he thought of the monster that was this boy's father. *I'd like to get my hands on him. I'd tear his head off.*

"Then Mommy and I left and came here."

"I'm glad you came here. I like you here."

"I like me here, too," Michael agreed solemnly.

∽∾

When she got the opportunity, Talley admonished Cole gently about the language Michael was picking up from his new friends. "Could you ask your brothers to please watch what they say around Michael. I've heard the cold compared to witch's breasts and brass monkey's privates."

"I'm sorry. I'll talk to them," Cole responded solemnly, suppressing a grin. "It's just the boy is so good and so quiet, they forget he's there."

"I don't want Michael taking that language into his classrooms," Talley insisted. She searched Cole's face to see if he was taking her seriously.

"I'll talk to them," he promised.

Cole sorted through the office mail that Talley had opened and placed neatly on his desk. "I see you ordered tickets to the Atlanta Business League Christmas Dinner. What's that all about?" he asked.

"You remember. I bought into the raffle for the Marketing Makeover. They're going to announce the winner at the black-tie dinner. I think you should go just in case TowMasters wins."

"I'm not going to this mess," Cole muttered. *What would I look like all by myself in a room full of "bougie" black people dressed up like the butler?*

Vickie, still clutching dispatch forms she'd brought to Cole's office, lingered, listening to their exchange. "Why don't the two of you go together? It only makes sense."

"Oh...I don't know..." Talley hesitated, objections flooding her mind. Since coming to Atlanta Talley had carefully avoided events and places where she might be recognized. This dinner for Atlanta's movers and shakers could be dangerous. *Still, it isn't as though I'm a famous rock star...she* argued to herself. *Surely I can get away with one evening.*

Then there was the frightening new direction this might take her relationship with Cole. Since that first night when Cole had invited her to dinner at his home and she had revealed her real name, except for their lunches which masqueraded as business meetings, Cole had steered clear of purely social interaction with her. They were constantly in one another's company at work and their friendship had warmed considerably but...*What about his fiancée?* she thought.

"You oughta go together," Vickie insisted. "It says there's dancin'. And Cole's a good dancer."

All of a sudden, Cole's mind was filled with an image of him holding Talley in his arms, her body pressed against the length of him, her cheek against his shoulder, his face buried in her soft curls as they swayed together to sensual music. He felt his rebellious body harden.

"What about Cole's fiancée?" Talley's question doused ice water on Cole's dream. Vickie rolled her eyes.

"Who are you talking about?" he demanded, astonished.

"Roberta."

"How you know her?"

"She came by and introduced herself last week," Talley said with a stiff smile.

"She shouldn't have done that. She's not my fiancée anymore. We broke our engagement a year ago," Cole insisted heatedly.

"Hmmm," Talley murmured doubtfully. "Roberta clearly thinks you two are still together."

"It's not true. I don't care what she thinks. Did she show you a ring?"

"Well, no…"

"She and I used to be engaged. But more than a year ago she gave me—no, *threw* the ring back at me and ended the relationship."

Talley's smile widened joyously, her eyes were bright with relief. *He's not engaged!*

Cole silently watched Talley's face change and began to feel hopeful. "Now that that's settled, what about this dinner? I'm not going by myself."

"And you don't have to," Vickie insisted, eyes shifting to Talley.

"It's been a while since I've dressed up…"

"We'd both have to get dressed up. I don't want to do it alone."

Talley heard the plea in Cole's voice. "Okay, I'll go with you."

Vickie gave a little skip as she left Cole's office.

Cole drove away from the building with a dazed expression on his face. *I have a date with Talley!* When he first mentioned the event, it was with no expectation that she would go with him. Then Vickie had butted in. When Talley hesitated, and he got nervous, there was Vickie, right on time. As hard as he fought it, he couldn't keep his heart from soaring with excitement. Maybe Vickie deserved a raise.

⁓

Joe and Alicia stretched out on opposite ends of the couch in her living room. She was reading a novel, he was watching ESPN on television. Her feet were tucked under his arm. Occasionally she'd wiggle her toes to get his attention and read him a passage from the book.

Joe had never felt so completely relaxed and at home with a woman. Lately he had been spending as much time as he could with her in her cozy house. He'd all but abandoned his sterile hotel room, only going there now and then to change clothes and to listen to the tapes he retrieved from Alicia's basement.

Teasing, he accused Alicia of putting some kind of Southern "mojo" on him, something that made him want to spend every free moment with her. He couldn't seem to get enough of her sweetness. Their lovemaking left him spent and dizzy with love for her. And then he wanted more. It was getting so he could not imagine his life without her in it.

Joe had been searching for Talley for two months. At the divorce hearing in Detroit, with Talley represented by her attorney, the judge had awarded Talley temporary child support and alimony of twenty thousand dollars a month—eighteen percent of Marshall's income. Jerome had talked fast and managed to delay the judge ordering visits for Marshall to see his son.

Recently, Joe had picked up a new local client. A buddy of his from the Marines now had a security job with a local insurance company, and Joe was helping him with a case involving an insurance scam. He was close to convincing his father that, even after Talley was found, there would be enough work in the city and the region to justify opening a branch office.

"Do you have a tuxedo?" Alicia asked him.

"Yep," Joe said.

"How 'bout you put it on and we go to the Atlanta Business League's Christmas dinner next week?"

He faked a Southern accent. "Sho' 'nuff, sweet stuff."

"I thought we understood you weren't to tease me 'bout the way I talk," she said.

"I can't help it, you talk funny." He grabbed one of her toes and brought it up to his mouth.

"No, honey, what you can't seem to understan' is down here, *you're* the one who talks funny. Leggo my toes!" she squealed as he planted wet kisses on them.

He pulled her to him, settling her on his lap facing him, her legs in their soft sweatpants wrapped around his waist. He kissed her deeply, then pulled her sweatshirt off over her head. She leaned her head back and thrust her breasts toward him. He licked and nuzzled her brown nipples until they were hard. Then putting his hands under her buttocks, he stood up and carried her, still wrapped around him, to the bedroom.

─ᘓ─

The next day, Joe listened to the tapes in his hotel room. He recognized most of the calls, since he'd been there when they came in. Then, a strange call startled him out of his doldrums.

Alicia had apparently received it earlier in the week, in the evening before he got to her house after work. The call was from a man.

"Alicia, sweetheart, how're you doing?"

"Tom! Where've you *been*?"

"I went out to California for a while after you broke my heart. I was putting down some tracks for Dallas Austin's new girl group. But I'm back now."

"Well, I'm glad you are!"

"You want to have lunch this week? See if you can mend my heart?"

"Silly boy, I didn't break nothing on you! But I'd love to have lunch with you. I want to hug your neck."

"If you say so. But I hope you hug more than my neck."

"You're so bad! Why don't you come by the office at noon on Wednesday?"

"I'm there."

Joe thought his head was going to explode. *This Tom is going to put his hands on my woman! Alicia is going to hug him. Tom hopes for more than a hug!* Today was Wednesday, which meant Alicia was going to see him today. Joe's forehead broke out in a cold sweat. *Maybe I'll turn up at noon today, too, and break both of Tom's arms!*

As he sat on the side of the hotel room bed, trying to calm down, it dawned on Joe that he'd begun to think of Alicia as his exclusive property. He needed to talk to her about what was going on with this Tom. It was eleven-thirty A.M. He called her at her office.

His voice quavered slightly when she came on the line. "Hey, what're you up to?"

"Kinda busy," she said, sounding distracted. "Can I call you back?"

"Want to go to lunch?" he asked.

"I've got a lunch already," she responded quickly. "I'll see you at home after work."

"Wait a minute. Who's your lunch..?"

"I gotta jet, I'll talk to you tonight."

She needed to get off the phone mighty fast, Joe thought angrily. "Who the hell is this Tom anyway?" Joe asked the hotel room wall. It took everything he had not to put his surveillance experience to work to find out what Tom looked like. But, he was already wrong for listening to her phone calls; it would be just too unfair for him to use the information to advance his own cause.

"Who cares about fair, she's *my* woman!" he said aloud. Then he sighed, "The woman has got me talking to myself."

Punching his arms into his jacket sleeves still left him craving a good swing at Tom. Slamming the door hard behind him, he headed for his office. The team was already working the phones. The sight of them didn't erase Alicia from his mind, but he had a job to do. There was a small private elementary school called Trinity in the Buckhead area of Atlanta. Joe was going to drive over and take a look when the schools let out around 2:30 P.M.

"We've pretty much exhausted the north side of town," one of the operatives had told him.

"Then it might be time to start looking south of the city," Joe said.

— ෙ —

Roberta could not shake the feeling she'd seen "Tallulah Parsons" somewhere before. Or heard that unusual first name in a different context. Sitting in her downtown office, Roberta was racking her brain trying to recall where she'd seen that face. The nagging feeling plagued her, but not as much as the fear that she might finally lose Cole. She'd been the only woman in his life for so long that she'd grown complacent.

Roberta didn't know what to make of Talley. That the self-possessed woman was not low budget was clear. The way Talley spoke, the way she carried herself, screamed education and class. Why would a woman like that be working for low wages in a towing business? And was she even interested in Cole? A truck driver?

The body language she'd watched between Talley and Cole seemed affectionate and friendly. Perhaps she only imagined that their touch lasted a moment too long for simple friendship. Was she making too much of the whole thing?

She'd placed several calls to Cole over the past few days but had missed him each time. There was this Atlanta Business League Christmas event. Her firm was buying a table. On the surface, it seemed like a good enough reason to call again. If she begged, perhaps he'd go with her.

She dialed the yard.

"TowMasters, this is Vickie. How may I help you?"

You could get the heck off the phone, Roberta thought and was tempted to say. Instead, she took a deep breath and said, "Put Cole on the phone. Now."

"Ro, Cole isn't here right now." Vickie's deep sigh was intended to aggravate and it worked.

"Did you tell him I called?"

"Yes, I told him you called twenty times," Vickie said.

"I haven't called twenty times," Roberta snapped.

"Feels that way."

Roberta heard a man's voice in the background. "That's Cole now, isn't it? Put him on the phone, Vickie. Don't you play with me, damn it!"

"You better not curse at me," Vickie spat. "That's Marcus you're hearing."

"Tell Cole to call me as soon as he gets in," Roberta said, slamming down the phone. Beside herself, Roberta got up and paced a five step circle. "The nerve of that half-witted, interfering brat. She doesn't know who she's messing with."

Still, if Cole wasn't in the office, she could always try his cell phone. She sat at her desk and punched in the numbers angrily. It rang and rang. She knew Cole would recognize her number when it appeared on his caller ID. She couldn't help wondering if he were screening her out.

Roberta was surprised Cole was being so unyielding. In the past when they'd had their little spats, he'd at least respond to her calls. But there was a way around even this. She flagged a colleague passing her office door.

"You have your cell phone with you?" she asked. He nodded. "Let me use it to make a quick call. I'll bring it back to your office."

Cole picked up on the first ring.

"TowMasters," he said, his deep voice sending shivers through her.

"Hey, baby, it's Ro."

"Oh." His voice turned flat and emotionless.

"I've been trying to call you all week."

"Vickie told me."

"Then why didn't you call me back?"

"Ro, I told you it was over between us…"

"Honey, you need to stop saying that. It can't be over so quickly. You can't just stop loving someone, just like that!" She was begging, she knew, but begging had worked in the past.

"See, this is why I didn't want…"

"But I still love you. Don't you care about that at all? Don't you care that you're hurting me so bad I can't stand it?" Roberta started to cry, whispering desperately into the phone.

"Of course I care. I don't want to hurt you. But…listen. I can't talk to you right now." Whenever Roberta had used tears in the past, Cole had caved. He was a sucker for women's tears. His sister, Lucy, rarely cried and he couldn't ever remember his mother having shed a tear, so he considered them rare and frightening. Besides, he had once genuinely cared for Roberta. But this time was different, the trust was broken and the care worn away. *There's nothing there now,* he thought. *I just want to be free of her.*

"Don't hang up. I want to just ask you one thing. Just one last favor," she pleaded.

"Okay, what is it?" Cole sighed.

Her voice was soft and sweet as warm chocolate pudding. "My firm is buying a table to the ABL Christmas dinner. Will you go with me?"

"Damn, Ro. I've already made plans for that dinner. I'm taking Talley."

"You mean you're going to rent a tuxedo and take someone else to a black-tie dinner, when I've been begging you for years to go to one with me?" Roberta shrilled. She stood and began pacing her office again.

"Actually, I'm *buying* a tux," he admitted.

"You bastard!" she screamed, throwing the phone across the room. Then with a gasp she retrieved the phone from a corner. It was mangled.

She collected herself, then buzzed her colleague on the office intercom.

"Listen, I'm going to have to buy you a new phone. Let's go to Circuit City during lunch."

The first thing Marshall did when he got to Atlanta was check in with the team at Joe's new office. He strode into the facility like a conquering general and began barking questions.

"Have you found her yet?" he demanded.

"Not yet," Joe said.

"Have you put any pressure on that lawyer of hers?" Marshall asked.

"As much as we can within legal boundaries," Joe responded.

"It might be time to start pushing some of those boundaries," Marshall snarled.

Marshall knew that if a copy of that tape ever got out, his life would be ruined. His father would never forgive him if he didn't find Talley and get that tape and Michael back. Marshall bit his lower lip. There had to be more than one way to find his wife and son. Talley was like a butterfly. She was probably flitting about right now without a clue about what she was doing, only succeeding because she didn't know how to fail. But she was bound to slip. Soon, he hoped, and he had to be ready.

In the underworld he frequented to acquire his drugs, it was easy to identify and pay men who would enjoy using violent force or larcenous subterfuge to get information. He was ready to put them to work.

CHAPTER NINE

Cole had expected to hear a lot of chin music from his brothers when he brought his new tuxedo home with all of its accoutrements—the pleated shirt, the black studs, the cufflinks, the patent leather shoes and the bow tie—which he was determined to master. But instead of teasing, they came to his room and discussed the various pieces with intense curiosity and eager support.

"Yeah, man, you can put it in high gear now," Winston enthused. "Y'know what I'm sayin?"

The whole family was determined he should represent them well if he was going to take Talley somewhere. They were all a little bit in love with her.

Talley had endeared herself to the brothers in various ways. She'd raved about Marcus' cooking and begged him to share his recipes with Narye. Then she had appealed to his neat freak instincts by joining with him to persuade Cole to hire a cleaning service to keep the office trailer sparkling.

She'd allowed Winston to flirt shamelessly with her and she cooed over his baby girl. She'd talked Tolkien with David, then found a beautifully bound copy of *The Hobbit* for his birthday.

But more than anything else, she had just been Talley—guileless and unselfconscious about her beauty and her background, eager to please, easy to be around.

"I hope you knuckleheads aren't making too much out of this," Cole said, looking at his brothers sternly. "Talley's just going with me to this dinner because she entered some kind of raffle, and she wants to see how it turns out," Cole told them.

They exchanged glances.

"You can be dumb as a post, man," Marcus said. "You can't see she likes you?"

"She has to like me. I sign her paycheck."

"Ain't nothing like that," Marcus said. "Her eyes follow you when you're in the trailer. She brightens up when you smile at her."

"Yeah," Winston said. "I know 'shorties' and that one wants her a juicy piece of big Cole, y'know what I'm sayin?"

Cole and David glared, and Marcus, closest to Winston, cuffed him hard. "Don't talk about Talley like that."

"I'm just sayin'," Winston whined, ducking away.

"Cole, you need to listen to someone besides yourself for a change," David piped up bravely. "If we could have someone like Talley in the family—it would just be…just…"

Cole gave David a look that silenced him. "Listen, this is my first date with Talley. I have enough trouble trying to talk to women, I don't need all y'all up in my grill."

The Friday before the Saturday night affair, Cole came into the trailer all smiles. He took Talley and Marcus into his office and closed the door.

"I've got some really good news," he said. "I talked to Greg over at the Porsche dealership and he said they've been having a lot of trouble with their long distance transporter. He said the Audi and Land Rover group have been complaining, too. They agreed that if I were to get an enclosed trailer, they'd give me all their long distance transport business!"

"Man, that's the dream, ain't it? That could add up to as much as ten thousand dollars a month in additional income," Marcus said excitedly. "If we can get a truck and trailer for fifteen hundred a month, we could net a nice profit."

"Don't forget insurance and maintenance," Talley added. "Gas and tolls…but even so, we could do well. It would be a start."

Cole looked at her eager, smiling face, his green eyes glowing with warmth. He loved it that she'd said *we*.

"So, even if we don't win the raffle tomorrow, we should still probably consult with a marketing firm about creating an image for TransportMasters," she continued.

"Now all I have to do is find the down payment for a new truck," Cole said. "I guess I'll have to go back to the bank for another loan against the land."

"No!" Talley insisted. "Please let me invest in the truck."

Marcus looked at her quizzically. "We need to put down about fifteen thousand dollars," he noted.

"I've got it!" she exclaimed. She now received more than that every month in alimony and child support.

"No," Cole said quietly, "that's out of the question."

Talley looked at his face. The warmth had drained from it.

"I just wanted. I thought…" Her voice was forlorn.

"No," Cole said harshly. He turned abruptly and walked out of the office.

What's wrong with him? Marcus wondered, looking at Talley's crestfallen face. "You just wanted to invest in the business. That ain't a bad thing. Cole has some weird moods sometimes."

"It's okay," Talley sighed. "I just wish he'd let me be a part of this. I think it has great potential."

Later Marcus took Cole out for a walk and broached the subject with him.

"What was up with that? Why'd you go all iceman on the girl?"

"You need to just stay out of it." Cole picked up a stick in their path and snapped it in half sharply. "There's stuff you don't know about."

"Is her money dirty or something?"

"No, that's nowhere near it."

"Well, what then?"

"We're not taking any of her money, that's all."

"I don't understand you, man. It isn't takin' if she's offerin'. There'd be papers and stuff to make it legal."

His eyes traveled to his brother's face. "I believe we can trust her, Cole."

Cole's head moved heavily. "It's not about trust."

The men strode together silently for a while.

"You still holding onto that thing against rich blacks, aren't you?" Marcus asked. "'Cause of that guy that killed Mom and Dad."

Cole sped up his pace.

"They were my parents, too, and I got over it. Why can't you? Besides, Talley isn't the villain here, just 'cause she's got some money. She wants to help out. Be a part of our business."

Cole stopped walking and faced his brother, furious. "She can be all the part of it she wants. I need her ideas and her marketing skills. I don't need her money."

Marcus backed away. He knew his brother's temper. "Okay, you be sure and tell her that stuff about needin' her ideas tomorrow night, okay?"

"Yeah, okay," Cole agreed.

Rigid with anger when Talley offered to buy a truck for his business, Cole hadn't been able to find the words to tell her that her money continued to overwhelm and intimidate him. His brothers had no idea of Talley's wealth. They thought she was from a "comfortable" family, like the girls from black doctors' families and black lawyers' families, the ones they went to school with. They didn't know what Cole knew.

The Pettifores and the Quincys were in a class by themselves. Bill Cosby had pots of money, Magic

Johnson had crazy money, Oprah Winfrey had money to burn. But Talley was even beyond that. Talley's family had money like white people had money. Like the Kennedys and the Rockefellers. She had generations of money bred into her very bones.

Talley could snap her fingers at the small change Cole's business was making. He knew that she was probably used to spending in one month the money he made in a year with three trucks working twenty-four hours a day, seven days a week.

His head throbbed with anguished humiliation whenever he thought about the hard life he and Lucy had lived for the last decade, pinching and scraping just to keep the family afloat.

How could a man ever hope to have a future with a woman whose *daytime* jewelry cost more than his house? That she'd agreed to be his date to this dance still astounded him. And she'd offered to buy him a truck. A truck! How could he ever look at his face in the mirror and see himself as a man if he let her buy him like that? The fact that Talley's offer was made with such ease and sincerity angered him even more. With her simple gesture of helpfulness, Cole felt Talley had unmanned him completely. His emotions were as raw and vulnerable as an open wound.

Damned if I'm going to be her gigolo, he thought, with his jaw clenched defiantly.

Talley sat in the office after Cole and Marcus left and tried to revive her spirits. She was surprised at how deeply involved in the business she had become.

"I love the satisfaction of contributing to a growing, thriving enterprise," she told Narye that night when the older woman chided her for coming home tired and late, night after night. "I can't wait to get to work in the mornings."

Charmed by the excitement, Narye smiled at her beloved charge. "I'm glad you're happy, Talley. But you need to get dressed for bed now."

"Narye, for the first time in my life I feel important to someone besides Michael. I love that my child needs me as a mother. But with Cole, it's different."

"Different indeed," Narye agreed gently. "For that one will never see you as his mother."

"Cole sees me as a whole person. Cole listens to me, he takes my advice," Talley enthused as Narye laid out her nightgown. "He lets me try new marketing ideas and they're working!"

"And perhaps those ideas will work even better if you are awake when you present them? Sleep now."

Talley climbed obediently between the sheets as Narye left her but found it hard to still her thoughts when she closed her eyes. *Cole needs that new truck…a new marketing plan…new business direction…extra money…ME! He needs me.*

Talley hadn't told Cole about the twenty thousand dollars a month alimony and child support order she'd received, along with a check for forty thousand dollars to cover October and November. She was afraid he'd fire her if he knew she no longer needed to work for him. She didn't want to leave.

I can help him with this business and I'm going to stay, she thought with fierce determination.

~ ෴

Talley dressed for the dinner dance with the giddy excitement of a teenage girl going to her first prom. She had rummaged through the bags of clothing that she'd tossed into the car the night she and Michael had run away and been delighted to find that she'd inadvertently included her favorite ball gown.

"I wasn't thinking, just throwing things into plastic bags, or I never would have packed a gown," she told Narye with a giggle.

"It was just back from the cleaners," Narye nodded, "in the front part of the closet."

The floor-length cream silk gown, woven with metallic gold threads, glowed against her creamy almond skin and golden hair. The short jacket had tiny mirrors sewn with gold thread around its stiff Mandarin collar. Tiny mirrors twinkled across the top of the low-cut neckline of the gown. Two years ago the outfit had cost more than three thousand dollars at Neiman Marcus.

She wore her gilded hair swept back into a sleek gold chignon, making her amber-fired eyes seem huge in the perfect oval of her face and accentuating her classically sculpted features and high cheekbones. She and

Narye searched through her jewelry box for just the right pieces and their diligence paid off. Simple two-carat diamonds studs for her ears and a single seven-carat diamond pendant seemed made for the dress. Now Talley stood perfect, wearing nearly forty thousand dollars in jewelry. Strappy gold two-inch heels, purchased at the mall earlier that day, put her at five feet, eleven inches, just the right height for Cole's towering frame.

She was also tall enough to be a stunning object of awe for a seven-year-old who still believed in fairy tales. Michael's eyes widened and his small mouth formed an "O" when she came into his room to say good night. "You look pretty, Mommy," he breathed. "Are you going to show Mr. Cole?"

"Yes, Mr. Cole is coming and he will see," Talley told the boy.

"I bet he'll want to kiss you. I do."

"He might. But I'm more interested in your kiss."

"You should let *him* kiss you, too," Michael insisted, giving her a wet smooch. "You smell nice. Can I whisper something to you?"

"Sure," Talley leaned in.

"I like Mr. Cole better than Daddy," he said softly. "Is that okay?"

"It's okay," she whispered back. "That makes two of us."

꩜

Cole was in purgatory. No one in the house knew how to tie this damned bow tie! What had possessed him to buy this piece of oddly shaped cloth instead of a neat clip-on bow tie? But the arrogant salesman at the store had lifted his eyebrow and turned down the corners of this thin, refined mouth when Cole picked up the loose tie. When the snide little man had suggested the little plastic package with the clip-on bow instead, Cole had been insulted. The mini-shrimp had a lot of nerve, treating him like he needed a course in remedial dressing. Cole twisted the ends of the tie again, to no avail. Hell, he was following the instructions that came with the damned thing, why did it keep coming out whopsided? Now he realized he should have swallowed his pride.

"Marcus, will you go next door to Miz Gardiner? See if she knows how to do this," he said to the brother watching his struggles from the doorway.

Marcus shrugged. "Why don't you just let Talley do it when you get to her house?"

Winston, sitting on Cole's bed, agreed. "Yeah, man. 'Shorties' go for that helpless thing."

"I don't want her to know I've never done this before," Cole admitted sheepishly.

"Oh, you think Talley believes you're always walkin' 'round the house wearin' a tuxedo?" Winston laughed.

Earlier that evening, the brothers had gathered around to watch Cole lay out the pieces of his attire. They admired the diamond cufflinks Cole had dug deep to purchase. Winston offered to loan Cole his prized Gucci watch. Lucy phoned to remind Cole to wear the onyx ring with "C" picked out in tiny diamonds that his father had left him. He'd taken it out of its blue velvet case and all the brothers admired it again.

Now, finally, Cole was ready to go out with the woman that he could barely bring himself to dream about.

David shouted from downstairs, "You better get your butt into the fancy Jaguar you borrowed from the dealership and go get Talley. You're gonna be late!"

"C'mon man, you look sharp enough to cut," Winston said as he hustled his brother down the stairs. "Put the crazy tie in your pocket. Just give Talley a pitiful look when you get there and she'll tie that bow for you. She'll get all up close and flirt with you. Just like in the movies. Y'know what I'm sayin?"

"Maybe you'll even get to kiss her!" David said, wiping his eyeglasses and grinning with vicarious relish.

Cole pushed the tie into his pocket and his hands went moist at the thought. Maybe he *would* get to kiss Talley tonight.

⁓⌒⁓

Joe was out in the living room leafing through a magazine while Alicia dressed. The deep bronze brocade dress she had been dying to wear was as flattering as she hoped it would be. The color brought out the tawny copper tones in her brown skin. The dark topaz jewelry was perfect with it. She gazed with satisfaction at the full-length reflection of her petite, rounded figure in the gown. The dress was sleeveless, fitted in front and with a becoming flare in the back. Matching bronze brocade shoes peeked out from the hem.

Joe would eat her up once he got out of this odd mood he was in. He'd been acting strange all week, grabbing and holding her tight one moment, going all cold and aloof the next. *Maybe he's having some strange male PMS problem,* she mused.

After nearly three months of being in his company almost daily, Alicia knew she loved Joe and wanted to marry him. She was pretty sure he loved her. The challenge was simply getting him to admit it and then persuading him to pop the question. She wanted *him* to bring it up—and soon. They weren't kids anymore and her clock was ticking.

It was time for Joe to take their relationship to the next level. She was going to have to broach the subject tonight somehow.

∽

Joe was in hell. He had waited for the past three days for Alicia to mention this guy Tom. When he had asked about her lunch on Wednesday, she'd said she lunched with an old friend. She hadn't volunteered anything else and he hadn't wanted to push. Now it was too late for him to bring it up again without sounding strange. He wished he hadn't been so honorable last week. He should have followed them, spied on them, at least gotten a look at his competition. It kept eating at him. If Tom was just an old friend, why hadn't she mentioned him before?

There was no question in his mind now, he was in love with Alicia and he wanted a future with her. But first he wanted to find out more about this Tom. Surely Alicia wouldn't be the type to two-time a man. He was going to find a way to bring it up tonight.

Roberta was trying too hard, and things just weren't working. The red satin dress was just a little too red for her skin tones, and the damn thing was pulling a bit too much across the hips. She'd wanted something bold, but this was bordering on shameless.

Hell, it was too late now. Her big round breasts were her saving grace. Full and heavy, they were beautifully showcased in the deep V of the ruffled neckline. Cole had always liked her breasts. That skinny, pale Talley had nothing like them.

Roberta took another deep drink from the glass of Chablis she'd carried as she dressed. Fuming over the irony of this evening, she refilled it from the bottle on her bedside table and drank again. How dare Cole take someone else to a black tie affair after all the times she'd begged him to go with her to the endless events that Atlanta offered. *How dare he make me go stag tonight?* She was going to have to have a conversation with him about it. She didn't plan to make a scene, but she was surely going to take Cole aside!

CHAPTER TEN

Talley fairly danced her way to the door at the sound of the chime. Finding Cole on the other side was her reward. The well-cut suit he wore enhanced his broad shoulders and slender hips. His white starched elegant shirt glimmered against the brown of his flawless skin and accentuated the scintillating glow of his beautiful blue-green eyes. Talley loved what she saw in those eyes.

Cole stared. "You look...I knew you would be beautiful, but...you look like a goddess...a golden goddess."

"Thank you," she murmured. Thrilled by his enthusiasm, she felt her knees go weak. "And you..." She searched for words. "You look positively dreamy." She couldn't take her eyes off him. His glowing good looks took her breath away. The formality of his clothes could not hide his blatant virility. And he was so large, he seemed to make the tiny living room of her townhouse even smaller.

"I don't know about all that," Cole said modestly. "I guess I look well enough, but this thing..." He held the tie aloft. "This thing is giving me fits."

"I can help you with that." Gliding closer, Talley took the tie from his fingers. Standing on tiptoe she fingered his collar and enjoyed the warmth of his closeness. Conscious of his awareness of her, she quickly and expertly worked the tie into place.

Inhaling the subtle scent of aftershave blended with Cole's special clean, healthy essence, Talley was dizzied by the force of her emotions. In the space of a breath, she knew she'd lived a lifetime waiting to feel like this, and she wanted to melt into the circle of his arms, but…She sighed, wanting…

She stepped away to admire her handiwork and his hand went to her back to steady her. For the briefest of seconds she dared to hope he was going to lean closer and take her parted lips for his own pleasure.

Watching the delicate flutter of her heavy dark lashes, Cole ached to kiss her. He wondered what gave her lips the tender lift that made him want to crush her to him. Those soft, tantalizing rosebud lips were enticing. The warmth of her tawny satin skin against his hand drew him, but he knew there could be no mere sampling what Talley offered. A single taste and there would be no turning back. That didn't stop him from wanting to take her lips, right there in front of the silently hovering Narye.

"We'd better go," Talley said softly, offering him her mirrored jacket.

"Yeah, go," Cole echoed, slipping the jacket over her shoulders and counseling himself toward patience. Before this night was over, he'd have his kiss.

━⟲━

"Oh, man…talk about gorgeous…" the cameraman angled his camera for a wider shot. "People that look like them, that's why I don't mind coverin' this stuff…"

Talley felt the swing of the camera's lens as it moved for a better shot of her and Cole. Carefully dropping her head, she managed to cover her face with the broad sweep of Cole's tuxedoed shoulder as they entered the lobby of the Hyatt Regency Hotel. She leaned a bit more on his arm and blushed when he smiled down at her.

They caused heads to turn as they made their way down the escalators and across the reception area in front of the banquet room. Cole was swollen with pride at the attention they drew.

"Now that dress…" a woman admired loud enough for Talley to overhear.

"Uhmm-hm," her friend agreed. "I'd do almost anything for that dress, but I would kill for that man!"

"She's talking about you, you know," Talley whispered.

"Nah," Cole demurred, delighted. "Couldn't be."

Talley was extremely nervous about the looks they were attracting and whispered to Cole that she wanted to hurry and sit down. They skipped the pre-event reception and went straight into the banquet hall.

At the door they received their table assignment. Unknowns with two "loose" tickets, they got stuck at a table in the back of the room, which was perfectly fine with Talley. Seated in a dark corner, she felt her comfort level increase.

Four young women joined them at their table as the banquet room began to fill. After they ogled Cole appreciatively and spoke politely to Talley, they began to excitedly spot local celebrities. The room was teeming with recognizable faces, faces of people who regularly showed up in the business, political and lifestyle sections of *The Atlanta Journal-Constitution*.

"Ohh, isn't that Andrew Young?" said one.

"Yeah, and that's Hank Aaron with him," said another.

"There's Senator Stanton and his wife, Sadonna. She's the one that did that crunk music video back before they got married."

"That's her sister with the basketball player, Big Mack Taylor. They're twins."

"I can see that, gurrl!"

Cole grinned at Talley and she winked. From their vantage point, they could see those who entered without being seen. It was a good thing they were inconspicuous since Talley had met and befriended Senator Maurice Stanton and Sadonna last year. Talley felt Cole and Maurice were very much alike and would enjoy each other's company. *One day, when I get these divorce and child custody issues solved, I'll introduce them,* she vowed.

Brightly clad multi-hued people peacocked into the room doing a social minuet from table to table. At one point, Cole put his hand over Talley's as it lay on

the table to call her attention to a particularly spec-
tacular outfit. He left it there in comfortable intimacy.

They dined on the broiled salmon entrée and
chatted amiably with each other and the young
women at their table about TowMasters, the Atlanta
Business League history, and the myriad Atlanta
celebrities in attendance. Then, just before dessert,
Talley went to the ladies' room.

Adjusting her lipstick in the mirror, she glanced at
the pretty woman in the bronze brocade dress
standing next to her. Alicia was staring at Talley.

"Talley, is that you? Is that my roomie?" Alicia
asked.

"Alicia!" Talley was thrilled to see her old friend.

"Honey! I been dyin' to see you! I heard you were
in Atlanta, but I didn't know where," Alicia said excitedly.

"I've been planning to call you. I have so much to
tell you! but…wait a minute. How did you know I
was here?" Talley asked, startled.

"Sugar lump, you got to get out of this hotel!"
Alicia said, her eyes widening as it dawned on her.
"I'm datin' the detective your father-in-law hired to
find you. The one that's in town lookin' for you. He's
here in the banquet hall!"

"Oh no," Talley gasped. "I was afraid of being
recognized if I came here."

"Where you sittin'?" Alicia asked.

"In the back of the room."

"Thank goodness for small mercies. We're way in the front. But you got to get out of here right now! Do you have to go back to your table? What're you doin' here anyway? Never mind, we'll talk about that later. Let's get you outta here."

"I have a date back at my table," Talley said.

"How'd you get a date in Atlanta so fast?" Alicia cocked an eyebrow.

"How is it you're dating the detective that's looking for me?" Talley demanded right back.

"Honey, it's a story. I'll tell you 'bout it. Give me your table number and you wait by the escalators. I'll go get your date. What's his name?"

"Cole. He's the only man at the table."

"And you left him there. Alone? Same ole naive, trustin' Talley," Alicia smiled.

"Here. I'll write my table number and my home phone number down. Memorize them, then swallow the paper," Talley said with a grin.

Alicia waved a hand at her as she rushed into the banquet hall.

As Talley stood in the recesses of the escalator, the minutes ticked by slowly and her fear welled up. *I cannot get caught tonight. If Cedric finds me, tape or no tape, I'll never get a divorce from Marshall. I'd have to go home with my tail between my legs. And Michael…and…and…I'd have to leave Cole,* she thought with growing panic.

"Why did I come to this thing?" she muttered, "This was a terrible idea."

She breathed a short sigh of relief a few minutes later when Alicia came back, pulling a puzzled and harassed Cole who was being followed by an angry Roberta.

"You can't just walk away in the middle of our conversation," Roberta complained loudly. "And who is this witch?" She indicated Alicia.

"Ro, I can't talk right now," Cole was saying over his shoulder. "I gotta go."

It was clear Roberta had had way too many glasses of wine, because she was determined to have her say. She continued to follow Cole, fuming.

"I brought you your big ole handsome man," Alicia said to Talley with an eyebrow cocked at Roberta, "but looks like he's draggin' some garbage with him."

"Who you calling garbage, bitch? I'll knock yo' black ass into the middle of next week," Roberta threatened.

Alicia shook her head in disgust. "Like I said, trash and garbage."

"Ro, please," Cole begged, embarrassed.

"Cole, we've got to get out of here, now, as quietly as possible," Talley said *sotto voce*. People coming out of the banquet hall were looking on curiously.

"Whachu saying now, you siditty yella dog?" Roberta slurred.

"Okay, that's enough out of you," Alicia snapped. She faced Roberta like a tiny bulldog, blocking her from talking to Talley and Cole as they hopped on the escalator down to the parking garage.

"Get outta my way," they heard Roberta shout.

Cole's borrowed Jaguar was parked in a row of luxury cars just outside the door. Once on I-85 headed south, Talley giggled nervously. Her giggles sparked chuckles from Cole. Chuckles grew until they were both laughing uproariously.

"Your friend is something!" Cole laughed. "Ro is twice her size."

"She was my roommate in college. She's a fighter. I actually feel sorry for Roberta."

"Why'd we have to leave?" Cole asked. "Besides the scene Ro was trying to make."

"I ran into Alicia in the ladies' room and we had a glad reunion. She told me she's actually dating the private investigator working for my father-in-law. She said he was in the banquet hall, her date for the dinner," Talley explained.

Cole let out a heavy breath. "Man, that was close."

They were silent for a while as the luxurious car slid silently through the night, headed south for Talley's College Park townhouse.

"Does Roberta have any right to be that angry with you?" Talley asked suddenly.

"Hell, *I* don't think so," Cole said. "But, you know, you women have different ways of looking at things than men."

"Looking at what, for example?"

"I've been telling Ro for more than a year now it's not ever going to work out for us. She wants a man who's finished college, who wears a suit and tie to work every day, and speaks perfect English. I'm not ashamed to put on my overalls and drive a truck in a business that I own and I *ain't* worried about how I talk as long as I'm understood."

"And she doesn't get that," Talley said, shaking her head. "Clothes don't make the man. My very well-educated, abusive husband puts on an expensive suit every day to go to work."

"Yeah, and I understand sometimes he puts on a dress after work."

Talley's breath came deep. "How did you know that?"

"Michael told me."

"Michael talked to you about it?" She was surprised.

"Yeah. He was pretty shook up seeing his dad like that."

"He hasn't spoken a word to me about it."

"He didn't want to bring back bad memories for you," Cole said. "I think he felt a lot better after he told me about it."

"What else did he tell you?"

"About the night he bit his dad's ankle. I said good for him!"

"I think I need to take him to a psychologist."

"Naw. My brothers and I will keep him sane," Cole grinned.

They were silent again as Cole pulled off the interstate at the Camp Creek Parkway exit.

"Getting back to Roberta," Talley said. "Have you been out with her lately?"

"I saw her at her place a couple of months ago," he admitted.

"You made love?"

"We had sex."

"It was love for her," Talley asserted, feeling a painful stab of jealousy.

"But I told her…"

"She didn't hear you."

"That's what I mean. I was weak that one time and she took it all wrong."

"Looks like you're going to have to join the ranks of dirty rotten scoundrels," Talley chided, shaking her head.

"Hey, I'll be one of those, if I can just get her to leave me alone."

"Here's a universal rule. Repeat it after me: Never sleep with a person you're trying to break with."

"I got it." He smiled sheepishly. "I'll never do it again."

"Better not."

"Listen, I don't want to go home. It's a nice night, want to go to the park and listen to some music? Maybe even find a paved spot and dance or something?" he asked.

"I'd love that."

"I'll stop at Green's liquor and get us some beers…or…or…some white wine. How about some Gallo?"

"Sounds delicious," she said with a smile.

With wine and plastic cups in hand, Cole pulled the Jaguar into John Adams Park and stopped near the deserted tennis courts. He found a mellow radio station playing oldies, then shook out the car's floor mats and set them on a nearby bench.

"Do you mind if I untie this bow tie?" he asked as they settled on the bench. He stretched his long legs out in front of him and poured two glasses of wine.

"Of course not," she answered, sipping the wine. He pulled the tie loose and unbuttoned the top button of his shirt with a grateful sigh.

They sat there quietly for a while, drinking the wine and looking up at the stars. Talley was intensely aware of the big man next to her. Even in repose he exuded powerful energy.

"You know, yesterday when I got mad at you for offering to buy a truck, it wasn't because I don't want you to be part of TransportMasters," he said. She nodded and looked down at her feet.

"I need your help with it. You've got a real talent for how things should be done, how to get business for it. I want to give you a title."

"How about vice president of marketing?" she suggested.

"Yeah, that's right," he said. "I'll even give you a raise."

"Now you're talking!" she said with a laugh. "But, let's wait until TransportMasters is actually making some money first. Though I don't doubt that it will happen fast."

"You don't really believe that," he said.

"Yes, I do," she insisted. "You've got the kind of drive and ambition that makes greatness. You're not afraid to work hard and you're very smart."

"Huh, me? Smart?" He laughed.

"Yes, you. Smart."

There was a chill in the air and when she scooted closer to him for warmth, he put his arm around her.

"It's a pretty night, isn't it?" he asked.

"Yes, it is," she said. "It's too bad we had to leave the dinner before we found out if we won the raffle."

"Did we have to be there to win?"

"I don't think so. I think they'll notify the winner by mail if they're not there. I'll call them on Monday. I have a very good feeling about this."

"Yeah, so you *do* think you can see the future?" Cole teased.

"Hush, or I'll make you dance with me," she said as Etta James came on the radio singing "At Last."

"You don't scare me, I love to dance," he said, standing and walking her to the tennis court.

As he pulled her close to him and wrapped himself around her, moving easily to the music, she enjoyed that feeling of complete safety that she'd had in his dining room not so long ago.

"This is the feeling," she whispered into the open collar of his shirt. "This is what I've been looking for."

"What feeling?" he asked gently, speaking into her hair.

"The safe feeling. Like nothing bad can get me or Michael." She sighed, rubbing a hand down his strong, broad back.

Stirred by the fluid caress of her long narrow hand, Cole's voice was husky with desire. "Nothing bad will ever get you as long as I'm with you."

"Promise."

"Promise." There was no hesitation in his answer. "I want...I need...." He stopped.

She leaned back and looked up at him. "What?"

"I just want to forget who you are for tonight," he said.

"I'm just a woman," she whispered. "A woman who wants very badly for you to kiss her."

He pulled in a small breath and touched his lips gently to hers. Her lips were soft and warm, her breath sweet, like the fruity wine they had been drinking. She sighed, a gentle sound, but it touched him to his soul, reverberating all through him.

He deepened the kiss and she stretched for more, her eyes actually tearing with the bittersweet yearning to take all of him inside her. She wanted to be a part of him and to stay in this warm sweet circle of trust and safety. His mouth was full and soft and moist and he licked her top lip with his tongue. She stood on her toes, melted into him and opened her mouth to let him in.

The devouring kiss seemed endless. His tongue entered her mouth and she welcomed it with her own. She sucked in a breath, and his hand came up to the back of her head, holding her steady while he probed deeper with his tongue. A small groan escaped his throat. She answered with a purr of her own. The kiss grew deeper and she felt him harden against her, the sexual excitement mounting uncontrollably in her. His hand lifted to cup her small firm breast and she gasped with the thrill of it.

Their tongues danced together, their arms tightened, their hands rubbed and clutched, pulled at each other's back and arms and neck. Their bodies strained to each other, frustrated by the clothing separating them. Their movements grew desperate; their breathing ragged and labored.

When they pulled apart at last, it was with a jerk. They stood back from each other and spoke silent volumes with their eyes.

He pulled her to him again. This time they just stood trembling in one another's arms as their panting eased.

"I don't know what to say," he breathed, finally.

"I don't either." She sighed happily.

"I don't know what this is, but it's so strong it makes me scared."

"I'm not afraid," she insisted. "Please don't be."

"I feel like you could really hurt me," he whispered. "I mean, do some damage."

"Or we could be the happiest people in the world," she suggested urgently.

"Yeah," he said, breaking the mood with a dry chuckle. "Like someone like me could make someone as rich as you happy."

"Someone like you could certainly try. We both could."

"People like me are always trying."

Suddenly he was a teenager again, seething with resentment against the rich Porsche drivers who had tossed him a tip without even looking at him. His insecurities and petty resentments were like evil fiends plaguing him unmercifully.

"Cole? What are you afraid of?"

"Nothing, Talley." There were no words, at least none that she would understand or accept.

He was afraid that Talley would have financial needs that he could never satisfy. He was afraid her money would take over his life, drowning his own self worth. He was afraid it would be only a matter of time before she, like Roberta, turned on him for his unpolished style. Except this time the betrayal would be devastating.

Talley looked up at him with puzzled and entreating eyes. "How can I make you know that money isn't everything?" she pleaded.

"You would say that, you've always had it." He thrust her away gently and turned his back to her.

"Exactly, I'm the expert on it," she argued, following him as he walked away from her with long strides

"Very cute. Try living without it," he snapped over his shoulder.

Talley lengthened her stride to catch up with him and then, facing him, she put her hands on his arms, trying to force him to look at her, to listen to her. "You get to a point with money where you realize there is only so much you need," she said. "That there is only so much you can buy with it and that it *doesn't* buy happiness. I've never been happier than in these past few months. With you and your family and my work. Michael and I have been safe and I have a purpose."

"Yeah," he said, shrugging dismissively. "Sure. You've been pretending to be poor and pretending to like it. And now you've got a purpose. That's nice, Talley. Real special. Come on, let's go. It's late." He walked away from her again.

"Cole, listen to me. I mean this. I want you. I want to be with you," she said urgently.

"You're just crazy. What did they put in this cheap wine?" he said, gathering the empty bottle and the floor mats.

She hung back from him for a moment, frustrated, then sighed and followed him to the car.

On the way home they sat silent until Cole said, "Well, one good thing. I got to kiss you. My brothers weren't going to let me back in the house lest I did."

"Your brothers are hilarious." Talley grinned, relieved to hear lightness return to his tone.

"They're crazy about you," he said.

"I'm crazy about them."

"Not too crazy, I hope. I don't want to have to commit fratricide," he smiled.

"You need to watch that Winston then," she smiled.

"Everybody has to watch Winston," he said ruefully.

⁓ↄ

After Talley and Cole escaped down the escalators, Roberta and Alicia stood eyeballing each other. Alicia had her tiny hands balled into fists straight down at her sides.

"Get the hell outta my way," Roberta said again menacingly.

Alicia stood her ground. "You need to just calm down and go back to your seat," she said. "Or better yet, you should go in the ladies room and look at yo'self in the mirror. You look broke off."

Roberta lunged at the small combatant. When Alicia sidestepped neatly, Roberta tripped and fell on the down escalator. It carried her, dazed, down to the garage floor, dumping her out at the bottom. As a valet rushed to help her up, she shrugged him off rudely. She spotted Cole and Talley just as they were driving off.

"Rats!" she said, stomping her foot and breaking the already bent heel of her shoe clean off.

The valet backed away from her with eyebrows raised.

Roberta limped around to the up escalator, her dress torn, her stockings ripped. When she got back to the banquet hall floor, Alicia had gone back to the dinner. Roberta stalked into the hall, got her purse from her table, made hurried apologies to the startled guests there and left.

On the way home she began to sober and images of her earlier performance made an unwelcome parade through her mind—her unsatisfying conversation with Cole at his table, following Cole out of the dinner, eyes ablaze, voice loud and raucous, shouting at that little witch in the brown dress…She burst into tears.

Talley had looked rich and aristocratic in a gown Roberta knew couldn't cost less than four figures. Where would a woman working for a towing company get such a dress?

All of a sudden came clarity. She knew where she'd seen Talley before. It was in a picture in *Vibrant* magazine! Talley was a famous, rich socialite! Roberta was sure she still had the issue at home. She pressed on the gas.

~ ❧ ~

Alicia returned to The Boyd Group table, none the worse for wear. Joe had noticed her lengthy absence, though. He'd just begun to wildly imagine "Tom" was somewhere in the room and that he and Alicia had snuck away to neck in the hall. He wanted to get out of his seat and track them down, but Alicia's boss, Christina Boyd, was watching his every move. He didn't think he'd made a good impression on Christina.

"Christina been givin' you the third degree?" Alicia asked Joe as she slipped back into her seat.

"Lord, yes," Joe said. "I don't think she likes me."

"Did she call you 'darlin' ?" Alicia asked.

"Toward the end of the conversation…"

"It's a start. She won't really like you 'til we're engaged. Then, she'll warm up nicely."

"Oh? Are we going to be engaged?" he wanted to know.

"Are you askin' me to marry you?" she responded.

"Stop playing games, Alicia. We need to talk about this."

"Sure, sugah, later. Not here. They've finally stopped the speechifyin'. Christina's gonna go up and pull the winnin' raffle ticket for the marketin' makeover."

Christina's graceful full-skirted black satin gown with its long-sleeved black velvet bodice made a nice swishing noise as she mounted the podium. Her black pageboy gleamed in the spotlight as she announced the winning ticket: "TowMasters, Inc. wins a marketing makeover valued at ten thousand dollars."

The crowd applauded while the spotlight searched for the winners.

"Not here? What a shame," Christina said. "But they'll be notified by mail."

When she returned to the table, Joe and Alicia got up to say their good-byes.

"What? You aren't staying to dance?" Christina asked.

"No, we gonna make our way home," Alicia said.

"All right, darling. I'll see you on Monday."

In the lobby of the hotel, Joe quickly pulled Alicia into the dimly lit seclusion of the hotel bar, seating her in a cozy booth. They ordered brandy and relaxed in the quiet and comfort of the well-padded high-backed cubicle.

Alicia sat close to Joe and slipped her arm under his.

"This is nice," she said, "cuddlin' with my sugar buns."

"Let's talk about this marriage thing," he said.

"Don't be nervous, honey," she giggled. "I was jus' foolin' with you. We don't need to go there."

"I need you to be serious about this," he said sternly. "I had planned to bring up the subject tonight myself."

"Did you now? That's surprisin'," Alicia teased. "Usually men avoid that subject."

"First, I need to know if you're seeing any other men."

"Good gracious, honey bunch, when would I have time to see anyone else? We're always together."

"What about that mysterious lunch you had this week?"

"Why are you harpin' on that lunch?"

"Why won't you say who your lunch was with?"

"I saw an old boyfriend. Okay?" She was defensive.

"And?" He prompted.

"And nothin'. We were catchin' up on old and new times. I told him about you and that was it. He doesn't mean anythin' to me anymore."

"Oh."

"Sweetie, there's nobody but you in my life now. Hasn't been since that night when we made love."

"Alicia, I've been crazy this week, thinking that there might be someone else. I haven't been able to eat or sleep. I guess I'm in love with you," he sighed.

She feigned dismay. "Or else you're comin' down with the flu!"

"No," he smiled, "I love you." He kissed her forehead.

"Sweetie, I love you too. But I haven't had any of the symptoms you describe. Mine have been more like a kinda blissful haze with occasional wild heights of joy." She nuzzled his neck.

"Maybe now that I know that Tom doesn't mean anything to you I can start feeling that way too."

"How'd you know his name?" Alicia frowned.

"You just said it."

"No, I didn't."

"Maybe you've said something before. Maybe Christina said something. I don't know. Forget it. Let's get out of here," he said quickly. He mentally kicked himself for the slip.

Alicia shrugged. "Yes, let's go home and play."

CHAPTER ELEVEN

Roberta awakened with a bad hangover. Her mouth felt as dry as old parchment, her head was pounding, and her stomach was knotted and churning. But she was on an emotional high, thrilled by her discovery.

The previous night she'd leafed through a pile of old magazines she'd stacked in a closet until she found the article that confirmed her suspicions. She'd fallen asleep with the *Vibrant* magazine beside her and as soon as she woke up, her eyes lit again on the photo:

Talley's golden hair was in a classic chignon and her face, in profile, was delicate and pure. "Mrs. Tallulah Quincy Pettifore, wife of Marshall Pettifore of Pettifore, Pettifore, and Quincy, LLC, was the hostess of the 2003 Detroit Alumni Chapter Delta Sigma Theta Debutante Ball," the caption said.

Talley Parsons is Tallulah Pettifore! Roberta exulted. She was clearly hiding the fact that she was a member of a class of African Americans for whom Cole expressed nothing but contempt! There was nothing Cole hated more than a liar. Wait 'til he heard the whopper "Mrs. Parsons Pettifore" was telling. *She was probably laughing at him and his dirty little business every day. What the hell was she doing there?*

Roberta hopped out of bed, hugging the magazine to her bosom. Then she fell back on the mattress when pain and waves of nausea hit her. She'd had wine before leaving her house last night, champagne and Scotch at the reception, lots more wine at the dinner table…and she hadn't eaten anything. Sore and bruised from her tumble down the escalator, she moaned out loud. Then, with a shudder of mortification, she remembered that whole evening. She crawled back under the covers and groaned some more. She'd wait until this afternoon to call Cole.

⁓

The weather finally turned cold in Atlanta, two weeks before Christmas. But it was a fresh, crisp cold and the skies were bright blue, so different from the gun-metal gray winter skies that colored Talley's memories of Detroit. Talley woke to the sun streaming in her window, her body filled with a feeling of languid well-being *Cole, big, bright-eyed Cole*, she thought, reliving their kiss. *I've fallen in love with him!*

She hopped out of bed and did a frenzied jig around the room, waking Michael, who came running into the room to join her.

"Why are we dancing, Mommy?" he wanted to know as he jumped up and down with her.

"Because we love Mr. Cole and we think Mr. Cole loves us!" Talley confessed, falling on the bed in a heap.

"Yes! Yes! We love Mr. Cole," Michael agreed, jumping up on the bed, too. Narye came into the bedroom and watched their antics with a worried frown. "We're going to *marry* Mr. Cole!" Michael told her.

"Mr. Cole is a good man and I agree that he loves you," Narye said to Michael, with a warning look at Talley. "But I would not be so quick to fly to marriage."

"Why not?" Michael asked.

"Mr. Cole has some personal demons to conquer first," Narye said enigmatically.

"Well, let's join him at church and help him get rid of those devils," Talley said cheerfully. "Come on, everybody, get dressed! We've got some exorcism to do!"

⁓

Alicia sent Joe away early Sunday morning, telling him she planned to go to church. He hadn't gotten into the Christian habit of going to church regularly, so she knew that would scare him off for now. *I fully intend to start indoctrinating him to weekly church service very soon*, she pledged to herself with a smug smile.

She dialed Talley's number quickly.

"Girl, you made my eyes so happy when I saw you last night," she said when Talley answered. "It was so good. You look just as gorgeous as you did at your weddin'—no, *more* beautiful!"

"And you! You're just breathtaking!" Talley said. "And just as feisty! What happened to Roberta?"

"Oh, her. She ran at me, the big lummox. I stepped aside and she went ass-over-teakettle down the escalator! I hollered!"

"That's terrible," Talley gasped. "She wasn't hurt, was she?"

"Not with all the paddin' she has on her butt and not more than she deserved, putting on a tacky performance over that poor man," Alicia said.

"Now, now, Alicia, remember, she's a woman scorned." Talley grinned.

"Who *is* that big hunk of manhood, by the way?"

"He's my boss. I needed a job when I first got down here, and he offered me one. I love working with him and his business so much I wouldn't leave for anything."

"Girl, tell me everything!" Alicia exclaimed.

"Not over the phone, we're on our way to church," Talley said. "I want to see your pretty face. Let's meet for lunch somewhere. You name a restaurant and I'll find it."

"How about Einstein's in Midtown on Juniper Street? I'll meet you there after church at about one-thirty," Alicia said.

～৲

Cole woke up remembering Talley's kiss. Her sweet mouth opening under his. Her curved form matching the hardened planes of his body. Her heat pulsing through her clothes. Her eyes looking up at him unfocused and her face flushed with answering lust. He rolled over and groaned, burying his face in the pillow to try and quench the images. When that didn't work, he forced himself out of bed.

Keeping busy and taking a good cold shower were the only cures for what ailed him. He roused his brothers for church, but over breakfast they all wanted to hear about "The Date."

"So, how'd Talley look, man?"

"You know she looked good. Like a queen." Cole smiled at the memory.

"She didn't mind about the tie, did she?"

"Naw, she whipped it into a bow easy," Cole answered.

"So did you dance with her?"

"We didn't stay for the dancing," Cole said. This raised a general howl and a chorus of hand slapping and nudges from the brothers.

"Took her right upstairs to one of them rooms, did ya?" Winston asked.

"Hell, no," Cole growled at him. "You know Talley isn't like that. We found out the detective that's looking for her was at the dance, so we had to get out of there. Then Roberta showed up. Started showing out."

"Ugh…Rozilla," Winston muttered.

"But I did get to dance with her," Cole went on.

"With big Rozilla?" Winston asked.

"No, dummy, with Talley." David shoved his brother.

"How?"

"We stopped at Adams Park on the way home. Had some wine, danced to the car radio on the tennis courts."

"That's good, that's good. Did you kiss her?"

"Yes," Cole said, feeling the print of Talley's lips tattooed against his own.

"Tell us about it," David demanded.

"No," Cole said curtly, holding his treasured memories for himself.

David was still trying to squeeze details from his closemouthed brother as Cole parked the truck in the church lot. It never failed that the four tall, hand-some, clean-cut brothers entering the Morning Star Baptist Church with their heads bowed reverently sent a tremor of yearning through the ladies in the congregation. Some sighs were even audible.

Cole was always embarrassed by the reaction. David found it amusing. Marcus usually just ignored it. Winston saw it as his due, strutting and preening, gathering all the love to himself.

I'm gonna have to pray for that boy, Cole thought, moving into his place in the family pew.

Just before the service began, Cole saw Talley, Narye and Michael slip quietly in the door and take seats in the back. Having overheard Marcus invite Talley to attend services at the southwest Atlanta church earlier this week, Cole figured it was a nice gesture, but he hadn't believed she would actually take him up on it. *She's probably Episcopalian,* he'd thought.

Seeing her now pleased him immensely and he joined her in the back row. Her lovely face brightened when she saw him coming, and Michael wiggled with glee.

Standing beside her, sharing a hymnal with her and hearing her sweet, light voice raised in song, Cole allowed himself to imagine for a brief moment that this was his family. That Talley was his wife and Michael, his son. It was a fantasy that made him tremble with excitement all the while he was trying to force it out of his mind.

Lord, help me get these crazy thoughts out of my head, he prayed.

—ଚ—

Talley and Alicia met outside the restaurant, both approaching at the same time. They hugged and chattered together as if no time had passed since they'd spent time together.

"I can't believe we went nearly eight years without layin' eyes on one another," Alicia said once they'd been seated and had ordered. "I've missed you."

"Our emails and phone calls have kept us close over the years," Talley said. "I don't know how I could have gone on without them."

"But you never told me what was happenin' in your marriage," Alicia sighed. "I knew you weren't happy, though."

"I couldn't find a way to describe what was going on. It was too humiliating and degrading."

"Can you tell me now?"

Slowly and sadly Talley described her life with Marshall over the past eight years—the devastating honeymoon, the discovery of his perversions, the degrading and painful abuse, the constant fear and anxiety...

With small gasps of horror and sympathy, Alicia listened, fighting back tears, reaching over occasionally to touch her friend's hand. When Talley finished by describing the incident she had videotaped, Alicia could only say, "That bastard! That bastard! I wish I could have been there to protect you."

"I'm learning to protect myself. Believe me. Having a child teaches you, toughens you up. I took the abuse from Marshall because I was afraid to leave and conditioned to put up with it. But when he laid hands on Michael...it was time to go."

The waiter came over to pour coffee for the women as they finished their meal.

"Alright, enough about me," Talley said. "Tell me about the detective you're seeing!"

"My Joe," Alicia breathed, her face glowing. Talley widened her eyes with surprise. "I'm crazy about him! I'm in love with him and he's in love with me," Alicia sighed.

"Uh, oh," Talley said faintly, stirring her coffee.

"No, you don't have to worry. He'd never use me to get to you. He's an honorable man! We met when he came to see if you had contacted me. I told him right then and there I wouldn't help him and that was that! He agreed not to try and question me."

"Hmmm," Talley said doubtfully.

"Really! We were attracted to each other from the first moment. It's been nearly three months now and last night he brought up the 'm' word!" Alicia said in triumph.

"Marriage? He brought up marriage?"

"Sure did. With only the *slightest* nudge from me."

"You're going to marry him? I wish I could meet him."

"Oh, you will, soon," Alicia assured her, reaching over to pat her hand. "Once Joe knows that Marshall was hitting you and your son, he'll be on your side, I'm sure of it. That's the kind of man he is."

Talley just shook her head and clutched her friend's hand tightly. "Please don't tell him anything I've told you today."

"'Course not!" Alicia said emphatically. "You know from our years at Spelman what a clam I can be. Now, you tell me about the man you were with last night."

"His name is Cassius Coleman. They call him Cole. He owns TowMasters, Inc…"

"Are you foolin' me?"

"No, why?"

"TowMasters won the marketin' makeover from my firm last night!"

"Oh, wow!" Talley was elated. "Will we be working together?"

"Abso-posi-lutely!"

"I can't wait to tell Cole! Oh, I am so pleased!"

"Tell me 'bout Cole, now!" Alicia demanded.

"He's…he's…wonderful! He's a real man's man. You know what I mean. All big boots and broad shoulders and voice like a roar. He's like Mufasa in *The Lion King*—forgive me, but I do have a seven-year-old, you know—big and bold and gentle as a kitten with those he loves."

"And he loves you," Alicia prompted.

"I think he does. But he won't admit it or act on it. He has so much trouble with my money."

"I can see that. It *is* somewhat dauntin', you know. So damn much of it."

"Stop, Alicia, I don't want to think it's hopeless."

"You care for him?"

"I love him something fierce."

"Go for it then, girl. Don't worry about the money thing. Have you slept with him?"

"No, no," Talley shivered. "I'm afraid of that."

"Lord, chile, what are you scared of?"

"I don't know if I'm any good at it," Talley admitted, lowering her eyes.

"I can't believe what my ears are hearin'," Alicia said, lifting her hands and bending her lobes forward.

"Marshall always hurt me," Talley said. "I haven't ever been really *loved*."

"I bet that big, pretty man could cure that," Alicia giggled.

CHAPTER TWELVE

Cole had never realized what a jealous nature he had. Ever since that kiss he'd felt proprietary toward Talley and even resented the smiles she gave male customers.

One evening when Cole towed in an illegally parked BMW sedan from toney Buckhead, the young and handsome African American man in brown suede jacket and tan gabardine slacks who came to retrieve it had flirted with Talley. She had been leaving the office for the day, unlocking her BMW SUV, when the man stopped to comment on her vehicle. As Cole watched, leaning against his nearby truck, they began an animated conversation.

The sleek young man, slender and loose-limbed with patrician features, was the same type who had carelessly killed his beautiful life-loving parents, Cole thought as he watched and seethed. And he looked so right with Talley.

Cole felt like a clumsy, lumbering clod as he edged closer, trying to hear their conversation. After one brief disdainful up and down look at Cole in his work pants and company shirt, the debonair young man dismissed Cole, and, grasping Talley's elbow, moved her away. Talley never even noticed. As the two stood chattering excitedly together, a feeling of utter despair washed over Cole, buffeting his entire body. Even though he had no claim on her, he couldn't help wondering what they were talking about.

~ ⸱ ᵔ ⸱ ~

"That's a good-looking truck," the man said, "You happy with it?"

"It's been good," Talley replied, smiling pleasantly.

As they discussed the merits of the expensive vehicle, the young man said, "I wish I could afford one, but on a tennis instructor's salary…"

"You give tennis lessons?" Talley asked, flashing the smile Cole thought of as his own. "Where?"

"I work at a new tennis club right near here with indoor and outdoor courts," he said. "It's called the Charter Club."

"I've passed the facility on my way here and wondered…"

"You should drop in sometime."

"My seven-year-old son was taking lessons before we moved down here and he was getting quite good," Talley told him. "I want to get him started again. Do you teach children?"

"Definitely," the man responded enthusiastically. "The earlier the better, I say."

"My son brought his racquet with him when we moved down here. I think he would sleep with it, if I let him."

"He sounds like a player to me. By the way, my name is George. George Thomas."

"And I'm Talley. Lessons would be a great Christmas present for Michael."

"Do you think I could persuade you to come to the club and sign up for membership?"

"Right now?" Talley looked dubious.

"I get a bonus if I bring in a new member," George confessed. "C'mon, ride with me now! I'll bring you right back."

"No time like the present, huh?" Talley flashed the smile again and agreed.

⎯⎯⎯ ᴄ⁊

Before Cole's stunned eyes, Talley hopped into the man's car and they drove off together. In the shadows where he stood watching them, Cole died a little. Though he wanted to wait and see when Talley came back, calls for service starting coming in from all over Atlanta and he had to leave the yard. When he got back late that night, her car was gone.

She told me she wanted me, but she was just shining me on, Cole thought contemptuously, his famous temper rousing to a fever pitch.

The next morning, Cole greeted Talley with a sneering look and growled, "How was last night?"

Confused by his tone, Talley gave him a questioning look. "What do you mean?"

"That guy you met last night," Cole said, his eyes narrowed and flinty. "Did you enjoy him?"

"Oh, that!" Talley smiled, relieved, "His name is George Thomas. He took me to a new club…"

"You don't have to give me the details," Cole interrupted, cursing himself for even starting the conversation. *I don't give a damn what nightclub they went to on their damn date.*

"But I…he…"

Cole brushed by her curtly and stalked out to his truck, insecurity eating his insides like acid. Hopping in, he spun out of the yard, spitting gravel. All that day he glowered and growled at his brothers until they whined at him.

It had never before occurred to him to wonder what Talley did with her time away from the office. He'd assumed it was spent quietly at home with her son and Narye. But now furious thoughts whirled in his mind as he pictured an imaginary life for her. It was filled with glamorous dates to Atlanta's expensive restaurants and nightclubs with handsome, stylish men like the one she'd driven away with. *While I'm plugging away like a drone, she's probably the queen bee of the South*, he fumed.

To bolster his spirits, Cole went to the bank and pledged some more land to get a down payment for his new truck.

Working with a friendly salesman at the local dealership, Cole ordered a Peterbilt 379 truck with seventy-inch studio sleeper and a three-car enclosed trailer.

"You're really in luck. I had a deal fall through on one already finished, so you can have it right after Christmas," the happy salesman told him. "It's a beaut, man. You're gonna love it."

But even the thought of his shiny new truck couldn't soothe Cole's soul.

When George dropped by the yard to bring Talley her membership card, Cole saw him driving away from the office and almost lost rational control. He fought the murderous urge to run the man's car off the road. The effort it cost him to stop his truck and let George pass left him breathless.

If Cole had talked to his brothers about his feelings and suspicions, they would have been able to help out. Marcus and Winston had met George and got treated to his pitch for new members to the club.

But Cole was not one to share his pain with others, particularly not with his brothers. The big dog in the household had a duty to swallow weakness and doubt, he believed. Besides, all that sharing stuff belonged on *Oprah* or someplace. Instead, Cole stalked around with a sour expression on his face, grumbling at anyone in his path.

When he roared at David for being ten minutes late picking up a car, Marcus pulled him aside. "What's wrong with you, man? You're like a bear with a sore paw. Cut it out! You bringing everybody down."

Talley didn't know what to think of Cole's new attitude toward her. In the office, he either ignored her or spoke to her in short terse sentences, not meeting her eyes. And he stayed away from the office most of the time.

Whenever he was near, her eyes followed him longingly, hoping he would look her way. She missed him terribly. Their shared lunches, the little private jokes, their conversations late into the night, his slow intimate smiles, the feeling of safety she had when she was with him. Frustrated, she was close to tears from his sudden coldness.

Finally she decided to confront him. Eyes narrowed, she made herself tall as she walked up to him.

"What? Are you angry with me even though I can't think of a thing I've done to cause it?"

Off guard, Cole's lips parted soundlessly as he backed away from her.

"No, you don't," she said to him as he edged toward the door of the trailer. She wagged a finger at him. "You need to tell me what I've done so I can apologize and we can get back to being friends. Can we do that, Cole? Can we get back to being friends?"

"Sure, we're friends," he muttered.

"Cole, what have I done to make you mad at me?" she asked.

"Nothing. You haven't done anything," he said in an icy voice as he eased out of the trailer.

I must have frightened him away with my passionate response to his kiss, she thought. *I'd do anything to have our friendship back. Christmas is almost here and I want everyone to be happy at Christmas.*

She was not to get her wish. With Christmas Eve upon them, Cole was still distant.

Talley, Narye and Michael joined Christmas festivities at the Coleman house. Instead of setting up a tree at their townhouse, they focused their creative talents on helping Lucy decorate the big Coleman house. They helped the brothers trim the tree and stock it with gaily wrapped gifts. Talley hoped the brothers would like the soft gray leather driving gloves she'd bought with the TowMasters logo embroidered on them. Cole's were silver with TransportMasters in black and electric blue, the colors they had selected for the new division.

Talley and Michael wove a length of spruce rope festooned with bright bows down the stairway banister and across the fireplace mantel. Narye and Marcus planned a huge Christmas dinner and produced popcorn balls, tree-shaped cookies and hot apple cider to bolster the decorators.

All through the weekend the house was filled to the brim with family, as all the aunts, uncles and cousins came through. Michael played riotously with the youngsters his age, torturing the older brothers and being teased and tormented in return.

On Christmas Day Talley revealed the secret she and Marcus had been giggling about for weeks. She'd taken the commercial drivers test and had her CD license. Cole's dismissive reaction to her news dampened her spirits.

"So now you think you can drive my new big rig?" he sneered.

"I sure can," she bragged. "I can't wait to try it."

"Whatever," he said, turning his back because it hurt to look at her. Talley had never looked more beautiful. In festive red velvet with her soft hair tumbling over her shoulders, she looked like a sparkling Christmas ornament. As she helped Michael open a gift, Cole watched her tuck a curl behind her ear and thought how lucky the gleaming tress was to be able to nestle so close to her smooth cheek. His hands twitched with yearning to grab her slender shoulders roughly, to smash his mouth against hers and get rid of the bright deceptive smile she was wearing.

Talley's smile widened when she saw the pretty pink cashmere sweater that was Cole's present to her.

"This is lovely," she told him with shining eyes. "You have exquisite taste."

Lucy agreed with a giggle. "I thought I was going to have to help Cole pick out something for you, but he went straight to that sweater. He said it looks just like you. 'Soft, sweet and warm,' he said."

Talley gave Cole a curious look. "That must have been before you got mad at me for something."

Cole's face was tight and blank as he turned away. *I'd like to just drag her out of here and…And what?* he asked himself. *And show her what it's like to be loved by a real man,* he finished in agony. He had finally admitted to himself that he loved her. *I love her. God, I wish I didn't.*

Michael was thrilled by his membership card to the Charter Club with the added promise of tennis lessons.

"Do you play tennis?" he asked Cole shyly.

"No," Cole responded, looking into the boy's eyes, so like his mother's.

"You should take lessons with me, then we could play together," Michael suggested hopefully.

"Maybe I will," he said, his heart going out to the child. He dearly loved the sturdy, handsome youngster. It was a shame that his mother was just another frivolous rich princess!

⟨∾⟩

The week between Christmas and New Year's was a bleak one for Cole and Talley. Lately she had begun responding to his coldness with a cool, distant air of her own. And it didn't help that Greg Carver, the manager at the Porsche dealership, had admitted to Cole that he'd gotten the transport contract because he and the salesmen had all been impressed with the style and professionalism of his new office manager.

"We'd been considering using you for a while," Greg said. "But when you brought Talley in, we knew you'd gotten where you needed to be in order to handle this work. She'll be great with our customers."

Cole fumed as he drove away from the dealership. *So my hard work and dependability aren't as important*

*as being able to phony up and schmooze the rich
customers,* he thought. *And now I gotta keep Talley
around. Every day. Looking like...like...a goddess.*

~ ❧ ~

Marshall didn't want to go home for Christmas.
He didn't want to be in that big empty house without
Talley and Michael. Staying with his parents and
looking into his father's angry eyes was out of the
question. Cedric seemed to be able to see the
shameful secrets in the crevices of his mind.

Marshall felt a need to redeem himself. *Granted, I
occasionally relax in women's clothing, but there's nothing
really wrong with that,* he thought. Instead of going
home, he'd go on the prowl for a woman. A big,
succulent, sexually charged female who would rein-
force his manhood.

He found the kind of woman he was looking for
at the bar at Club Velvet on Peachtree. She was all
female animal and stared at him with smoldering eyes.
Her sleek black hair, long healthy legs, rounded hips
and generous bosom oozed sexual heat.

As he stared at her, her plump lips curved into an
inviting smile.

He walked over and sat on the bar stool next to
her, his leg touching hers.

"You have a beautiful smile. Can I buy you a drink
to celebrate?" he asked.

"Sure," she said, flipping her long, braided pony-
tail over her shoulder. "Gin and tonic."

Marshall checked his watch. It was ten forty-five. He hoped to be in bed and inside her before midnight. He raised his arm to catch the waiter's attention.

"Goodness," she said, "is that a Rolex?"

"Yep."

"It's a pretty one."

"Thank you."

"You must be doing well at whatever you do."

"I'm a lawyer. Corporate law. What do you do?"

"I'm a financial consultant."

"You here alone?"

"With some girlfriends," she said, nodding toward two pretty girls talking to some guys down the bar.

When he looked at her silently for a few minutes, she looked back brazenly. There was some chemistry between them.

"What's your name?" he asked.

"Roberta," she said. "What's yours?"

Marshall ignored that. He had no intention of giving this woman his real name. He was looking for anonymous sex.

"Listen, Roberta, I like you. I like the way you look. How about going somewhere quiet to get to know each other better?"

Roberta gave the privileged-looking man the once-over. He was slimmer than she liked her men, with narrow hips and shoulders, but he was tall and wore his expensive clothes well. He had that special sheen of wealth and good breeding. The package smelled like money.

"How do I know you're not Jack the Ripper?" she asked.

"I'm not. I'm an easygoing guy that's being turned on by everything you do," he grinned. "How do I know you're not Cat Woman?"

"I could be."

"Well, I know how to make you purr," he bragged.

Roberta considered the situation. For a night, maybe two, this man would distract her from the pain and resentment she was feeling. She had not been able to get in touch with Cole. His family had circled the wagons against her. With the arrival of the holidays, she'd decided to deal with Tallulah Pettifore later. Her time would be better spent trying to find a new man. "The best way to get over one man is to get under another."

So Roberta had begun frequenting the bars and clubs with a group of girlfriends on the hunt. And now she'd met this promising stranger.

If they were good together, it might turn into something. If not, well, he looked as if he could afford to buy her several lovely parting gifts. Why not be optimistic?

"Tell you what," she said. "Why don't you follow in your car to my apartment? We can talk there."

Outside, Roberta noted that the valet brought him a sleek Ferrari. *Very nice*, she said to herself.

Roberta knew she was taking a chance inviting a strange man into her home and inevitably into her bed, but the four gin and tonics she'd drunk had her feeling a bit reckless. Besides, she had condoms and a pistol beside her bed, and she knew how to use them both.

As soon as they entered her apartment, Marshall was on her. He buried his mouth in her neck, groped her breasts, and squeezed her buttocks. She pushed him away from her firmly, saying, "Calm down, fella."

"What's wrong?" he snapped. "Let's get it on."

"You know, you look a lot smoother than you act," she said with a lifted eyebrow.

He backed away, then sighed and slumped down on the plump pillows of her oversized couch. Roberta came out of the kitchen with wine and two glasses. When she sat beside him on the couch, Marshall reached for her again.

"You in a hurry?" she asked. She backed him off with a tight smile, beginning to regret her decision to bring him here.

"You're so lovely," he said. "I can't help myself."

That's better, she thought.

Damn, he thought, *she's going to make this a chore*.

"How come a beautiful, sexy creature like you is not already taken?" he asked.

"I was," she said. "I'm going through a breakup."

"I'm sorry to hear that," he said, inching closer to her. "His loss," he added, reaching for her.

This time she came to him. She put her glass of wine on the table and leaned into him, letting him undo the pearl buttons on her cream silk blouse.

He clawed the blouse off her shoulders and pulled one plump breast out of the bra cup it was nestled in. He put his mouth on it, sucking at the dark nipple greedily. She felt her insides melting, her juices flowing. She reached for his manhood, expecting to find it full and throbbing. It was not.

"Let's go into the bedroom," she said, standing. He followed her willingly.

Undressed, they stretched out on the bed. She put her head on his stomach and began to ring the tip of his flaccid shaft with her tongue. When she got a reaction, she took it all into her mouth where it began to grow. Her breathy sigh of relief stirred the hardening rod and she flapped blindly in the drawer of her bedside table until she found a condom.

Roberta was disappointed. His member wasn't very big to begin with and it didn't seem to be getting much bigger. He was not helping, lying there stiffly with his eyes squeezed shut, letting her work at him. She climbed on top of him, trying to guide the shaft into her moistness. The thing went limp. She rubbed herself on it, hoping the friction from her hot, wet opening would create a reaction. Nothing.

She rolled onto her back with a sigh.

"It ain't working," she said.

"Suck it again," he demanded.

"Why don't you suck me first?" she suggested.

She heard him make a disgusted noise.

"You know what," she said, standing up. "This just might not be our night."

He came up from the bed suddenly, his face a distorted mask of rage and slapped her, hard. Grabbing her arm, he spun her around until her back was to him.

Then, twisting her arm behind her, he kicked her legs out from under her, pushing her down on the bed. Roberta screamed in pain and tried to fight him. With his manhood as stiff as a board, Marshall grabbed her by the hair and yanked her head up, pushing himself into her roughly. She screamed louder until he hit the side of her head with his fist, dazing her. Her face dropped on the bed.

Holding her fast with his knees bent into hers, her arm twisted painfully behind her, he thrust again and again, ignoring her muffled cries of pain. With his free hand, he slapped her buttock hard with each push. Until, with an exultant animal cry, he emptied himself.

When he pulled out, he pushed her forward onto the bed. "Thanks for the ride," he said, ignoring her weeping. He dressed quickly and left the apartment.

⁓꙳

Cole's truck was delivered on New Year's Eve, but he could take no real joy in it. As he sat in it at the yard, he looked at the empty passenger's seat and imagined Talley sitting beside him, smiling at him as she used to. He'd never been so low in his life and he wondered how he was going to survive seeing Talley every day, knowing he loved her and had lost her to another man. Then, as though he had conjured her, she tapped on the window.

Preparing to leave for the evening, Talley had seen Cole sitting alone in the truck. She and Narye and Michael were planning to spend a quiet New Year's Eve watching DVDs. She had promised her son that he could stay up long enough to watch the Peach Drop at Underground Atlanta on TV.

Cole's attitude toward her had been so consistently brusque and unreasonable in the previous two weeks that she had given up trying to win him over with kindness and put a little ice in her manner, too. *Well, two can play that game,* she'd thought. But she was miserable. There was no explanation for the angry and contemptuous looks he gave her.

Maybe if I show him how much I share his joy in his truck, he'll come around, she thought. She was the only one on the yard who had not examined the inside.

"Can I have a tour?" she asked with a sweet smile when Cole leaned over and pushed the door open on the passenger side.

With a grudging shrug, Cole took her hand and pulled her up into the truck's cab. His heart swelled with pride while he watched her reaction to the enormous, expensive machine.

"It's beautiful," she enthused. "And this is just the beginning for you, Cole. I predict that you will soon be able to buy a second and then a third…Can I see the sleeper part?"

Cole nodded and followed her into the area behind the seats, her apricot scent addling his senses as she brushed past him. They were standing close together in the truck's tiny sleeper when Cole snapped. For ten years he had sacrificed everything he'd ever wanted for his family and their future. He'd put everybody's wants and needs and wishes ahead of his own. He'd always put business ahead of pleasure. Enough! It was time for *him* to have something he yearned for. He was going to have Talley. *I'm just going to have to try and make her love me!* he decided. *And to hell with the consequences.*

Turning suddenly, he gathered Talley into his big arms and crushed her against him passionately. His mouth silenced her as he drank in her lips like a thirsty man. With her tight against him, he could feel her heart hammering wildly and it excited him to a fever pitch.

"I don't care if you are seeing someone else," he hissed at her startled face. "I love you and I want you."

"But I'm not…"

"Shut up," he said, staring into her eyes. "Just listen to me. Whether or not you love me back doesn't matter. I just have to tell you this now and see what happens. I love you, and I want to be with you."

He pulled her to him and kissed her again fiercely, his mouth and tongue working. The urgency of her response was gratifying. She pressed herself against him, her hands clutching his arms. He could feel her nipples tightening against his chest as her breath came in short pants. *She wants me too,* he realized with an overwhelming joy. His touch gentled on her, his mouth softening.

"I've missed you," Cole whispered.

"I've missed you, too," she responded with a soft moan. "Just tell me why you were so angry with me."

"How did you think I would feel, watching you go off with that dude in the BMW, knowing you were seeing him?" Cole sighed.

"Dude? You mean George Thomas?" she said, backing away from him with an incredulous cry. "He's the tennis pro at the Charter Tennis Club. I hired him to teach Michael. I'm not dating him. He's engaged!"

"Oh," Cole said, stunned into an embarrassed silence. He suddenly remembered Michael excited about his new racquet at Christmas, talking about his tennis lessons.

"Is that why you've been so ugly these past weeks?" she demanded. "You thought I was with George?"

"Well, I…"

"Is that all you can say after you've put me through hell?" she demanded, grabbing Cole's shirtfront.

"I…ah…"

"You what?" she spat like an angry kitten.

"I'm sorry," he said. "I don't know what got into me. I just can't bring myself to believe…I just…"

"Believe this, Cassius Coleman. I want you as much as you want me," Talley said, surprising herself. "And no one else."

"You do?" he asked slowly.

"Yes! Damn it! I'm in love with you, too."

Cole realized he had never heard her curse before. *Maybe she does care some after all,* he thought in amazement. "Oh, Talley." He pulled her to him again and felt her straining against him, trying to get closer through their clothing. His hardened body ached with wanting her.

"When...how...can we be alone?" he wanted to know.

She sighed and buried her face in the soft hairs that curled on his chest just above the V-neck of his wool sweater. With flat shoes, her head fit neatly under his chin.

"I don't know," she moaned.

He leaned down and kissed her mouth again, a warm, moist nuzzling. She melted closer into him, standing on her tiptoes to nibble on his full, soft lips. Suddenly he stood straight up and pushed her back from him, holding on to her shoulders.

"Listen, I got an idea," he said with a wide grin. "I have to take two Porsches to a dealer in Boston next week and bring two back. "Why don't you go with me?"

"Of course! I can help you drive!" she suggested eagerly.

"Oh, yeah, uh huh, that's right," he said with a skeptical grin.

"No, really, I can," she insisted. But his mind was elsewhere.

"We can spend the night in New York City after we deliver the cars," he said excitedly. "I have a buddy with a secure lot in New Jersey. We can leave the truck with him and go into the city. Stay at a really nice hotel. Go to dinner…"

He squeezed her shoulders tight, shook her vigorously and asked, "What do you think?"

A little dizzy from the shaking, she bobbed her curls and said, "It sounds good, Cole."

"I can hardly wait!" He sounded like a kid with a treat ahead. He planted soft kisses all over her face.

⌒♋

The first thing Alicia did when she got back from Alabama after New Year's was to call her friend Talley and arrange to meet her.

"I've got something to show you!" she said. "Can I come right over to your place?"

"You bet," Talley said. "I've got things to tell you too!"

Alicia was wearing a two-carat diamond engagement ring. She waved the sparkly thing in Talley's face as soon as she opened the door.

"You're engaged! Wonderful!" Talley squealed. "How'd it happen?"

"It was actually quite hilarious," Alicia said. "Joe went home with me and we were stayin' at Mom and Dad's house, you know, and I was sleepin' upstairs in my old bedroom, Joe was sleepin' on the pullout couch in the den. That was okay for the first few days, but then Joe and I took to missin' each other, you know. So one night, he crept up to my room and we were goin' at it on my old creaky bed and I think I gave a loud shout when…you know. But then Dad slams open the door and Mom's behind him and they switch on the light!"

"Omigod!" Talley hooted.

"So the first thing Joe says to him is, 'Sir, we're engaged to be married!' Then he looks at me. And I nod. And we were engaged. Isn't that somethin'?"

"How romantic," Talley laughed.

"Well, he asked me again later over dinner and champagne out at Montgomery's finest restaurant. And then we bought this ring."

"You look happy, Alicia," Talley said to her glowing friend.

"You better believe it," she said adamantly.

"Have you set a date yet?" Talley asked.

"In the spring.

"And you think you've known him long enough?"

"I've known him for three months, Talley. That should be long enough, don't you think?" Alicia was a little defensive.

"I'm not saying a word. I knew Marshall all my life. *All my life!* I've only known Cole a few days longer than you've known Joe."

"How's it goin' with the big man?" Alicia wanted to know.

"He got his new truck. We have to get it lettered with the name TransportMasters. It's enormous. And it has this cute little sleeper part in the back."

"Oh, does it?" Alicia said with a salacious grin.

Talley reddened and dropped her eyes, quickly changing the subject. "We need to get started with our free marketing plan!"

"I'll talk to Christina on Monday. We should plan to meet at my office soon," Alicia said quickly, eager to get back to the more important subject. "What's happenin' with you and Cole?"

"I'm going on a trip with him," Talley said shyly. "We're driving up to Boston in his new truck to deliver some cars. We're going to stop in New York on our way back."

"Uh oh. Y'all gonna' be getting busy all the way up I-85, aren't you?"

"Oh, hardly," Talley said, embarrassed. "He'll be driving!"

"Oh, it'll be hard all right, and he'll surely be drivin' it."

"Stop, Alicia!"

"They have all those truck stops where you can pull in for a quickie in the sleeper of his truck. Those people in Boston aren't *ever* gonna get their cars!"

"I'm sure I will be able to contain myself," Talley said primly.

CHAPTER THIRTEEN

For the rest of their lives, Cole and Talley would remember that slow trip up I-85 and I-95 north to Boston and back down to Atlanta.

The trip took two days longer than it should have because they could not stay out of the truck stops. Fortunately, Cole's customers weren't in a hurry for their cars. He was able to blame his tardiness on the weather, which had been cold and blustery all the way.

They were less than a hundred miles outside of Atlanta just inside Georgia at the South Carolina border when Cole looked at Talley, cleared his throat, and said hoarsely, "There's a Flying J truck stop up ahead. Wanna stop and get a soda or somethin'?

"Yes." She hoped she didn't sound coy. "I could use a drink."

From the moment Cole lifted Talley into the big truck, his hand lingering on her tiny waist and then patting the toe of her boot as she settled in, he'd had a hard-on. The vibrations of the truck hadn't helped.

Sexual tension in the cab had shimmered in the air between them as the truck roared up Interstate 85. Both of them were too intensely aware that just a few steps behind them was a small, dark room where they could be alone and undisturbed for as long as they liked.

Talley's mouth was dry. She had to hold her hands clasped together tightly in her lap to keep from reaching out to him. Her voice quavered when she spoke.

At the truck stop Cole parked the truck away from the others in the lot, jumped down from the vehicle, and strode over to the restaurant. When he returned, sodas in both hands, Talley was in the sleeper. Barefoot, she was sitting on the side of the pulled-down bed looking down at the floor.

Cole set the sodas in the small refrigerator. Then he turned and looked at her, his blue-green eyes naked with hunger and longing.

"You sure you want to do this?" he whispered.

"Oh, so sure," she said tremulously, standing up.

He took her into his arms gently. She was shivering.

"You cold, baby?" he asked softly, rubbing her back and arms.

"No," she said, "I'm afraid."

"What you afraid of?" he asked, surprised.

"It's just a reflex," she said. "I've come to associate sex with pain."

He groaned and hugged her hard to him, kissing her face, her hair, her neck and her hands.

"You've got nothing' to be afraid of," he said, his voice deep and husky with intense emotion. "Never, not anymore."

Slowly, in the warm, dimly lit cabin, he undressed her. He pulled her sweater over her head and planted kisses on every bare spot he could find. She was braless under the heavy wool and the pink nipples of her small round breasts hardened under his touch. He fondled the perfect globes, warming them with his callused hands.

Unbuttoned blue jeans slid easily down her slender hips. He held her steady as she stepped out of her silky underpants. Then he stood back from her and loved her reverently with his eyes. Her pale willowy body glowed in the dark room.

"You're so…so…you look…I haven't got the words."

"Cole," she said, reaching out to him shyly.

He drew her to him and held her so tightly he took her breath away.

"I can't believe this is happening at last," he said softly. "I wanted you so much sometimes it pained me."

He knelt in front of her and wrapped his arms around her waist, his face pressing into her stomach, his mouth loving her small belly button. Her knees weakened and she had to sit down on the side of the bed. She began to unbutton his shirt, kissing his forehead, his cheeks and his mouth.

He stood to take his jeans off and her eyes widened at the size of his rigid, revealed manhood. He saw her startled look and was quick to reassure her.

"I know," he said, his brow furrowed, "but I promise I won't hurt you. I'll go real slow."

Tentatively, she put her slender hand on him at his root and he sucked in a deep breath. Like mahogany wood with a satin finish he filled her palm. She looked up at him as he towered over her, his broad muscled chest and flat belly tapering to slim hips. His thighs rippled with power. She was mute with lust for him, the emotion overpowering her fear. She wanted him, all of him, deep inside of her.

"Come inside of me," she whispered, lying back on the bed, her arms reaching.

But Cole was determined to take his time with her, to travel a road of adoration down her body. He lay down beside her on the bed and began his journey with her mouth. He explored it thoroughly with his tongue, while his hands rubbed up and down her body.

He kissed and fondled each breast, one at a time, paying special attention to the sensitive, swollen nipples. She put her hand out to touch him and he pinned her arms gently.

"Relax," he said, gruffly. "Just let me love you."

She lay back and sighed with anticipation. He kissed her rib cage and her stomach, the muscles jumping as he edged his way down toward her mound. Kneeling between her legs, he kissed each inner thigh, his lips grazing the sides of her soft, hairy core as she arched toward him.

He held her delicately boned feet against the hair of his chest, then lifted them one at a time to kiss the arch of each and to put the toes in his mouth. She shivered with the strange feeling and snatched them away. He chuckled.

"Put it in," she begged again.

"Not yet," he whispered.

He leaned forward suddenly and, startled, she closed her legs against him.

"Come on, baby, open for me," he said, gently massaging her trembling thighs.

Slowly, she opened her legs and he leaned into her, his tongue searching for her nub of pleasure. When he found it, he suckled gently as she gasped and groaned. It was a pleasure like she'd never felt before. She bucked and arched against his wet, licking tongue. His touch deep into her core made her cry out with the joy of it. Slowly and patiently he licked and sucked at her secret crevices, bringing her to the brink of climax. Just as she thought she could bear no more, that she'd explode, he moved again easing his massive shaft into her.

Talley flung her legs into the air and stretched them wide, determined to take all of him into her. She was so wet he was sliding in easily. She could feel every inch of him, the fierce heat of his erection pulsing inside her.

She looked up into Cole's face, loving the look of him loving her. His eyes were heavy-lidded, blue-green fire gleaming through the slits. His mouth was open, contorted with lust, and his neck muscles bulged with the effort to control himself so as not to hurt her.

"Oh, Cole," she whispered, her voice throaty, "I want, need, all that you have for me."

With that, he plunged deep inside her, holding nothing back. Her legs wrapped around his waist and moved her against him in cadence with his slow, rhythmic thrusts. She loved the feel of him, his muscular length heavy against her. She reveled in the incredible power of his surging body. She ran her hand down the sides of his arms, marveling at the rock-hard muscles. She laid her hands on his chest, touching his nipples delicately.

The thrusts came faster and more demanding as he began to mutter her name in a deep voice. His breath a hot imperative against her skin, he pushed his manhood deep into her center, until she could feel him touch her womb. At that moment Talley knew real passion for the first time. Though a married woman, Talley was a spiritual virgin. Her essence was now touched by love and passion for the very first time. This was the feeling she'd been searching for. This was what the poets and bards wrote and sang about. She completely gave herself up to the feeling.

He bore down on her, their bodies meeting in seamless harmony. The searing heat welled up inside her and she cried out in ecstasy, her climax jerking her body violently. At that same moment, Cole let out a wild, breathy moan and they fell in a heap on the bed. Senses shattered, souls eternally mated, they held each other tightly.

The sensation of release opened a well inside Talley and she began to cry. Deep quaking sobs came from her chest and fat tears ran down her face. Cole stared in terrified amazement.

"I'm sorry, baby, I'm sorry. Did I hurt you? What's wrong?"

"No, no," she told him, trying desperately to stifle the sobs. "I'm just so happy."

He pulled her to him and she buried her face in the soft hairs of his warm chest. She could feel his heart beating against her ear. The steady sound warmed and comforted her.

"I love you, Cole." Clinging to him, Talley knew no other words.

"No, you don't," he said in a quiet voice.

"Yes, I do," she insisted. "Do you love me?"

"Yeah, I do. I wish I had the words to tell you how much."

"Why do you say that I don't love you?" she asked.

"I just know better, that's all." His gentle finger touched her cheek.

"Well, you know wrong," she said, sighing and stretching against his length. "This was more than sex for us. This was a covenant. A blessed union."

"Yeah, that sounds real pretty. But saying doesn't make it so."

"You *will* learn to trust me, Cole. I *will* make it so. I love you."

Cole silently searched her face, looking for what he needed to wipe away his long-held doubts and prejudices. Though the answer was there in the depths of her eyes, he could not recognize it. *How could someone like her love someone like me,* he wondered, his insecurities as sensitive as exposed nerve tissue.

"We better get back in the cab," he said finally. "People want their cars and the road doesn't drive itself."

Cole and Talley stopped at each of the five Flying J truck stops between Atlanta and Boston. Their hunger for one another was endless. A look, a word or a sigh would set them off and they would count miles to the next truck stop. Again and again they would park in a spot far from the other vehicles and rush back to the sleeper, tearing clothes off. Just past New Jersey, exhausted, they fell asleep in one another's arms.

In the morning, inside the sleeper's tiny combination shower and toilet, the fall of water washing over them, Cole held Talley straddled on him, her arms wrapped tightly around his shoulders, holding him a willing captive deep inside her. She heard him whisper and strained to hear his words: "Now I know what they mean when they say a man is whipped. I'd crawl on my hands and knees across burning coals to get to you."

She just covered his smiling mouth with hers and sucked in his bottom lip, straining for another glorious climax.

～∽

From the moment they stepped out of the taxicab in front of New York City's Plaza Hotel and the uniformed doorman beamed with enthusiasm and said, "Mrs. Pettifore, welcome back!" Cole knew he had made a mistake.

When he asked Vickie to make reservations at the best hotel in New York, it hadn't occurred to him that it would be Talley's regular stomping ground. When he told Talley proudly that they were going to the Plaza, she'd knit her brow slightly, but said nothing. Now, to his embarrassed dismay, she was recognized, welcomed and cosseted.

"Nice to see you again, Mrs. Pettifore," the concierge bowed as they passed. "Let me know if you need theater tickets this time."

"Mrs. Pettifore! It's been a while. Will you be wanting your regular suite?" the reception clerk asked with a sycophantic grin.

Talley nodded shyly, afraid to look at Cole. It was a measure of New York sophistication that no one acknowledged the peculiarity of Mrs. Pettifore being accompanied by a strange large man in flannel shirt and big boots. Except for the small tussle he had when the bellman wanted to take their bags from him, Cole was completely ignored.

"I hope everyone seeing us together won't create a problem," he muttered as they entered the luxurious white and gold high-ceilinged suite of rooms that was to be their home for the weekend.

"Of course not," Talley soothed. "The staff is very discreet. Besides, I don't need to leave this suite again. Do you?"

"I can't think of any good reason," Cole agreed, taking her into his arms and looking around the huge, elegantly appointed room. "I think this place is big enough for me to do the job right."

"What job?" she asked.

"You know," he said. His smile was so intimate it made her blush.

At first Talley had let Cole control the direction of their lovemaking. He'd lift her and turn her and set her willing body where he wanted her. He'd kiss and lick and suck and enter her at will, his aim to please her, to make her eyes glaze with passion, to hear her breath come in gasps. She was amazed at how unselfish he was, at his willingness to meet her needs and take her further in their sensual dance. He'd strain to hold back until she reached her peak.

As time and familiarity emboldened her, Talley became more aggressive and adventurous. Cole's big, hard, brown body with its rippling muscle and sinew, its tight curves and hard planes, became Talley's playground, her personal ship on a sensuous voyage of discovery. She crawled all over him, tasting and testing, stretching and flexing.

There seemed to be no end to their sexual need for one another, but their pleasure in one another's company when they weren't making love was just as strong. Despite their widely divergent backgrounds, their basic values of honesty, integrity and duty and devotion to family were identical. And, lying in the wide bed trading jokes and dirty limericks, they discovered a shared silly sense of humor.

One area where they could not agree, however, was Cole's prejudice against the African American upper class. After listening quietly to one of his diatribes against snobs and phonies and wanna-bes, Talley couldn't contain herself.

"Cole, *you're* a snob," Talley told him as they lay naked together. Her stern tone was softened by the way she nuzzled his broad back.

"Me? A snob? You're crazy," he laughed.

"You're a reverse snob. Just as prejudiced and bigoted against black people with money as the worse Georgia redneck is against blacks," she said.

"I don't see it."

"You lump us all into one big group and then make judgments against us," she pointed out. "We're not all alike. Some of us look at money as a tool to make things better. To effect positive change in our communities."

Cole grunted. "Some. Not many."

"Besides, aren't you fighting as hard as you can to become one of us?"

"The hell I am," he shouted, sitting up abruptly in the big bed.

"What is all this obsession with growing your business then?" she demanded. "Don't you make enough money now to live comfortably with the trucks you have? Why do I always hear you talking about adding trucks and getting more clients?"

"That's different. It's like you said once before. I want to build something."

"You just want to be *rich*. You want to join the 100 Black Men and buy a big house in Lithonia," she teased.

"That's just crazy," he growled, covering her laughing mouth with his own.

Happy as they were in the gilded cocoon of the Plaza suite, ordering room service, sleeping nestled together and loving each other to distraction, they knew it would eventually have to end.

"Damn, we gotta get those cars back to Atlanta," Cole sighed on Sunday night.

"Can't we stay another day?" Talley asked, burying her face in a feather pillow. If Talley had seen Cole go quietly into the bathroom and check the cash supply in his money belt, she would have been overwhelmed by guilt.

"We can't afford to stay up here another night, baby. I'm broke."

"But I have *lots* of mmm…" she started. Then, seeing his face begin to turn stormy, she stopped and turned away, pulling the soft sheets over her nakedness.

"You've got to stop holding my money against me," she told him. "It was just an accident of birth. You wouldn't resent me if I had been born with green eyes instead of brown…"

"Your eyes aren't just brown, they've got little flecks of gold in them," he responded to change the subject.

"You know what I mean, Cole," she pressed.

He silenced her with a look.

The next day they picked up the truck and cars in New Jersey and headed back. "I gotta keep the left door closed, baby," Cole told Talley. "I gotta make good time."

"The left door?" Talley frowned her confusion.

"The driver's side door, honey," Cole grinned. "Gotta keep it closed. No stops."

At the last truck stop inside Georgia, Cole relented and they made love with passionate abandon, aware that soon they would be back in the real world. Talley would go back to being hunted by her husband's family. Cole would have to work like a madman to make up for the extravagance of this trip.

At some point, Talley knew, Cole would have to come to terms with the fact of her money. If they were to continue their relationship and take it to its logical conclusion, they would have to reach an understanding on her inherited wealth. On her own, without Marshall or her parents, Talley was worth millions. Her money was in trust funds, in stocks and bonds and property in her name. Her son Michael, at age seven, was worth more than one hundred million dollars and he'd inherit more upon the death of his grandfathers.

For now, floating down I-85 in a protected bubble of love and sexual satiety, the future was only to the end of this trip. But Talley knew that someday soon she and Cole would have to go to that uncharted territory and make hard decisions. It could be a difficult, dangerous place. She likened the future to what she had read on old English maps which marked area beyond a certain point in the ocean with a warning: "Here be dragons."

CHAPTER FOURTEEN

Talley's divorce proceedings dragged along slowly. Jerome was doing the best he could, but the Pettifores kept throwing up roadblocks. Talley was granted permanent custody of Michael once the judge had viewed the shocking tape. But, Cedric was fighting to set up a liberal visitation schedule. He wanted Talley to come out of hiding.

"The judge won't allow you to hide for much longer," Jerome said, "If Cedric prevails in his suit for grandparents' rights, we will have to at least let them come to see Michael."

"You don't understand. Once Cedric knows where I am, he'll kidnap Michael. I'll never be able to get him back," Talley argued.

"He can't steal the boy out from under everyone's nose," Jerome insisted.

"You don't know Cedric," Talley said.

Jerome was silent while Talley paced the office.

"Tell them if they don't leave us alone you'll release the tape to the Detroit media," Talley said.

"I've already hinted that, of course, which is why they've held off for these many months. But I don't want to carry the bluff too far."

⎯⎯ᧁ⎯⎯

At the yard, Talley threw herself into the business of building up TransportMasters. Talley and Cole had tried to conceal the change in their relationship, but no one was fooled. They touched each other with more familiarity and more frequently now and their smiles held shared secrets. More and more, the brothers and Lucy began to treat Talley and Michael like a beloved sister and nephew. Everyone expected daily to hear that she and Cole would marry once the divorce was final.

Narye watched this new closeness with concern.

"Have you given thought to how your family will react to Mr. Cole?" she asked Talley one evening.

"Oh, I'm not worried. Mother will adore him. She's so softhearted, she'll react to his sweetness and kindness. And Daddy just wants everyone around him to be happy—or at least pretend to be."

Narye nodded her agreement.

"I'm more concerned about how Cole will react to *them*," Talley went on. "Especially my sisters-in-law. They are the epitome of the class that Cole rants against all the time."

"Mr. Cedric will be a problem," Narye reminded her.

"Cedric will hate anyone that might have some influence over Michael," Talley said with a worried frown. "I'm not sure how to handle that."

"It must be handled if you are planning to speak of marriage."

But neither Talley nor Cole had brought up marriage. It was too complicated a subject. Dragons abounded.

～♋

Roberta spent the month of February with her arm in a sling doing some serious soul searching. The experience with the strange violent man, whose name she'd never learned, made her wary of frequenting bars to find Cole's replacement. She was going through a miserable dry spell.

She was having a tougher time getting over Cole than she'd expected. For one thing, in the past she'd been the one leaving. She'd never doubted for one moment that all she had to do was crook a finger to get him back. She'd felt that Cole knew how fortunate he was to have an educated and refined girlfriend like her. She also knew that he wouldn't settle for less than that in his woman.

Now she was beginning to realize what *she'd* lost. Men like Cole—honest, loyal and steady—didn't grow on trees. So what if he didn't want to finish college? So what if he drove a truck? She missed his gentleness and his thoughtfulness. She missed his big arms around her and his narrow hips between her legs. She missed his giant manhood buried deep inside her.

Perhaps it was time for her to meet with Cole and tell him she was ready to take a whole new approach to their relationship. She'd tell him that she would be happy to accept Cole just as he was. And, while she was at it, she'd expose that high-yellow slumming snob-bitch Tallulah for the phony that she was!

She left a very calm message on Cole's cell phone saying she needed to talk to him alone to share some very surprising information about his business. She begged him to come by her place that night to discuss it. The reference to his business worked. Cole left a message that he'd drop by that evening.

Roberta prepared for him as though it was their first date. She dressed in a filmy, curve-hugging gown with her long black hair loose and flowing. She sprayed herself and the apartment with her most expensive perfume and dimmed the lights in the living room. Her heart leaped into her throat when the doorbell rang.

But her heart sank to her heels when she opened the door and found Cole, Marcus and David standing there. Cole gazed at her steadily while Marcus and David looked her up and down with knowing grins. Their smiles widened when she led them into the softly lit living room. She sharply flicked on the lights.

"You brought your brothers for protection from me?" she hissed at Cole as Marcus and David took seats on the comfortable couch.

"You said it was about the business and Marcus is the new president of TowMasters now. David just came along for the ride," Cole said calmly. He sat in an armchair by the couch.

Roberta perched uneasily on an ottoman and looked at the three faces, so much alike.

"So what is it about our business that we need to know?" Cole asked.

"It's actually about one of your employees," Roberta said snappishly.

The men looked from one to the other.

"They're all family," Cole said.

"Oh, I know you don't consider that yellow-haired girl family." Roberta's voice got a little shrill.

"Almost," Marcus drawled, with a wink.

"That's because you don't know who she is," Roberta said smugly.

In that moment, Cole knew where she was going. He hadn't yet told his brothers about Talley and he wasn't prepared to let Roberta blurt it out. He stood up abruptly.

"Let's go," he said roughly to his brothers.

"Wait a minute," Marcus said to Roberta, angry challenge in his voice. "You tryin' to say somethin' about Talley?"

David stood up quietly, his fists clenched, his eyes flashing fire behind his glasses.

"Her real name is Tallulah Quincy Pettifore," Roberta said quickly before Cole could hush her.

"And she's been playing all of you for big dumb jack-asses!"

The name rang in the air. Marcus looked confused, but light dawned almost immediately on David's face.

"She's a Pettifore?" he said with a gasp. "She's *that* Tallulah?"

"Wait a minute," Marcus said again. "Quincy. Pettifore. From Michigan. Ain't they some majorly rich black aristocrats?" He looked at Cole, who was standing silent near the door.

"Did you know this?" he demanded of Cole.

"Yeah, I did," Cole said.

Roberta whirled around and stared at Cole.

"You knew?"

"Well, what the hell is she doing at your yard?" Roberta asked indignantly as Cole.

"It's a long story and none of your business," Cole said. "C'mon, guys, let's go. Marcus and David moved toward the door. As they passed Cole, David started: "But Cole, what *is* she doin'…?"

Cole cut him off. "We'll talk about it at home," he said. "Keep moving."

As his brothers moved toward the truck parked in front of the building, Roberta stopped Cole with a clutching hand on his arm.

"I did want to talk to you alone," she said, begging him with her eyes. "I wanted to tell you how much I miss you. How I don't care anymore whether you go back to college or not…"

"Roberta, it's too late now. I'm in love with someone else," he said.

"That rich bitch?" she asked incredulously.

Cole said nothing.

"You think she could love *you*?" Roberta said her voice getting loud. "You're jus' crazy. You think she's gonna give up her life among the high and mighty and settle for a no-count strugglin' *truck driver*?"

Roberta's careful diction was slipping with her mounting agitation.

Cole stared at Roberta. Her face distorted as she spewed her jealousy and hatred.

"I don't know why I ever thought you had class," he said, shaking his head and walking away.

As soon as Cole got in the truck he looked at his brothers, who were staring back at him with round eyes, and said, "I don't want anybody treating Talley any different, you hear me?"

"But, damn, Cole. You knew who she was all along and you didn't say anything. That's not fair," Marcus said.

"What difference would it make?" he demanded.

"We just shoulda known."

"She asked me not to tell," he said, "for two reasons. One, because she's hiding from her husband and she didn't want anyone letting anything slip. He's got a team of detectives looking for her. The other is that she liked the way you all treated her, just like a regular girl. She doesn't want you to change, and I don't either."

"That's why you didn't want to take money from her," Marcus said, comprehension dawning. "That little bit of money we needed was jus' chump change to her!"

"That's why that Michael is so well behaved," David said. "He's one of them double-comma kids!"

"What you mean?" Marcus asked.

"Like the commas between the zeros. His money's got two."

"I'm going to have a family meeting and set some ground rules for y'all," Cole said. "We don't want to mess things up for Talley and Michael. You can't tell anybody!"

"Wait until Winston hears," David said excitedly. "We gotta tell Winston and Lucy!"

Winston was beside himself when he heard the news. They were in the family room at their house.

"Man, you *hot!*" he exclaimed, touching Cole on the shoulder with a finger and snatching it back. "Ow! You burnt my finger. And when you marry Talley, I ain't goin' be pullin' nothin' but heiresses!"

"Now sit down, all y'all," Cole roared at his brothers.

The men recognized that voice. It was Cole's "take no prisoners" voice. They tumbled over one another in order to sit down. At one time or another they had all been on the bad side of Cole's slapping arm, and even now, in their twenties, they could remember the blows.

"First off, I mean it when I say y'all can't be acting different to Talley and Michael, " he said. "Do you hear me? I'm not gonna have them feel uncomfortable or put in any kind of danger."

He looked at the chastened faces of his brothers.

"Man, you don't have to worry 'bout that. We all gonna look after Talley and Michael's feelin's. They're our friends," Marcus soothed.

"Second," Cole continued, "we can't tell anyone outside the family who she is. Her father-in-law wants to kidnap her and Michael and get them back. Her husband used to beat her and the child and she doesn't need him finding her."

"Why would anybody want to hit Talley?" Winston asked, his jaws tight. "That's some *crap*, man, y'know what I'm sayin?"

"And, third, we got to keep an eye on them now. I don't know what Roberta is going to do with the information. But mad as she is at me, she might do anything."

That part hadn't dawned on the brothers.

"Someone needs to stay close to the yard and someone close to Michael's school all the time," Winston insisted.

"But we got to do it without letting our business slip," Marcus warned. "We need to set up a schedule."

⟋⟍

Joe spooned against Alicia in the bed they now shared in her house.

He nibbled on her ear, waking her.

"You awake?" he asked.

"Ummm, yes," she answered.

"Then gimme some," he said, poking her soft rear with his stiffness.

"I gotta get up," she murmured. "I gotta get to work."

"Won't take but a minute," he said, pushing against her.

"That's what I'm afraid of," she said. "And I'll be at the office all day wantin' some more."

"Baby, I wouldn't do you like that," Joe promised.

"Sho' you would," she said with a pout. "You did it yesterday."

"Okay, here," he said, turning over on his back, making a tent of the covers. "You get on top and take all this hot thang."

Hot thang? She gave a little jump and stared at him as she recognized the phrase she had used on the phone to her sister. He had his eyes closed. She shrugged.

"Now you talkin'," she said, climbing on him.

Later, as they stood at the double sinks in her bathroom, he asked her, "Have you heard from Tallulah yet?"

She stuck a toothbrush in her mouth and brushed vigorously.

"Well?" he asked again.

"None of your beeswax," she said adamantly, spitting out toothpaste.

He, of course, knew she'd heard from Talley. Indeed, he knew she had an appointment with Talley at her office today and he intended to be outside the office to follow Talley after the meeting. But, he dearly loved teasing Alicia. He loved that she had such a hard time lying to him.

— ☙

Talley left The Boyd Group office well pleased with the results of the meeting. She got her car out of the parking lot on International Boulevard and headed toward the impound yard. On the highway, she excitedly reviewed all the things for TransportMasters that had been promised by the marketing firm as part of the package they had won: A new logo using the black, silver and blue colors she and Cole had decided on; a print ad with a slogan and tag line; a direct mail brochure and a suggested mailing list; a completed web site. She didn't notice the nondescript brown Toyota following her.

Joe was humming along with Luther Vandross on the radio as he tailed Talley. It had taken him almost five months, but he'd finally found his quarry. The hard part was over. Now all he had to do was find a way to get her and Michael to come along nicely back to the bosom of their loving family.

Joe didn't think that would be too difficult a task. Surely by now Talley was tired of living undercover and eager to get back to her beautiful estate and that lovely peach bedroom. He was troubled by his suspicions that her husband had hit her, but he forced himself to put them aside. *I've got to do my job,* he rationalized.

He watched her turn onto a newly paved road off Camp Creek Parkway. A sign, TowMasters, marked the business inside.

"Jesus," he muttered to himself. "She's been working for a wrecker service. No wonder I couldn't find her."

CHAPTER FIFTEEN

Although Alicia had been down to her basement many times to wash clothes in the past few months, she'd had no reason to move the heavy old oak desk in front of the phone line to her house until Joe's ball of socks rolled under it. When she did move the desk, she immediately saw the odd wires coming out from her phone line and going into an electronic device.

With a shock she realized it was a tape recorder. She stared at the thing for a few moments before the enormity of the betrayal struck her. Then she sank down on the basement floor, clutching the socks to her chest.

Her mind was awhirl with half-remembered phrases from Joe:

"Now that I know Tom doesn't mean anything…"

"Have you heard from Tallulah yet?"

"You love this big thang, don't ya?"

He had been laughing at her all this time. Listening in on her most private conversations, learning how to manipulate her, using her to find Talley. Omigod! Talley!

Alicia raced up the stairs to her bedroom to call Talley. Then she stopped. She raced back down the stairs to the recording device and smashed it to pieces. Then she ran back up to the phone to call.

"Talley," she gasped when her friend picked up the phone. "It's awful! Joe had a tape recorder on my home phone. He probably knows where you are by now…"

"Wait a minute, sweetie," Talley said. "Let me think. I don't think I've ever said where I was when we talked on your home phone."

The women carefully reviewed their conversations.

"But he did know we were meetin' today. He could have followed you from my office," Alicia said.

"Then he knows where I work and if he waited and followed me home tonight, he knows where I live." Talley gasped. "God, he's probably told Marshall by now. I've got to get out of here. Where's Joe now?"

"He's at the gym. Came home late and went right out. Talley, don't do anythin' until I ask him. He may not have told anybody yet. I may be able to talk him out of it."

"How are *you* feeling, honey?" Talley asked.

"Betrayed, miserable, angry, hurt. I don't know what to do," Alicia wailed.

"It's pretty bad," Talley said. "But don't do anything rash."

─ ᑲ

When Joe came in from the gym, Alicia was waiting for him in the bedroom with the smashed tape recorder on the bed. It was the first thing he saw when he walked in.

"Oops, cold busted!" he said with a sheepish grin. "You got me, girl."

Then he looked at her face, and his smile froze.

"Hey, you look really mad," he said.

"How could you? I trusted you. You've been lyin' all this time," she spat.

"Honey, please don't be mad."

"I'm not mad, Joe. I'm disappointed and hurt. And, I've come to a decision."

"What do you mean?" he said, moving toward her and reaching out.

Alicia put her hands up to push him away and got off the bed where she'd been sitting. He noticed she had his bags packed beside the bed.

"What is this?" he asked. "You going to kick me out because of a little tap on your phone?"

"Yes," she said calmly.

"C'mon," he said, moving toward her. "I'm sorry 'bout that, but you knew I was a detective. It's what I do for a living."

Alicia's jaws were clenched as she fought back tears. "Yep. I knew you were a snake, so I shouldn't be surprised you bit me. That's what a snake does." She turned her back on him and leaned on the bureau. He could see her face in the mirror.

"So you want to break up?" he asked.

"You lie far too easily for me. We need to be apart for a little while so I can think things over."

"You're breaking us up. When someone says they need time apart, it means they need some time to look for someone else!"

"That's not what *I* mean," Alicia said, turning around to face him again.

"Why are you making such a big deal over this...I love you. You love me. We're going to get married. I know I was wrong to listen in to your private conversations, but I didn't use them to hurt *you*."

"It was deceitful, Joe. It was connivin'."

He shrugged. "I don't see it that way."

"That's part of the problem," she said.

"I'd have to stop doing business if it was up to you," he grumbled.

"It was *us*, not business. Surely you see the difference," she said forcefully, her eyes searching his face. "We had a promise."

Joe couldn't look at her.

"Have you told anybody where Talley is?" she asked.

"I just found out where she works and lives today. I left a message with my dad that I'd found her but I didn't say where."

"Can I believe that?"

"Sure, you know you can trust me..." He stopped when he looked at her raised eyebrow.

"You know, technically, I didn't lie to you about..." he started.

"Jus' hush, Joe. I want to tell you somethin'."

Very slowly she recounted what Talley had told her about her life with Marshall. She told him in vivid detail what had occurred the night Talley left with Michael.

Joe listened to her quietly, the deep creases in his jaws twitching with suppressed anger. When she finished he looked at Alicia's somber face and shook his head.

"I suspected he had hit her. But I didn't know it was a regular thing," he said.

"You suspected he was abusive? And you still came after her?" Alicia squeaked.

"I didn't know for sure. I don't think my father does either. I need to give him all the facts."

"Just please don't tell the Pettifores where Talley is."

"I hear you. I need to talk to my father."

They were silent for a few moments, looking at each other.

"Honey, please forgive me about the phone...," Joe started.

"Joe, it jus' made me realize that we rushed into this engagement without really knowin' each other. The man I thought I was marryin' couldn't have been this deceptive with me. And he wouldn't drag a woman back to an abusive husband."

"Maybe you're right." Her words hurt. "The woman I thought I was marrying would be more understanding about my commitment to my profession."

"You see," Alicia said, taking a deep breath. "We need some time apart."

"So you're kicking me out."

"Yes," she said.

"You're mighty calm about it," he said. "You're a lot tougher than I thought."

"See what I mean? Time to learn."

Joe picked up his bags and moved slowly to the door.

"You know there's no guarantee I'll come back," he said.

She flinched. "Then it wasn't meant to be."

She followed him as he moved slowly out to the small foyer.

"Can I kiss you good-bye?" he asked in the doorway.

She started to lean toward him, her eyes glazing, her lips parted and ready.

He put his hand on her waist and she stiffened.

"I can't let you, Joe," she said, her quivering voice betraying weakness for the first time that evening. "You need to get out of here now." She shut the door quickly.

Joe stood outside the house for a few minutes looking up at the windows, then walked to his car.

⟞ჟ

Paul Griffin was a stocky man the same height as his son. Muscular in his youth, he had thickened with age. He had deep, dimpling creases in his cheeks, like Joe's, but his had sagged into jowls.

"I held off calling Cedric Pettifore to tell him the good news, as you asked," he said to his son, "I'm ready now to hear you explain."

The two were sitting in the office of Joe's father at Griffin Investigations in Southfield. Joe had gotten back to Detroit late the previous night and after a few sleepless hours had hurried to the office to confront his father.

"Did you know when you sent me after Tallulah Pettifore that she was running from an abusive situation?" Joe asked his father.

"No, I didn't."

"Would you have sent me if you had known?"

"I'm afraid so, Son," came the uncompromising response.

"So I guess telling you about the stuff that went on in that woman's life won't make a difference."

"I don't need to know it," Paul said. "We would have gone after her no matter what."

"Why?" Joe asked. "Why would we do that?"

"We're private investigators, we ain't judges," Paul said.

"So we just follow orders, like Nazi soldiers."

"Why do you care all of a sudden?" his father asked. "Never bothered you before. Listen, boy. We *have* to do whatever the Pettifores say. Cedric Pettifore set me up in business and we've built everything on their contracts. For thirty years I've been prosperous because of them."

"Cedric needed someone to do his dirty work," Joe said in disgust. His father nodded.

Joe stood and paced. "Well, *I'm* not doing it. I've decided I'm not going to give up the woman. I figured out we've been paid about $75,000 in fees and expense on this chase. I'll send them a check from my savings right now. It's my decision. I'll take the hit."

"They don't care about the money. They want that boy," Paul said.

"They ain't getting him through me," his son replied.

"You'll destroy this firm," his father said tiredly.

"I can't help that. I can't carry this load, Dad. It's too heavy for me."

———∽———

Talley didn't know what to make of the situation developing with Cole. It seemed the deeper their love got and the more intimate they were with one another, the more time she had to spend convincing him she loved him.

Every time they saw a particularly distinguished-looking man in a business suit or a fancy car, he'd say to her, "That's the kind of man you need to be with, Talley."

"But I love *you*, Cole," she'd say.

"No, you don't," he'd respond.

"Yes, I do."

It got to be kind of a game. Only neither of them was really amused.

When Narye would take Michael out to play dates or to tennis lessons, Cole and Talley would seize those precious moments to be alone together at her town-house and make love.

"I love you," she'd say, lying stretched out against his body, her legs wrapped around his.

"You love makin' love with me," he'd say.

"Definitely."

"But that's about all I'm good for."

"So you think I'm just using you for sex?"

"Yep. You don't really need me."

"Yes, I do."

"No, you don't. How can you say you need me when you got all the money in the world? What do you need me for?"

"Money isn't everything. I need you to complete me. We are two halves of a whole and without each other, we're just fractions."

"Maybe me, but not you."

And so on.

Whenever she'd try to turn the conversation serious and question whether he really doubted her love, he'd change the subject or the mood.

"You really must stop saying that I don't love you, Cole," she'd start. "It hurts me."

"I don't mean to hurt you, baby. I hate to see you frown like that," he said, walking away.

"What am I going to do about him, Lucy?" Talley complained to his sister one day.

"Just keep on lovin' him. He's not a word man, you know. He's a show and do man," she said.

Narye agreed.

"Mr. Cole is a man who trusts his eyes, not his ears," she said while brushing Talley's hair one evening. "It will take time, I think, to convince him. Even after everyone around him knows for sure."

"But I believe *him*. I know he loves me."

"You don't carry the burden he does," Narye said.

"What burden?" Talley wanted to know.

"He has put you on a high marble pedestal and he is carrying it around on his back," she said.

Then she added with a sad smile, "He has a very firm perception of life's social strata and what people belong on each level. It's odd to find that kind of caste prejudice in America. Or anywhere outside of Victorian India."

~ુ૭

"The good news is that you can come to my house and comfort me now that Joe's gone," Alicia said to Talley, leading her into the bright yellow kitchen. "The bad news is that I desperately need comfortin' because my Joe's gone."

"You shouldn't have sent him away," Talley said. "You love him so much."

"He listened in on all my private and personal conversations. With my sister, with you, with old boyfriends that called. He made fun of me to my face without me even knowin'!" she shouted, slamming the white enamel teapot on the stove. "He teased me about what I told my sister about his willy!"

"That's just your pride hurting," Talley said gently, taking the teapot from her with a smile.

"He lied to me, and he deceived me, Talley. He promised he wouldn't use me to find you, and he did," she said quietly. Alicia sank down on a stool at the kitchen counter. It was noon on Saturday and she was still in her pajamas. Her eyes were shadowed, her hair wrapped in a scarf.

"He had a job to do," Talley tried.

"No. This was bad."

"But…forgivable, don't you think?" Talley filled the pot with water and set it on the stove.

"Forgivable? How can *you* say that? After the danger he put you in…"

"We don't know that yet," Talley soothed.

Well…," Alicia hesitated. "I have to learn to trust him again."

"He had a job to do, Alicia. If I can forgive him, you should."

"I don't want to be with a man whose job overrode his personal scruples."

"I thought you said he didn't know what I was up against."

"He suspected that Marshall had hit you."

Talley was silent.

"He went home to talk to his father. If he comes back and says he wants no further part in it, then maybe we can start again."

"For your sake and my own, I hope he does," Talley said. She turned the gas burner on under the teapot and began searching for cups.

Alicia indicated a shelf for Talley and reached into a canister on the counter for chamomile tea bags.

"I see you didn't give up the ring," Talley noted.

"I took your advice. I didn't do anythin' that rash," Alicia said with a crooked little grin.

"I took mine off the minute I got out of that house," Talley recalled.

"Is that big trucker gonna put another one on?" Alicia inquired.

"I don't know. I don't know what to make of our relationship at this point," Talley said. "It's like he's waiting for another shoe to drop."

"What do you mean?"

"He thinks any day now I'm going to come to my senses and leave him. I can't make him believe I'm here to stay."

"Give him some time, sugar lump. Talley Pettifore is heady stuff for a man like him. He's probably still pinchin' himself."

"See, even you're doing it."

"Honey, the truth is the light."

"*He* is my truth. *He* is my light. He's worth more than gold to me."

"Alright, sugah, I'm convinced." Alicia put her arms around her friend. "Give him some time."

━━━━ ᧤

Roberta was in the dentist's office, leafing through an old Ebony Magazine, waiting to be seen for a tooth that had been aching ever since her violent encounter, when she saw Marshall's picture in an article on "Legal Dynasties."

The exquisite irony struck her immediately. The twist was so bizarre that she laughed out loud, a harsh raucous sound that startled others in the waiting room.

Marshall Pettifore. Talley's husband. Her rapist.

In short order Roberta found Marshall. He was registered at the Ritz Carlton in Buckhead. She left an anonymous message at the desk for him to meet a woman wearing a red hat at The Tavern Restaurant, which was across the street from his hotel, if he wanted information about his wife.

She didn't have to wait long. As Marshall entered, searching the restaurant, his aristocratic good looks and elegant bearing drew glances from every direction. His face fell into an expression of disappointment and distaste when he spotted Roberta in her red felt hat seated in a darkened booth.

"How did you find me?" he wanted to know as soon as he sat down.

"You're not that hard to find, Mr. Pettifore. If you want to stay anonymous, you should fire your publicist."

"What do you want? What about my wife?" He was short, impatient.

"You should relax and be more pleasant with me, considering what we've shared," Roberta taunted.

"My wife," he insisted.

"I know where she is. And I know who she's sleeping with."

"What are you talking about?"

"Your uppity little Talley is sleeping with my trucker." Roberta sneered. "And judging from what I saw of your little prick, she's finally getting filled up!"

"I don't need listen to your trashy mouth," he said savagely. "Just tell me where Talley is."

"Talk to me like that again, and I won't tell you anything," Roberta threatened.

Marshall was silent for a moment, assessing the woman.

"Okay. I'll pay you. How much do you want?"

"Keep your stank money. I just want you to go get that yella-haired bitch away from my man," Roberta said.

"I'll gladly do that," Marshall said.

"I don't know where she lives, but I know where she works."

"I need to know where she lives."

"You'll just have to follow her home then. She gets off at six P.M."

CHAPTER SIXTEEN

From his car, parked unobtrusively at the edge of the yard, Marshall watched as Narye and Michael picked up Talley. Talley walked out of the office with a huge brown-skinned man, who had his hand on her arm. He helped her into the passenger side of the BMW and patted the toe of her shoe. She kissed him and smiled into his eyes. Marshall felt an absurd stab of jealousy at the loving intimacy. He followed as they drove off.

Narye had groceries in the back of the vehicle and Marshall watched from the shadows while she and Talley unloaded them at the door of her neat little townhouse. At one point, Narye shivered and looked around. He thought she'd spotted him.

He could hear the murmur of their voices. Talley's familiar lighthearted giggle sent waves of longing for the days when they had been children together and he had been her favorite playmate.

He had coke in his wallet. He decided to hit it just once before he faced her. It would give him the confidence he needed to be persuasive. He hadn't seen her or his son since that night and he was nervous.

When the doorbell rang, Talley, Narye and Michael were at the dinner table. Narye gave Talley a perplexed glance as she went to the door.

"Miss Tallulah, it's Mr. Marshall," Narye said urgently, looking out the peephole of the door. The ringing had become more persistent.

"Oh, God," Talley gasped. "Michael get in the bathroom, lock the door."

"Is Daddy going to hurt you again, Mommy?" Michael shrilled. "Should I bite him?"

"Get in the bathroom."

Marshall was pounding on the door in addition to ringing the bell. "Let me in, Talley," he was shouting. "I just want to talk to you."

"Call 911," Talley said to Narye as Marshall began kicking at the door. She raced back to the bedroom and opened a locked suitcase where she kept the gun she'd taken from the safe. Her hands were trembling as she handled and loaded the unfamiliar object.

She heard a huge cracking noise at the front of the townhouse as the wooden door gave way. As Talley ran to the living room, the gun in her hand, Narye was on the phone giving their address to the 911 operator. The door had splintered at the lock and Marshall was inside. Talley hid the gun behind her before he saw it.

"Why wouldn't you let me in?" he said with a little whine in his voice. "You forced me to break your door."

"What do you want, Marshall?" Talley asked, her voice firm.

"I want you and Michael to come home."

Talley looked closely at Marshall. His eyes were wide and red, but he seemed calm. Her rapid heartbeat began to slow down.

"We're not going to do that," Talley said. "I'm getting a divorce."

"I don't want a divorce," Marshall said petulantly, chewing on his lip.

"Well, I do," Talley said quietly. "I've been a coward for eight years, but I'm strong now, Marshall. You and Cedric can't touch me anymore."

"But we're supposed to be together, Talley. That's the way it's always been."

"I'm with someone else now."

"That big loser you were with tonight?" Marshall spit out.

"Cole's a good man."

"I want things back the way they were!" he cried out in anguish.

"So you can rape me, and beat me and our child at will?" Talley said, her voice beginning to vibrate with anger.

"No. So we can be together like we're supposed to be. Like when we were kids," Marshall whimpered.

For a moment Marshall looked like the charming little boy he had once been and Talley let down her guard. Suddenly, Marshall's face changed, hardened, and he grabbed her arm and pulled her to him, holding her in a vise-like grip.

"You bitch! You come with me or I'll break you in half," he snarled.

Talley tried to lift the gun she had concealed behind her back, but Marshall wrested the gun from her and then struck her head with the barrel. She sagged in his arms. Narye ran at him, flailing her arms, kicking and screaming at the top of her lungs. She tried to jump on his back, but he twisted around and flung her off. No sooner had she pushed herself up than she flew at him again. Marshall turned and shot wildly at her. Narye dropped to the floor at his feet.

Michael came running out of the bathroom to see Narye on the floor and his father trying to drag Talley's unconscious body to the door.

"Where are you taking Mommy? What's wrong with Narye?" he cried.

Marshall turned around quickly and smiled stiffly at his son. "C'mon, Michael, you're coming with your mother and me." Marshall began backing away, dragging Talley with him.

"What's wrong with Mommy?" Michael wanted to know. He held back.

"C'mon, Michael. We're going home."

"I don't want to go," Michael cried. "You hurt Mommy again."

Narye was slowing pulling herself up behind Marshall. Michael's tennis racket, which had been beside the door, was in her hand. She used all the force in her small, wiry body to strike Marshall on the back of the head with the racket frame.

When he dropped Talley and fell backwards out of the door, Narye shut the door and she and Michael leaned against it determined to hold it shut despite the splintered lock. Outside Marshall groaned, got to his feet and began to pound and push at the door. From the distance came the wail of police sirens, and when Marshall stopped abruptly they heard the neighbors screaming at him.

"This isn't finished, Talley," he shouted through the door. "I'm going to take care of that clod you've been with, then I'm coming after you!"

Marshall ran to his car and peeled off. When the police pulled into the complex, both Talley and Narye were unconscious. Blood from the wound in Narye's side had soaked her clothing. Sitting on the floor between them, Michael was petting first one and then the other, and weeping. He had his mother's cell phone in his lap and had pushed the programmed number for Cole.

The boy wept into the phone when Cole answered. "Daddy was here. He took Mommy's gun. He hurt Mommy and Narye."

"Let me talk to your mother, Michael," Cole said, his voice low and intense.

"She can't talk. She's not moving."

There was a silence on the line as Cole grasped the enormity of the situation. He asked, urgently,

"Michael! Can you tell if she's breathing? Go feel her chest. Is she breathing?"

"I think so."

"What about Narye?"

"She's breathing too, but there's blood all over her."

Cole told him to sit still and wait for him or one of his brothers to get there.

Winston was in the area and arrived before Cole. He pushed his way through the crowd in the parking lot and told the police officer Talley was his sister.

When he saw the scene through the doorway of Talley's apartment, his mouth dropped. Michael ran to him, and he clutched the little boy in his arms. Police officers were kneeling beside each of the two women and Talley began to revive.

"Michael. My son," she moaned, her hands reaching out.

"He's here, ma'am. He's okay," one of the officers said.

An ambulance was pulling into the lot.

"Narye?" she asked.

"She's hurt bad, but there's an ambulance here to take the two of you to South Fulton Medical Center."

"Where's my son?" she asked.

"He's here with me, Talley," Winston said. "Michael called Cole. He's on his way."

"Oh, Winston, thank goodness. I want Cole," she said with a catch in her voice.

"He's on his way." Winston was soothing.

"Call him. Tell him to meet us at the hospital," she said.

"Okay. Don't talk anymore. I'll take Michael home and put him to bed. I'll make sure the door to your house is secure. Don't worry about anything, Talley."

— ᴄ᷉ —

After being treated for a slight concussion Talley was released from the hospital that evening. Narye, though, remained in the hospital overnight. The bullet had passed through her side, luckily without damaging any organs.

The police questioned Talley and traced Marshall to the Ritz Carlton, but he had checked out when they got there.

When Cole rushed into the emergency room and found Talley at last, he took her into his arms as though she were a fragile wounded bird and held her to his chest gently, murmuring soothing phrases into her hair. She clung to him, sighing deeply, and all the fear went out of her in that breath.

"You and Michael and Narye are going to stay at our house. The boys can double up. I'm never going to let you out of my sight again," he said.

"Umm," she murmured.

"C'mon, let's go home," he said.

Cole put Talley to bed in Lucy's old room and sat in a chair beside her bed until she fell asleep, then stayed home with her the next day. He was the first thing she saw when she opened her eyes.

"How's your head?" he asked.

"It hurts. It's throbbing," she said.

"The doctor gave me these pills for you to take," he said, holding them out with a glass of water.

She took the pills obediently, then asked, "Where is everybody?"

"We decided to take Michael out of school for a few days until the police find Marshall. The boy's spending the day with Marcus in the truck. Everybody's out," he smiled.

"My head would feel better if you would lie beside me and rub it," she suggested with a seductive smile.

"Okay, but I'm not rubbing anything else," he said sternly. She inhaled the scent of his skin and his soap when he got under the covers with her, then slipped his arm around her and molded the curves of her body against him.

"How do you suppose he found you?" Cole mused.

"Joe, that detective who's dating my friend Alicia, must have told the Pettifores," Talley sighed. "It'll break Alicia's heart."

"I guess Ro could have found him and told him," Cole muttered.

"Roberta?" Talley asked with a startled little jump.

"Yeah, that's her kind of dirt. She figured out who you were," he admitted. "I didn't say anything because I didn't really think she'd go that far."

"I wish you'd told me anyway."

"I'm sorry."

"Still, it was probably Joe. There would be no reason for Roberta to track Marshall down, would there?"

"I don't know," he said. "She can be spiteful."

"Those pills are making me sleepy," Talley sighed.

"Just relax and let me hold you."

⁓⟋

Talley talked to her mother later in the day and carefully explained the situation to her, calming Claudia's worried cries.

"I'm fine, Mama, just a headache. Narye gets out of the hospital today. We're going to take care of her. Michael is taking a few days off from school so we can keep an eye on him. And the police are looking for Marshall."

"Cedric is going to be furious that Marshall created a scandal down there," Claudia said.

"The newspapers haven't made the connection yet. Maybe they won't."

"I wouldn't count on it, dear."

"Are you sure y'all are gonna be alright?" Alicia asked when Talley called her next. "And you think Joe told Marshall where you were?" she asked, a hint of tears in her voice.

"It's possible. Though there is the chance Roberta could have searched him out and told him for some reason," Talley said.

"That could be it," Alicia said, brightening. "Truly! Roberta was awfully mad at you. And once she realized who you were, she was probably dyin' to know what the hell you were doin' here!"

"She wouldn't know Marshall was here looking for me," Talley said.

"Yeah, but she coulda called his office in Detroit. She coulda been thinkin' she'd get your husband to come down here and get you. Believe me, that heifer would do anything to get that big, bright-eyed man back!"

"I guess I would too," Talley admitted. "Have you heard from Joe?"

"He called from Detroit a couple of times. I haven't taken his calls. I'm still stewin'."

"You're a tough cookie," Talley said.

"It's my future. I've gotta be sure I can trust the man I'm gonna spend the rest of my life with. He's gotta know I'm serious about this."

CHAPTER SEVENTEEN

When Cedric heard that the Atlanta police were looking for his son for assaulting Talley and shooting Narye, he was enraged. He decided it was time that he took a look at the videotape. He found it locked in a bottom drawer of his son's desk and brought it home with him.

After his wife went to bed, Cedric went into the library and inserted the tape into the player.

Every moment of the short, brutal video hit Cedric like a vicious blow to his own body. When he watched his son punch Michael in the face, sending the small boy spinning across the room, Cedric let out a gasp of horror.

When the tape finally clicked off, he sat alone for the rest of the night among the tall, dark shelves filled with antique law books. He remembered the first time he had surprised Marshall at age fourteen wearing one of Martine's many wigs and sashaying around her dressing room in an Yves St. Laurent gown. He'd immediately made the assumption that his son was gay.

"I will not have a sodomite for a son," Cedric told him. "I will beat the black off you."

"I'm not like that, Daddy," Marshall insisted. "I just like putting on Mom's clothes. I'm not having sex with men."

"Of course you aren't. Because I would kill you," his father said in fury. "You're going to marry Tallulah and give me a grandson I can be proud of. I don't have any other use for you."

Cedric was not a man to doubt himself or his decisions, but through that night he wrestled with the demons of remorse and culpability. Marshall had displayed a timid, whiny nature at an early age and Cedric's bitter disappointment had always been obvious. He recalled all the times he'd been harshly dismissive when the boy had run to him for attention. Try as he might, Cedric could not remember a time when he'd had a kind or encouraging word for the child. *Did I do this to my son? Did I drive him to this perversion?*

As the pink fingers of dawn edged into the library through the heavy brocade curtains, Cedric made the decision to wash his hands of Marshall completely. No matter how big a role he had played in the making of his son, it was too late now. Cedric realized that he could no longer think of Marshall without seeing him punch Michael in the face.

At the office that day, quietly and methodically, Cedric went about the business of erasing his son from his life. His jaws tight with suppressed anguish, he had Marshall's office cleaned out and his name taken off the company letterhead. He revised his will, leaving Marshall nothing.

Then he had his secretary phone Marshall and inform him that if he came back to Pettifore, Pettifore and Quincy, company guards would escort him off the property.

"Mother, how could you let him do this to me?" Marshall demanded of Martine after he received the call. Marshall was hiding out in a room at a Holiday Inn outside Atlanta while he tried to decide what to do. He was still determined to force Talley and Michael to come home.

"There was nothing I could do," Martine wept. "You went too far this time. The police are going to arrest you for attempted murder!"

"But where will I go? What will I do?"

"I don't know," Martine wailed. "Cedric is adamant. Marshall, your father watched the tape!"

Her words struck terror in his heart. He had never felt so frightened and despairing. *He saw the tape. He saw it all.*

The images his father had seen spun around in Marshall's head.

"Is it Halloween, Daddy?"

"Marshall, your son is in here. Please. Don't. Can't you see?

"I'll do what you want. Just let me get Michael to leave the room."

"Mommy! Mommy!"

Marshall twisted and turned around the room, holding his head, trying desperately to rid himself of the sights and sounds that tormented him.

This is all Talley's fault, he thought. *If she hadn't made that tape and then run away, none of this would be happening to me. If I can get her to come back, make her tell Dad she's forgiven me, it'll be all right again.*

"You need to stop dicking around with this," he said to his image in the mirror. "You need to act like a man for once in your life and take some real action."

⁓

Joe noticed when Junius "June Bug" Wilson got on the flight to Atlanta behind him. June Bug was one of Detroit's more notorious thugs, with a history of arrests for all manner of assaults with weapons ranging from firearms to pool cues to ice picks. But when four of June Bug's tattooed homeboys followed him, sporting skullcaps and do-rags, jangling gold chains and flashing gold teeth, Joe was sure trouble was brewing.

When the flight landed, Joe hung back to see if he could tell where they were going, and he saw Marshall meet them at baggage claim and lead them across to the parking deck. Marshall was so uncharacteristically disheveled, his face unshaven, his hair wild and unruly, that Joe almost didn't recognize him. *He looks terrible. Why is he meeting these characters?* Joe wondered as he followed them to the parking deck and watched them get into a big black SUV.

It didn't take Joe long to realize that this could mean danger for Talley. He pulled out his cell phone to call Alicia immediately. Alicia would help him find Talley and warn her.

"Joe! Did you tell Marshall where to find Talley?" Alicia demanded as soon as she heard his voice.

"Marshall knows where Talley is?" Joe fired back.

"Yes. Didn't you tell…?"

"No, I didn't. I promised you I wouldn't, remember?" Joe said. "I love you. I sold my house and quit my job in Detroit. "

"What…"

"I can't talk now. Quick, do you have Talley's number at work?" When she gave it to him, Joe hung up and called TowMasters.

"Is Talley there?" he asked hurriedly.

"May I ask who's callin'?" Vickie queried musically.

"Put her on! Right now!" Joe shouted.

"Just a moment." Vickie was miffed, but she got Talley to the phone.

"Talley, this is Joe Griffin. You have to get away from there," Joe said when she picked up. "Marshall just picked up a gang of thugs from the airport and I'm pretty sure he's heading your way. Bounce! Now! I'm on my way there."

"But…I thought…"

"Hurry!" Joe said, hanging up.

"Vickie, come on," Talley said. "We've got to get out of here. Grab your coat. Call Marcus and Winston on the radio. I'm phoning Cole."

Vickie used a 911 code to call the truckers and tell them to get to the yard. Then she and Talley hopped into Talley's truck and raced down the driveway onto the parkway. The women pulled into a Burger King parking lot down the street from the yard and as they got out of the car, watched Marshall pass them driving a big black Escalade filled with tough-looking men.

A few minutes later Winston and Marcus came barreling down the parkway in their trucks. Talley and Vickie, standing on the sidewalk outside the restaurant, flagged them down and the men pulled into the fast-food lot.

"What's going on?" Marcus wanted to know.

Just then, Joe spotted the two big TowMasters wreckers in the Burger King parking lot and pulled his rental car in. He joined the little clutch of people talking excitedly beside the trucks.

"Hey, you must be Talley," he said to the tall, slender beauty with gold curls. "I'm Joe Griffin."

The two big men turned to look suspiciously at him. "You that detective?" Marcus asked.

"Yeah, but I swear I never told the crazy man where Talley was," he said quickly to the brothers.

Marcus assessed the earnest honesty in Joe's face and nodded at him.

"It must have been Roberta," Winston said.

"I need to tell you what Marshall's up to now," Joe said. "He's imported some Detroit thugs and apparently they're at your place now looking for Talley."

"Cole should be here any minute. David's got Michael with him."

"Tell David to keep Michael away from here," Talley said.

"Aw, no," Winston wailed. "David would never forgive me. Y'know what I'm saying? I'm gonna tell him to drop Michael off at our house and c'mon."

Marcus picked up a tire iron and weighed it in his hand. "I haven't made a head roll in quite some time," he said grimly. "I'm about ready."

Vickie giggled nervously.

Talley fretted, "What are you guys going to do? What are you going to do?"

Vickie's boyfriend Jamal pulled up in his truck. The parking lot was getting full and the restaurant manager peered out the window at them.

When Cole came down the street in his big Peterbilt and pulled in, the manager came out. Cole waved at him and pulled around to the back of the lot. The others got in their trucks and joined him in the back.

"How many?" he asked Joe immediately.

"Six, counting Marshall."

"And there's six of us," he said, nodding at his brothers and Jamal as David came speeding around to the back of the restaurant and hopped out of his car. "A fair fight."

"Whaz up, whaz up?" David asked eagerly.

"Aren't you going to call the police?" Talley asked Cole.

All the men looked at her as if she'd lost her mind.

"Do they have guns?" Cole wanted to know.

"I doubt it," Joe said. "They just got off the plane. Besides, Marshall doesn't want to kill Talley, just take her and Michael back to Detroit."

"Marshall has my gun!" Talley exclaimed.

"Oh, that little pea shooter can't hurt us," Cole said, grinning at her.

"You guys can't be planning to…," she started.

"Baby, why don't you and Vickie, go on to the house. We'll be along in a little while," Cole interrupted with a raised eyebrow.

"But you might get hurt," Talley wailed.

"Somebody's gonna get hurt, but it ain't gonna be us," Marcus said, pumped.

"Like the man said, 'Let's roll,'" Cole said quietly to the group. The men began getting into their vehicles and pulling off.

"I'm so sorry about all this," Talley said to Vickie who was watching Jamal drive off.

"No need to be sorry," Vickie said with a sad smile. "Jamal and I both hate bullies."

"I appreciate it," Talley sighed. "Let's stop by the drugstore on the way home and get some first aid supplies."

⸻ ❧ ⸻

Talley called Alicia from Cole's house.

"I think you should know your fiancée has gone off with Cole and his brothers to fight some thugs on my behalf," Talley said.

Alicia was thrilled. "He has? For sure?"

"For sure," Talley said.

"Wonderful!" she exclaimed. "Whacha doin'?"

"Vickie and I are at Cole's house with first aid supplies waiting for them," Talley said.

"I want to be there!" Alicia said excitedly. "Can I come too?"

"You certainly may. Come on."

⟿

When the trucks pulled into the yard, the thugs from Detroit were sitting in the car arguing with Marshall. They had already kicked down the door of the trailer and trashed the offices. Papers and file folders littered the walkway and chairs and the old TV lay askew in the parking area. The gangsters got out of the Escalade and eyeballed the big truckers headed toward them with tire irons, chains and two-by-fours.

"I thought you told me the bitch would be alone," Junius hissed at Marshall. "You set us up!"

"No. I didn't," Marshall hissed back. "How was I to know that all these guys would be coming here?"

Cole spotted Marshall immediately and saw red. He surprised the thugs by ignoring their shouted threats and striding straight up to Marshall. Without a word, he delivered two swift punches, then in one lightning-fast round-house move, kicked the startled man's feet out from under him. Marshall howled and collapsed, fumbling in his pocket for Talley's gun. Cole pulled him to his feet and then knocked him unconscious.

Cole's brothers stood solidly to keep the thugs from interfering. When Cole was finished with Marshall, he turned his attention to June Bug and then everybody joined in.

David and Winston fought as a team. David, eyeglasses safely stowed in his truck, would hang on to a combatant's arms long enough for Winston to get in his jabs, then they'd trade places. Jamal, catching on, sent men spinning their way.

Marcus fought neatly and methodically, carefully placing his punches where they would do the most damage, all the while keeping an eye on Cole's back.

Cole, fueled by his rage at anyone who would threaten his beloved Talley, fought like a man possessed. At the center of the fray, he jabbed and whirled as though channeling Mohammed Ali.

Grunts and groans and the thuds of flesh meeting flesh filled the air. When Marshall came to, he crawled dizzily into the Escalade and hid.

Ultimately, the truckers prevailed. When the thugs jumped into their SUV, Cole and the others chased the black truck out of the yard with triumphant howls and brazen threats. Then, in typical male fashion, they celebrated by slapping high fives with each other.

The victors weren't undamaged. Jamal lost a tooth. David had a shiner growing and there were numerous bruises, scrapes and cuts evident throughout the group. But, on the whole, the six exultant men who presented themselves to their women at Cole's house were easily mended.

Cole grabbed Talley and Michael in a bear hug and Jamal did the same to Vickie. Joe was surprised and delighted to find Alicia at the house, even though she pointedly ignored him after checking that he was all in one piece.

The women swabbed, bandaged and splinted, then dispensed Excedrin and Tylenol.

Afterward, the men, still fired up, toasted each other with shots of Crown Royal and tried to out-brag one another. The women flashed skeptical grins at one another as the stories of physical prowess got wilder and more farfetched.

"I sent this one hardhead flying so high, I thought he was going to land on the trailer roof," said Jamal.

"They couldn't get off our land fast enough," David said.

"They looked like they were shot from a cannon," Marcus agreed.

"You and Vickie are going to be pretty mad when you see what they did to the office," Cole said.

"Oh no, they didn't trash the place, did they?" Talley groaned.

"Our files are all out on the sidewalk," Cole said sadly.

"I'll help you clean 'em up," Marcus offered. "Don't worry."

Joe caught Alicia as she was coming out of the kitchen with a bowl of potato chips.

"Girl, do you still love me?" he demanded.

"Yes," she admitted shyly.

"You going to marry me?"

"I guess so," she said, eyes down.

"Look at me," he said, lifting her chin. "Alicia, I'm sorry about the tap on your phone. I put it on there before we fell for each other, and I didn't take it off 'cause I was doing my job even though I knew it was wrong. But I hope I can make it right with you from now on."

"Did you really quit your job with your dad?"

"Yeah. I'm going to set up here. I have a few clients already I can bank on. I've got some bucks put away. We won't starve."

"Okay," she said meekly, not objecting to the 'we.'

"My bags are still in the car. Can I come home with you?"

She nodded and he pulled her to him and whispered in her ear, "You want some of this thang tonight?"

"Joe, you cut that out. Don't you ever, do you hear me, *ever* refer to that conversation again!"

⁓ᘒ

Marshall and June Bug argued bitterly all the way to the airport.

"Man, you said they didn't know we were coming."

"I don't know how they found out."

"We weren't looking for no ten or twenty guys to be coming at us. We shoulda had our guns."

"I expected you to be able to handle yourselves without guns."

"Not with twenty guys coming at us!"

"If you want to stay in Atlanta, you do it at your own expense," Marshall told the gangster as he stopped the car at Delta Ticketing. "And I hope you don't expect to get paid the rest of your money."

June Bug was not taking that. He got out the Escalade, snatched Marshall from the driver's seat and proceeded to beat what little stuffing Cole had left in the man out of him. He pulled Marshall's wallet out of his pocket and he and his riders drove off in the Cadillac before airport security could stop them.

June Bug's last words to Marshall were, "Everybody in Detroit knows you're a faggot. Don't come back there."

Marshall took a cab back to his hotel, stopping off at a liquor store first to buy some vodka with a few bucks he found in his pockets, along with the pistol he still carried.

Sitting on the side of the bed in his room, the TV blaring, Marshall downed drink after drink. The gun was held loosely in his hand between his knees. Periodically, he would put the barrel into his mouth and strain to pull the trigger. Each time his courage failed him, he would curse at himself and take another drink.

After he downed the last drop in the bottle, Marshall put the barrel against the side of his forehead, squeezed his eyes shut and pulled the trigger.

CHAPTER EIGHTEEN

When Talley's attorney notified her of Marshall's suicide, Talley's first emotion was guilt. Then she felt a deep sense of relief. Then she felt guilt for feeling relieved.

"Oh, Narye," she wept to her friend. "We loved each other so much when we were children. We didn't have any other friends and we leaned on each other for everything."

"I remember," Narye soothed.

"How could he have changed so much?"

"His father was quite brutal to him. I never understood why," Narye recalled.

"He told me once when he was a teenager that his father knew a secret about him. Do you suppose Cedric knew about…the cross-dressing?"

"Perhaps."

"I want to remember him as that sweet boy who used to chase frogs with me in the garden. Who brought me donuts that he'd filched from the kitchen. Who painted a face back on my doll after she got soaked in the rain."

"It's best to remember him that way," Narye said as the phone rang.

When Talley answered the phone, her mother's quiet voice helped to soothe her guilt.

"I always felt an incredible sadness in Marshall for most of his adult life," Claudia said. "Even before the two of you were married, he couldn't find peace in himself. He's found it now."

"Michael and I will be coming home for the funeral," Talley told her mother. "But, I still don't trust Cedric not to try something."

"The wind is out of Cedric's sails," Claudia said. "It's as though he aged twenty years overnight when he heard of Marshall's suicide."

"I'm surprised. He treated his son very badly when he was alive," Talley noted.

"It was a strange relationship. Very strange indeed. Martine, of course, is devastated."

"I expected that. She loved Marshall so much."

"Your Grandfather Quincy is very ill too," Claudia told her. "We don't expect him to last the month."

"We'll be in Friday night and go straight to my house. I'll call you when I get there."

The night before Talley left, Cole came to her bed in his house and loved her as though he were putting his seal on her. He thrust himself deep into her with hungry intensity. She responded to his passion with an urgency of her own, clung to him with trembling limbs, matched his tempo. When she climaxed, she had to muffle her cries with a pillow for fear she'd wake the household.

Cole didn't want to tell her how afraid he was to let her go.

"You're not coming back, are you?" he asked huskily, kissing her forehead and cheeks.

"Of course I am," she said.

"Why should you?" he asked. "You don't have anything to worry about up there now. Your home and your life are with your family."

"You're here," she said.

"That's nothing." He turned his back to her.

"It's everything to me." She pressed her breasts against his hard, warm back and caressed his shoulders.

"No, it's not," came the muted response.

"Yes, it is."

"No, it's not."

"Stop, Cole. Michael and I will be back right after the funeral, right after I make arrangements to sell the house and Marshall's things. Unless...Do you want the Ferrari?"

"What?" Cole turned back around and peered at her in the darkness.

"There's a brand new Ferrari. Do you want me to keep it for you?"

"No, sell it. You can probably get as much as $100,000!"

"Cole. Please understand. I don't need $100,000."

"Well, hell, I don't need a Ferrari. What would I look like in a car like that?"

"It's the big coupe. You'd probably look quite good in it," she said with a laugh.

"Naw, I don't want that asshole's car."

"What about his…"

"I don't want any of his stuff." Cole turned back on his side, his back to her. She snuggled up to him again.

"Well, I'll ask Marcus."

"He'll say the same. But don't you dare ask Winston! You hear me?"

"We'll see," she teased.

"I mean it. That boy's got no morals," Cole groused.

"Speaking of morals, we *are* fornicating," she responded with a giggle.

"I hate that word," Cole said.

"I'm a free woman now," she said hopefully. She raised a bit and leaned her chin on his arm, trying to peer into his face.

"Yeah, I know," he said softly.

"Michael needs a father badly," she hinted.

Cole sat up abruptly. "I better get back to my room," he said.

"Cole? What's wrong?" she asked, distressed by his reaction.

"I'll see you in the morning," he said.

But in the morning, he was already gone.

"He had to pick up a couple of Porsches to go to Miami," Marcus said. "He asked me to take y'all to the airport this mornin'."

"Oh." Talley was disappointed.

"When are you comin' back?" Marcus asked on the way to the airport in Talley's car.

"As soon as possible," Talley said.

"Cole doesn't think you're coming back, y' know," Marcus confided.

"He's being silly. As soon as I get all of Marshall's affairs settled and can see to our houses…"

"Houses?"

"Yes. We've got villas in Spain and the Bahamas, a lodge in northern Wisconsin and I've got a flat in Paris."

"What do you do with all them places?" Marcus asked.

"We have a management company that rents them out when we're not using them. I'm probably going to sell the estate in Farmington and the lodge in Wisconsin."

"Yeah, you need to keep the other places," Marcus said with a grin. "I wonder if I could use your villa in the Bahamas for my honeymoon? What do you think?"

"Of course! When are you going to get married?"

"Soon as I find a woman like you."

"Oh, Marcus, you flatter me." Talley patted his arm shyly and Marcus shrugged.

"When are you and Cole gonna hook up?" he wanted to know.

"I don't know. He hasn't asked."

"What?"

"No, not a word."

"What's wrong with the damned idiot?" Marcus exclaimed. "I'm sorry, I'm sorry," he said quickly, glancing in the rearview mirror to see if Michael had overheard the mild profanity.

"That's okay," Talley said, checking the backseat. Narye and Michael were playing a travel checkers game.

"I'm gonna talk to Cole as soon as I…"

"I wish you wouldn't. If he's going to ask me to marry him, I don't want him pressured to do it. He's got to feel it."

"I know he feels it. He's crazy 'bout you."

"It's my money. He sees it as an obstacle, not an advantage."

"Yeah, he's got some weird hangups 'bout people with money. And, he's real independent. He likes to make his own way."

"Everybody needs help sometimes."

"I know that. But not Cole. It used to piss us off when we were kids. He and Lucy were strugglin' to make ends meet and folks wanted to help us out. He'd tell us that if we started lookin' for help all the time, next thing Social Services would be wantin' to take us away from him and Lucy."

"He did have a point."

"Maybe then, but now he takes it too far."

⟡

Talley stood in the huge marble foyer of her house in Farmington and inhaled deeply. The tall floral arrangement on the table in the center of the room was fresh, thanks to the service that came in twice a week. The household staff hadn't missed a beat, despite the fact that Talley hadn't been home in six months. Her home was still beautiful, sparkling clean, and smelled of tiger lilies.

This was testament to Narye's efficient training of the men and women who worked under her supervision. Narye liked to say she ran the house as if it were the Ritz Hotel in Paris. "There are always fresh flowers in the bedrooms, meals on demand, overnight laundry and fresh water in a crystal pitcher next to the bed," she boasted.

The sun was streaming in from the huge window at the top of the stairs, but it was still a chilly March in Michigan. In Atlanta the air was warming and the dogwoods were starting to bloom.

Talley walked down the hall to what had been Marshall's room. It was wood paneled, heavily masculine. A large oak bed dominated the sleeping area; a huge roll top oak desk filled an adjoining lounge.

Talley had rarely entered this room. Marshall had always come to her space when he wanted to see her. There had been times when those visits hadn't been painful and frightening. Sometimes he'd crawl in her bed just to have her hold him. She tried to remember those times.

Narye had followed her into Marshall's room.

"We need to start getting rid of all his clothes. Give them to Goodwill. We'll keep his good pieces of jewelry. Michael will want them someday," Talley said. "I'll call Marshall's sisters. There might be some things they want. I'll go call them and his mother now."

⁓

The funeral was a very private family affair with just a sprinkling of dignitaries and a handful of celebrities. The fact of Marshall's suicide could not be kept from the media, and Cedric decided not to make a display of his son's last rites. Nonetheless, there were many famous Quincys and Pettifores, so the spotlight could not be entirely avoided.

Bouncers stood at the door to the church and ringed the gravesite, keeping media and the simply curious away.

Later at the house, Talley and Michael clung to each other and received condolences. Martine was a shrunken shadow of herself. A tendril of hair dangled from her normally immaculate coiffure. She huddled in a huge armchair and met expressions of sympathy with dazed and confused nods. Cedric stood beside her chair, occasionally leaning on it for support, his eyes deep and shadowed.

Claudia gently pulled Talley away to the library for a quick update on her Grandfather Quincy's situation.

"I know you said you wanted to get right back to Atlanta, dear, but please stay with your father and me until his father passes. We need you here with us."

"Mama, I have to get back to Cole," Talley protested.

"Tell me about this Cole," Claudia suggested, taking her daughter's hand and patting the leather sofa cushion beside her.

"I love him so much, Mama, I can't tell even begin to tell you." Talley's eyes gleamed softly. "He's big and strong and safe. He's kind and loving and generous. He's so different from Marshall."

"And you can't bear to be away from him for a few extra days?" Claudia's smile grew tender at her daughter's enthusiasm.

"He's insecure about me. Nothing I do seems to help with that. He doesn't believe I'm coming back at all."

"Just call him and tell him you must stay with your parents for a bit longer. That your grandfather is dying. Please?"

"Oh, Mama," Talley sighed. "All right."

"Besides, you can't just run away now. You have so many things to take care of here. And…well…Cedric wants to see you."

"Cedric wants to see you," her father repeated that evening.

"I don't want to see him," Talley snapped. "He hounded us in Atlanta."

"He wanted you to bring Michael back."

"So Marshall could beat him? So he could take him away from me? Don't tell me you condone that?"

"Of course not, Talley."

"You never helped me," she spat at her father, surprising him with her intensity. "You knew Marshall was hurting me and you didn't do anything."

"I couldn't," Derek said, reaching his hand out to his daughter.

She shrugged away and turned her back on him.

"Why couldn't you stand up to the Pettifores? Why did you let them hurt me?"

Her father could not meet her eyes. "Cedric can't hurt you anymore," Derek asserted. "Now that Marshall is dead, he has no control over you and your son."

"And now I've finally found a man who will stand up for me," she said. "It took me twenty-eight years, but I found Cole."

"Go and see Cedric. Tell him that."

~ ⌒ ~

"She's going to be up there a little while longer," Cole told Vickie when she asked about Talley. "If she comes back at all. Her Grandfather Quincy is dying, she says." They were out at the yard and Cole had just gotten off the phone with Talley.

"What do you mean 'if she comes back at all'?" Vickie snapped at him. "Of course she's comin' back."

"Why should she?"

"'Cause of you, you big dummy," she replied.

"Yeah, sure."

Cole went out and got in his truck. He climbed into the sleeper and looked around, then quickly backed out and sat behind the steering wheel. After a minute, he put his head down on the wheel and closed his eyes.

He was still sitting there when Marcus pulled into the yard and went into the office trailer.

"He's pitiful, ain't he?" he said to Vickie, looking out the window at the big man slumped over his steering wheel.

"I feel real bad for him. Talley called to say she's gotta stay another week or so."

"Aw hell, you know what he's thinkin' now, don't you?"

"She ain't coming back," they said in unison.

"Why don't you see if you can find him a load going up to Detroit?" Marcus suggested. Vickie peered at him for a moment until comprehension dawned.

"That's a great idea. I'm on it!"

⎯⎯ ૭

Cole decided he couldn't turn down the trip to Michigan that Vickie had arranged, even if he didn't have a confirmed load coming back. The trip was paying real well. And it was going to Detroit.

Cole's brothers hung around his room while he was packing, offering their suggestions.

"Take that suit you bought for Granddad's funeral," Marcus said. "You only wore it once. You can meet her parents in that."

"Yeah, and take your tuxedo in case they dress for dinner," said Winston.

"Man, you been watchin' too many of them old movies on TV," David howled.

"I was jus' foolin'," Winston said sheepishly. "I know they don't do like that anymore."

"Y'all are crazy. I'm dressing just like I do all the time," Cole said.

"You don't need to be wearin' your TransportMasters shirt goin' up to her house," Marcus fretted.

"I hadn't planned to," Cole replied angrily. "Why don't y'all get outta here?"

"He's nervous, that's why he's so grumpy," David said loudly as they left his room.

"I would be too," Winston agreed, equally as loud, "goin' up to be inspected by all them Quincys and Pettifores, y'know what I'm saying?"

—☙

Talley and Michael waited for Cedric in his library. Talley had ignored Cedric throughout the funeral rites and Michael had not had a chance to do more than just speak to his beloved grandfather.

When Cedric came into the room, Michael raced to give him a big hug. While Talley watched, standing stiffly by the sofa, the distinguished old man's haughty features softened and he slowly and painfully knelt to return the boy's bear hug.

"Michael, I missed you," he said, his normally commanding voice breaking with emotion.

"I've missed you too, Papa Cedric," Michael enthused, "but I have so many adventures to tell you about!"

"We'll talk for a long time later," Cedric said, looking at Talley for confirmation. She nodded curtly.

"Michael, why don't you go visit with Grandmother Martine?" Cedric suggested. "She has a surprise for you."

"So, you've not turned him against me," Cedric said to Talley, nodding gratefully at her. "I thank you for that."

"He loves you," Talley said as Michael ran out of the library.

"He's the best of both the Pettifore and Quincy lines," Cedric said. "You should never have taken him away from here."

"Don't pretend you don't know why I had to leave. Marshall was out of hand. I was afraid of him. He hit Michael!"

"I didn't know until recently that he had hit the boy." Cedric turned and stared into the fireplace.

"You saw the tape."

"Not at first. I was afraid to look at it. Once I did, I disowned him. I think that's why he killed himself."

"He was unhappy all his life. And he was getting worse."

To Talley's surprise, Cedric picked up a porcelain ornament on the mantle and crashed it into the fireplace.

"He made me sick! But, maybe if I'd paid more attention to him as a child he wouldn't have…Martine says I was always cruel to him. Could I have been the cause of his perversions?" Cedric paced in front of Talley as the words spilled out of him. "No, no," he answered himself. "He was all wrong from the beginning."

"You tried to force him to be something he wasn't," Talley said coldly. "I won't let you do that to Michael."

"Tallulah, you must understand. I would never…"

"You'll never have the chance. I'm going to marry a man who will protect us from you forever."

"What man is this?" Cedric asked, turning away from Talley in frustration.

"His name is Cassius Coleman. He's a truck driver in Atlanta."

Cedric's head snapped around like a cobra's. "Are you insane?"

CHAPTER NINETEEN

If the tall wrought-iron gates with the "P" in the center weren't sufficient to impress Cole, the long oak-lined driveway, the five-car garage where he parked his truck, the massive white columns and the tall, arched windows of the huge house were.

But it was his Talley who raced out of the big double doors and flung herself into his arms, wrapping her legs around his hips. He dropped his bag and clutched her to him.

She inhaled the smell of his leather jacket and his tangy aftershave and reveled in the feel of his strong arms around her again.

"Baby, I missed you," he said in her ear. She covered his face with kisses, stopping only to nibble his lips.

Michael came bouncing out of the house after her, yelling Cole's name.

"Hey, kid," Cole said huskily, swallowing a lump in his throat.

"Can I call you Daddy now?" Michael wanted to know.

"Michael!" Talley said quickly. "Hush!"

Cole lifted an eyebrow at Talley and she just shook her head, embarrassed that Michael had been so bold.

"Kids…you know," she said.

She led Cole into the house. He stopped in the foyer and looked at the drawing room on the right that seemed to stretch off into infinity, at the huge staircase in front of him, at the tall double doors leading to the library.

"Damn, Talley, this is beautiful."

"It's listed with The Registry. I should be able to get ten to twelve million for it."

"So you're really selling it, huh?" Cole said.

"Yes, Cole. I'm selling it. So I can move to Atlanta to be with you," she said emphatically.

"Hmmph," he grunted.

"I thought we'd just have a quiet dinner at home tonight," Talley said. "We can dine with the family tomorrow. And you should rest before we eat. I know you must have kept 'the left door closed' all the way up here. You probably need a nap."

"Let me show you my room," Michael said, grabbing for Cole's hand. "I'm picking out the things I want to take with me to Atlanta. You can help."

"Why don't you go with Michael," Talley suggested. "I've got to go talk to the cook. I'll be up in a minute."

A distinguished-looking older man in a dark suit came to the front of the house. For a moment, until Talley called him Jack, Cole thought he might be Talley's father.

"Jack, take Mr. Coleman's suitcase up to the burgundy guest suite," Talley said.

"I can carry it," Cole said, startled.

Talley just smiled and left Cole and Jack eying one another, while Michael pulled on Cole's hand.

Later, Cole slipped between satiny soft sheets and lay back on down pillows in the big oak bed in the suite. He had showered in the huge black ceramic bathroom, noting the 14-carat gold fixtures and the shower with nozzles spraying water at various heights from all directions.

"Damn," he'd muttered to himself, "it would be too easy to get used to this."

He was luxuriating in the feel of the mattress—not too soft, not too hard—when he heard a small sound and Talley came in through a side door hidden in the paneling.

"Hi," she whispered. "Want some company?"

He reached out his arms to her and she came into them immediately, discarding the filmy wrap she'd been wearing. She stretched out on top of him and every curve of her body molded against his. A mutual shudder ran along their length as he ran his hands up and down her back and buttocks.

Talley straddled him, rubbing her hands over his chest and arms. He sighed and gave himself up to her ministrations, stretching his arms above his head at her bidding.

She planted tiny kisses all over him, inching herself down his body, feeling the muscles in his stomach jump as she lightly kissed that concave part of his body. Exploring, she tasted the soft hairs where his manhood rested. He quivered with the pleasure of it and let out a small, whimpering sound. Tasting the heavy, thick shaft, she lapped at the drop of moisture at its tip.

He leaned up on his elbows and wordlessly made her shift her body around until her cleft was trembling above his mouth. He raised his head hungrily and buried his lips in her softness, his tongue searching and flicking until he found her sensitive nub. She plunged her mouth down on his rock-hard manhood in response. They filled the air with the sounds of their passion and their gasps of pleasure.

At the brink of climax, Talley turned and eased herself down on him, taking the whole of his hot hardness into her. They surged and thrust in perfect harmony until they both cried out simultaneously in final ecstatic release.

She collapsed on his chest, stretching her legs out behind her until she was lying on top of him again, length to length. He held her there, his manhood still buried inside her, their hearts beating together as though they were one person.

Sighing, she rolled off him and curled easily into the curve of his body. His breathing slowed and steadied as he dropped off to sleep.

When he awoke finally, it was the next morning. He was alone in the bed and he was ravenous.

Talley came in, dressed in jodhpurs and jacket, and smiled at his nakedness.

"Come on, get dressed and get some breakfast. You missed dinner last night, so I know you're starving. Let's go riding after you eat. Do you want to?

"Where are you going to get horses?" Cole wondered.

"We've got stables on the estate," Talley said.

"I haven't been on horseback since I was a boy," he said nervously.

"It's like riding a bicycle, it comes right back," she smiled. "Come on, get up! I have the perfect horse for you!"

After breakfast in the cozy dining area off the kitchen, they headed out to the stables. Looking back at the house, Cole asked. "How many bedrooms have you got?"

"There are eight suites of rooms," she said.

"So eight bathrooms," he said.

"Actually fourteen," she replied. He whistled.

"What's Michael doing today?" he asked.

"Since we're here for a little while longer, I've hired a tutor for him to coordinate with his teacher in Atlanta and be sure he keeps up," Talley said.

"Money solves every problem, doesn't it?" Cole commented wryly.

Talley ignored him. Instead, she sped up to greet a beautiful golden stallion her stableman was bringing out to her. The horse whinnied in recognition and Talley petted and nuzzled his nose. "This is Sunrise," she said to Cole. The stableman was also leading a large black mare that he presented to Cole. Cole and horse eyed each other warily.

"Her name is Sultan's Granddaughter," Talley said. "We call her Sultie. She's real gentle. Go ahead, pet her. Here, give her this lump of sugar."

The horse took the sugar from Cole's outstretched palm and tossed her head.

They mounted the horses and walked them gently out of the stable yard.

"I'll show you around the estate. We have a little over twenty acres. There's a pond and a small copse where Michael and I picnic sometimes."

"What's a copse?" Cole asked.

"A small stand of trees," she said lightly.

"Damn," Cole said faintly.

When they came to open fields, Talley let Sunrise have her head, and golden horse and golden girl took off at a gallop. Cole held Sultie back and watched Talley melding with the bounding horse, her hair flying, sparkling in the sun.

He sighed and shook his head, his heart swelling at the sight of the beautiful pair.

Eventually she turned and rode back to him.

"What's wrong?" she asked. "Come on!"

"I can't keep up with you, Talley. I never can and I never will," he said, a wealth of meaning in his words.

"It's not a competition," she said, leaning forward in her saddle. "Just let go and enjoy it. Enjoy it all. Why not?"

"It's not right," he said. "*I* didn't earn it."

"But it's here and it won't go away. It comes with me. Please, Cole. Take it. Take me," she said, her eyes pleading and searching his face.

Cole turned away, unable to meet her eyes. He urged Sultie back toward the stable yard and the mare obediently sped up, eager to trot back to her stall.

"Sunrise, maybe the riding wasn't such a good idea," Talley mused to her horse, stroking his neck. "And I don't imagine swimming in our indoor pool is going to make him any happier."

A handsome, muscular young man met Cole and Talley at the back door of the house. The man astounded and irked Cole by giving Talley a thorough up and down look and shaking his head sorrowfully with a "tut tut" noise.

"I know, I know. It's been months," Talley said to him sadly. She didn't seem to mind the stare.

"Simmer down, sweetie," she said to Cole, noting his annoyed look.

She introduced Cole to Marcel, her exercise trainer, and suggested Cole join them in a session in the weight room in the east branch of the house.

Marcel walked around Cole, looking him up and down, and nodded his approval. "You have a naturally good body," he said. "Great bone structure. We could do some enhancements with the dumbbells."

"I didn't bring any workout clothes," Cole muttered.

"Just put on your boxers and a T-shirt. We're at home," Talley giggled.

The weight room was set up like a regular gym with mirrored walls and all the newest equipment. Talley went to work on the Stairmaster immediately, and Marcel put Cole to "running the rack" of dumbbells, lifting ever heavier and heavier weights at each set.

Later Cole and Talley sat naked together in the small sauna room off the exercise area, the tenseness easing out of their muscles.

"How often do you do this?" Cole asked Talley.

"Marcel comes to me for an hour four times a week."

"I bet he's expensive," Cole said.

"I don't know. My accountant pays him," Talley said quickly. "Speaking of accountants, I've got to meet with them this afternoon to go over some things relative to the sale of some property. Do you have enough to keep you busy?"

"I thought I'd wash my truck."

"Oh dear, I had Bennie, the guy that takes care of our cars, arrange that this morning."

"Why the hell did you do that?" Cole fumed.

"It was sitting there. It was dirty," she said meekly.

"I'd better go look at it," he huffed.

Later before they dressed for their dinner with Talley's family, Cole was in better spirits.

"Your guy Bennie is pretty nice," he said.

"That's good," she said. "You bonded with him over vehicles, did you?"

"He admired my truck," Cole said. "Said he liked our logo."

"It is pretty, isn't it?" she agreed.

"I drove the Ferrari," Cole went on. "I really didn't want to, but you know how weak I get around a beautiful piece of machinery. And Bennie insisted."

"Oh he did, did he? That was nice of him," Talley said with a little chuckle.

"That's a great car. Bennie thinks I should drive it to your parents' house tonight," he said.

"Whatever Bennie says."

On the drive to Grosse Pointe from Farmington, Cole waxed almost poetic about the feel and the ride of the Ferrari.

"This is smooth as silk, responds like a willing woman," he enthused.

"If you like it that much, I won't sell it," she said. "We can pop it in your trailer and you can take it home to Atlanta with you."

Cole was silent. "Naw," he said finally, "I don't wanna do that."

Talley rolled her eyes in exasperation.

"Okay, so tell me why I have to meet your family tonight?" he asked. "Why do I have to meet your ex-husband's family at all?"

"I'm sorry, but they insisted. They know I'm in love with you. They're interested in how you might influence Michael. Michael is both Cedric's and my father's heir."

"A double-comma kid," Cole muttered.

"Pardon?"

"Nothing, just something Winston said. Michael is a multimillionaire at age seven."

"Yes, he is," Talley said calmly. "When Michael is an adult he will have enormous responsibility. He will have to run the law firm, the family foundation and be accountable for the future of the family. *If* he's willing to take the duties on. I want Michael to have a choice. Cedric insists my son has no choice."

"I see. That's why your father-in-law wanted him back up here so bad. So he could get him ready to take on all this stuff."

"Exactly."

"Poor little dude. He doesn't know what's in store for him."

"Marshall was crushed under the weight," Talley said. "I can't, *I won't* have that happen to my child."

"If you ask me, Michael is a different kind of kid. He's happy, strong, loved. He's got you for a mother."

"He's a good boy, isn't he?" she smiled. "And he loves you and your brothers."

At Talley's direction, Cole drove the car up a long winding driveway until they reached a mansion twice the size of Talley's at the top of the hill.

A white-gloved butler opened the door and took their coats. Talley drew Cole into a room where a number of people were chatting and sipping drinks around an enormous blazing fireplace. They all turned to stare.

One by one Talley introduced Cole to her parents, Claudia and Derek; to Marshall's parents, Cedric and Martine; and to Marshall's three older half-sisters: Claire, Michelle and Della.

After the flurry of introductions there was a small embarrassed silence until Claudia said graciously, "Cole, come over here and sit next to me." She patted the seat beside her with a small, delicate hand. "We're so happy to meet you. Talley told me how you rescued her on the side of the road, then took her and Michael under your wing."

"We all owe you a huge debt of gratitude for that," Derek agreed with a nod.

Cole looked at the petite blonde older woman with Talley's amber eyes and was easily drawn to her. He walked over and took a seat on the small settee next to Claudia. She smiled warmly at him and engaged him in conversation.

"I understand you're a businessman with a trucking concern," she fluttered.

"Yeah," he said with a smile, "but I'm not concerned about it. It's doing real well."

Claire snickered and turned away to whisper to Michelle. Talley glared at her.

"How many trucks do you have, dear?" Claudia asked, smoothly gliding over Cole's bad joke.

"Four. Three Nissan flatbeds and the Peterbilt I drove up here."

"The Peterbilt is the biggest one, isn't it?"

"Yes, ma'am," he said and went on to describe in detail the various features of his beloved truck. Claudia held up well under the onslaught of information about air brakes and horsepower, asking questions and smiling gently into Cole's beautiful eyes and animated face. At one point she looked at her daughter and nodded her approval. Cole had gained a fan.

Cedric stood stiffly and silently by the fireplace, scowling at Cole. The waves of animosity pouring off him were so intense that Cole almost felt their physical impact. Several times the younger man looked up defiantly at him.

At dinner, Cole was seated at Derek's right hand, with Claire across from him and Talley at his side. He was stiff and silent through most of the dinner, listening to them talk about perfectly matched pearls and trouble with landscapers and a private party at Le Côte Club in Paris. He felt as if they were speaking a foreign language. Talley took his hand in hers under the table.

But when Derek asked Cole how he went about getting clients for his truck, Cole relaxed and talked about how Talley was helping him build visibility and branding for the two divisions of his business, local towing and long-distance transport.

After dinner the sisters adjourned to the media room to watch television. Claudia, Martine and Talley put their heads together over a catalogue of fine art in the drawing room. Cole fell into Cedric's clutches in the billiards room, with only Derek to mediate.

"Do you play billiards?" Cedric asked.

"That's like pool, isn't it?" Cole wondered, looking at the pocketless green table and the three balls on it.

"Similar skill sets are required," Cedric said.

"Why don't I just watch for a while?" Cole suggested.

"So." Cedric chalked his cue stick and examined the table. "You're in love with my son's widow." He leaned in for his shot.

"Yeah, I love her. My whole family loves her."

"And she loves you." Cedric took his shot neatly.

"She *says* she does," Cole said.

"Why do you put it that way," Cedric asked. "Do you doubt her?"

"Yep," Cole responded. "I do."

Derek made a little "tsk" noise and turned to stare at the young man. Cedric paused at his next shot and looked up with a smirk. "That's very interesting. Do you think she's leading you on?"

"She been with only two men in her life, sir, me and your son. Your son made her unhappy, but I'm as different from him as a man can be. Maybe that's why she thinks she loves me. It could just be a reaction."

Both Derek and Cedric put their cues down and stared at Cole.

"Are you saying you don't want her?" Derek demanded.

"I'm not saying that. I'd be crazy not to want her. But I don't want her to do anything she'll regret."

"Very sensible," Cedric agreed emphatically. "So you haven't asked her to marry you?"

"No," Cole said.

"But you plan to," he said.

"I haven't made any plans."

"You do know that my daughter is selling her property, uprooting her life here and moving down to Atlanta with the expectation that you will marry her," Derek sputtered.

"Calm down, Derek," Cedric said, grinning widely. "The man doesn't have to marry Talley if he doesn't want to."

"I didn't say I didn't want to. I just want to give it some time," Cole insisted.

"Then there's no real reason for her to move to Atlanta right away, is there?" Cedric insisted.

"Except I think long-distance romances are really hard," Cole said, getting Cedric's drift.

"That is true, but if the bond is strong…"

"You don't want her to move to Atlanta *or* marry me, do you, sir?"

Cedric's response was dry. "How perceptive."

"Yeah?" Cole challenged. "Why not?"

"You don't want to get me started on the obvious. It'll take several days." Cedric smiled tightly.

"Why don't you just give me the highlights."

"If you marry Talley, I will do everything in my power to get Michael away from you and back here where he belongs," Cedric said. "As a grandparent I have rights. You don't want to go up against what I can offer him."

"Talley is his mother. There's no judge in the world…"

"I eat judges for breakfast," Cedric interrupted. "And I spit out family court judges. Young man, you are so far out of your league here that you might as well be in another galaxy," he went on. "I don't want my grandson tainted by your Talley, I morality and values."

"That's enough, Cedric," Derek fussed. "Both of you are guests in my home…"

"Naw, it's okay. No need for him to piss on my head and call it rain. He's just telling it like he sees it," Cole said defiantly, his eyes not leaving Cedric's face.

"How colorful," Cedric murmured derisively.

"Only thing," Cole continued, "my morals and values are pretty good. A lot better than your son's were. So come on with it. No judge, chewed up or spit out, will let you touch Michael after Talley tells them what you did to your own son and shows him what you let him do to her!"

Cedric gasped and stepped back, a look of horror on his face at the point that Cole had made.

"You ignorant trash," he spat. "How dare you…"

But Cole had already turned on his heel and stalked out of the billiards room. On his way to find Talley, he got lost in the maze of hallways and ended up outside the media room. For a few moments he stood there, unseen, hearing the conversation among Marshall's three sisters.

"You need to take an example from Talley," said one sister. "Get a big, black, truck driver to service you when your husband can't get it up."

"A big, *dumb,* truck driver," said another, "So he doesn't catch on right away that he's being used."

"Even if he knew, he wouldn't care. I'm sure the jerk is just loving it. In Marshall's house. Driving Marshall's car. Porking Marshall's wife. Like a leech."

"How can Talley stand to be with someone so coarse?"

"It won't last much longer. What on earth could Talley find to talk about with him when they aren't rutting? Do they have anything at all in common?"

Cole turned away, feeling dirtied by the sneering tones, the crude language, and the bitter jealousy. He stalked the corridors until he found the drawing room and saw Talley and her mother sitting together in a halo of light, the rays from the lamp glinting off their hair. They were talking quietly. Claudia had her hand on Talley's arm. They both looked surreal, untouchable. He blinked at the sight, forcing himself to remember that less than twenty-four hours ago he had been buried to the hilt inside that glowing girl and her serenely beautiful face had been distorted with passion.

"There he is now," Claudia said, looking up with a little smile.

"Let's get out of here," Cole said abruptly to Talley.

"What's wrong?" she asked, startled. She looked at his face, tight with suppressed rage and said, "Of course. You've been talking to Cedric. Mama, we need to make a quick getaway."

On the way home, Cole was silent. It was brooding silence full of tamped-down, boiling anger. His sister, Lucy, had spoken of his temper, his hyper-sensitivity, but Talley had never seen it at its height before and it frightened her.

When they got into her house, Cole went straight to his room and started packing. Talley followed and watched him with huge eyes.

"What are you doing?" she asked.

"I'm leaving. What does it look like I'm doing?"

"Why?"

"This isn't right. I'm a big, dumb, truck driver with nothing in common with you, Talley. I might as well be on another planet. You need to stay on this planet and me on the other."

"Cedric," she said, sighing heavily. "I never should have left you alone with him."

Cole turned with ferocious force, causing Talley to back away. "It's not just Cedric, Talley, it's everything. This house, the cars, and the butler—he's wearing white gloves, for God's sake! Then, there's the horse-back riding. You looked good on that horse. How can I afford to give you a house with a…a…stable?"

"You don't have to. I can support my own horses," she said.

"I'm not going to live off your money like I'm some leech."

"Cole, listen to me. Don't do this. We love each other…"

"Then they're talking about regular trips to Paris to some nightclub and finding some pearls in Japan…like it's no big thing."

"They just don't know anything else…" she started.

"It was people like your family that killed my parents," he shouted.

Anguished by the pain in his voice, Talley reached out to touch him and he jerked away from her as though she burned him.

"I told Cedric I wasn't going to marry you, so you don't have to worry. He'll stop threatening to take Michael away from you. It's just me. He don't want me to 'taint' the boy…"

"Wait a minute, Cole," she interrupted sharply. "Did you just say that you're *not* going to marry me?"

"I wasn't planning to ask you right now," he spat furiously.

"Well, when, then?" she wanted to know.

"*If* and when it felt right to *me*," he shouted, anger and despair welling up inside of him.

"But now you're not going to do it at all," she said quietly.

"Now I'm just getting the hell out of here before I *taint* some damn somebody," he snarled, picking up his bag.

Talley stood aside.

"Go ahead, then. That will make you just like all the other men in my life. Coward!" she shouted after him.

Cole walked out of the house and drove away.

CHAPTER TWENTY

"I love you very much, Joe, but I can't get married without Talley. It's that simple," Alicia said.

"Will she come?" Joe asked, trying to get past the emphatic "no" behind her gentle Southern tone.

"It's been more than a month since she and Cole broke up, and she still says she doesn't want to come anywhere South. She says it hurts too much."

"Then we'll go to her. Get married in my hometown, the Motor City."

"No way. I want to have my weddin' in Montgomery so I can show you off to all my friends and family. I wanted to get married in June, but that's just four weeks away. We'll just have to put it off. In the meantime, we're gonna have to figure out a way to fix things between Cole and Talley," she mused.

"Oh now, we shouldn't meddle," Joe said warily.

"Oh pulleaze, Mr. 'Tap-on-the-Phone,' that's what you do for a livin', isn't it?"

"Snooping. Not meddling."

"I'm gonna go 'head and call Marcus and see if he knows what's goin' on with Cole," Alicia said. "All Talley will tell me is he 'objects' to her 'lifestyle.'"

"Too rich?" Joe said incredulously.

"Too rich. He got up there and saw how Talley *really* lives, and it blew his mind."

"Alicia, I really don't think you should call Marcus or Cole. If Talley wanted you to do something, she'd have asked you to."

"I suppose you're right, but it's hard to just sit here and watch your best friend so unhappy."

"I can certainly see how Talley's lifestyle might be overwhelming for a guy," Joe said. "But Talley doesn't expect him to try and match that, does she?"

"Of course not. I don't know what Cole is thinkin'. But it's clear he doesn't know my Talley. She's as honest and unpretentious as they come. The money doesn't mean anything to her. She'd give up everythin' for the man she loved."

"She'd better not give up all that money," Joe said.

"No. She won't, for Michael's sake. Cole's the one has to change."

⸺ ๑๑

"He's just stubborn and ornery, that's all," Lucy said to Marcus about their brother. "I honestly believe he doesn't *want* to be happy. He wants to feel all gloom and doom and bring everyone around him down."

"And he's pushin' himself like a crazy man. He's been taking longer trips and goin' without sleep," Marcus worried.

"Has he heard from her since he's been back?"

"He won't call her and she ain't callin' him. He told me she got mad when he said he wasn't ready to get married."

"He needs to go ahead and marry the girl. They were made for one another. Anybody can see that. Stevie Wonder could see that!"

"He says she's just got too much money. That he can't support her the way she's used to."

"She hasn't asked him to, has she?"

"He said he wasn't up there two hours when he started liking the lifestyle. It scared him."

"So he thinks he's going be Talley's stud. That people are going think she's his sugar mama…like he ever could be. It isn't in his nature."

"He says they got nothing in common."

"Oh, give me a break," Lucy groaned. "If I know Cole, he went up there and got his feelings hurt by at least one of her relatives. You know how sensitive he is. He needs to get over it and get her back here. I miss her."

Marcus sighed ruefully. "We all miss her. And the office is a mess again."

⁓

"She's taken the house off the market and put Michael back into his private school here," Claudia said to her husband with a sigh.

"Cole wasn't what I would have chosen for my daughter," Derek said, "but he did hold his own that night. Showed some guts. I could tell that even Cedric was impressed. But, I guess Cedric ultimately did what he set out to do. He ran the boy off."

"Talley loves Cole. She breaks my heart. All shadowed eyes and skin and bones."

"She needs to get out among people of her own age," Derek suggested. "All she does is hang around that house."

"I liked him, you know," Claudia said, "He had honest eyes and passion for his work. Like you when we were young."

⁓

Talley came into her house in drenched and mud-splattered riding clothes after a gallop in the rain with Sunrise.

Narye caught her as she was going up the back stairs.

"What were you doing out riding in this weather? Do you want to get sick?"

"No, I was just restless. I've been having trouble sleeping, so I thought I'd ride to exhaustion."

"I hope it works. Your eyes look so tired."

"I know."

"Your mother called. She wants you to go with her to a fundraising dinner for the Museum of African American History."

"Oh, I just can't," Talley said tiredly, sitting down suddenly on the stairs and covering her face with her hands.

Her friend sat beside her on the stairs and put her arms around her.

"Miz Tallulah, why don't you call him?"

"I want to so badly. I think about it all the time. But what good would it do? I'd just be begging him for something he doesn't want to give me."

"What's that?"

"I want him to trust me and our love. I want him to marry me."

"It might make you feel better to hear his voice," Narye suggested gently.

"Not unless he's going to say what I need to hear."

—ᴄ

Cole was in the Peterbilt plowing down I-85 in a dark rainstorm, hungry and exhausted. He knew he had been pushing himself hard these past few weeks, but he was having trouble sleeping in anything but fits and starts. Besides, he had to get the two Aston Martins he was carrying to Atlanta by eight A.M. Nearly a half-million dollars in cargo.

He was staying on the road more than he should, but it was hard to be home in Atlanta. The office trailer still had some of her things in it, and a hint of apricot scent lingered in the room she slept in at his house. His family was giving him a hard time. David barely spoke to him and Winston badgered him.

"You need to talk with her, man," Winston argued. "Y'all need to *fix* this. Y'know what I mean?"

Marcus had been the worst. "You'll never get me to understand why you let her go," he said angrily, confronting Cole in the parking lot at the yard. "I know how you feel about rich people, but they ain't always as bad as you make out. Talley's different."

"I know."

"You love her, don't you?"

Cole began climbing into his truck. "I'm crazy about her, man. But I can't live in her world with the people she's used to dealing with, and I can't make her live in mine. I can't give her anything near what she's used to."

Marcus gave him a disgusted look. "Last I heard, she never asked you to. You two need to create your own world to live in. No need to worry about anyone else."

"Nothing I give her would be good enough."

"That's just…some junk! You can't be that insecure and distrustful."

"That's not what it is…"

"That's exactly what it is, man," Marcus shouted at him. "You're scared of takin' a chance and trustin' Talley. I would not have believed you could be such a snivelin' coward."

"A coward. That's what she called me, so I guess I am." Cole shrugged, defeated.

"So what are you gonna do now? Stay a coward?"

"I'm going to focus on work. I'm going to grow my business."

~ ⌒〇 ~

The new division is doing well, Cole thought groggily as he pushed the big machine down I-85. He had enough work to keep two trucks busy. *Maybe I ought to go ahead and get a second truck and put Uncle*

Winfrey's middle son Malik in it. Malik is a promising young...

"Hey TransportMasters, you're weaving across the zipper," the voice crackled over the CB radio. "Get back between the lines!"

Whoops! He'd blacked out there for a moment. Maybe he'd better pull into a Flying J. Take a nap in the sleeper. It was hard to be in that bed, though. His mind raced every time he lay down on it. *How she looked with her hair spread out on the pillow. How her legs felt wrapped around his...*

Cole didn't see the huge sinkhole that sent his truck jackknifing across traffic. He only caught a glimpse out of the corner of his eye of the Kenworth truck that skidded into him, pushing him into oncoming traffic across the median. His cab hit a concrete bridge pylon and toppled over. Then everything went dark.

⌒♋

"The police just called the office. Cole is at Grady Hospital in the intensive care unit. He was in an accident just outside of Atlanta. He's unconscious," Marcus sputtered at Lucy over the phone. "I'm on my way over there now."

"I'll meet you there."

Cole's brothers and Lucy gathered to hear the news about their brother from the doctor who had been treating him since he was brought in off the highway.

"Simply put, your brother is in a coma. Both his legs were broken, but those have been set and they should heal. And he's had some kidney damage. Once again, that should heal. We just don't know when he's going to regain consciousness."

"But he will, won't he?" Lucy asked.

"I can't say for sure. I don't have all the information I need. I'm waiting for additional x-rays."

"But there's no real damage to the brain?

"There may be bone fragments. His skull was cracked. He's lucky to be alive, though. They had to use torches to cut him out of his truck."

"Can we see him now?"

The doctor looked at the crowd of tall men and the woman who seemed to be riding herd on them.

"Sure, but no more than two at a time."

"Marcus, we'll go in now," Lucy said. "We'll be out soon so Winston and David can go in."

The sight of that big vigorous man lying still and helpless, hooked up to tubes and wires, was appalling. Lucy began to cry immediately. All Marcus could say was, "Ah man…ah man…"

Cole's face looked shrunken and ashy. There were cuts and bruises all over it, bandages on his neck and around his head. His big hands were limp and dark against the white covers. His legs were in casts from thigh to toe. When Lucy touched his hand and said his name, he didn't stir.

Grateful for Cole's survival, the family unit tightened after the doctor sent them all home, saying he'd call if there were any changes. The men sat, despondent, in the family room of the house.

"What are we going to do?" David wanted to know, wiping moisture from his glasses.

"We're gonna keep goin' until he gets well," Marcus said.

Winston fiddled nervously with the magazines on the coffee table in front of him. "He looks pretty bad."

"At least he's alive," David snapped at him.

"Yeah, that's good," Winston agreed quickly.

"What about the truck?" David inquired.

Marcus shook his head. "It's just about totaled but we had insurance on it. We need to either get it towed to Peterbilt and see if it can be fixed or junk it."

"And the cargo?"

"That's the problem. The two cars were completely torn up. We had cargo insurance of $200,000 per car. We're about $100,000 short."

"Oh no," Winston said.

"Then there's the folk who were injured or whose cars were damaged in the pile-up. They're coming after TransportMasters. Apparently other trucks saw him bobbing and weaving down the road before the accident. They said they thought he was drunk. He was just too sleepy."

"Damn," David said.

"The other thing is the sorry health insurance we've got. It ain't for long-term care. If Cole has to stay in the hospital longer than a month, we're up a creek."

"We need to call Talley," Winston said immediately.

"Cole will kill us," David said.

"If he gets strong enough to kill us, that would be a good thing. Y'know what I'm sayin'?" Winston asked.

"We shouldn't call her yet," Marcus said. "Let's just wait and see what happens. Cole might wake up tomorrow."

⁓

"Mama, I think I'm pregnant," Talley said abruptly, sitting in the sun-drenched solarium of her home, having a late breakfast with her mother.

"Oh dear, oh dear," Claudia fretted, putting down her fork. "How should I feel about this? Should I be happy?"

"You can feel however you like, Mother," Talley laughed. "I'm happy." She leaned back in the ornate white wicker chair.

"Then I'll be happy, too," her mother replied with a sweet smile. "That's always best, anyway. How far along are you?"

"It must have happened when Cole was up here. In all the excitement of his visit, I missed taking the pill for a couple of days. I didn't think it would matter, but I guess it did." She sipped from her delicate teacup and gave her mother a wry smile.

"So will you tell Cole?"

"The last thing I want is for him to think this is some kind of ploy to get him to marry me."

"Oh, no, oh, no," her mother agreed, reaching across the glass and wicker table to pat her daughter's hand.

"I've been disappointed too many times—my father, my husband and now Cole." Talley played with a leaf on the ficus plant next to her.

"But Cole is different," her mother argued. "Even *I* see that. Marshall grew into a monster…and—well, I do hate to say it—but your father is a *weak* man. Your Cole is very strong, even if he is being stubborn."

"I know what I want to do," Talley said.

"What is it, dear?"

"I want to go confront Cole and demand that he take care of me and Michael and our unborn child."

"Perhaps you should," Claudia suggested shyly.

"Yeah," Talley said, warming to the idea. "I'll sue him for child support."

"That's right," her mother added with her tinkling laugh. "Make him pay your hospital bills."

"Perhaps I will."

CHAPTER TWENTY-ONE

"Marcus, you've done all you can," Lucy argued. "We have to call Talley."

Winston agreed. "Cole's been in a coma for six weeks. It's just costin' too much."

The family met at the office to come to some hard decisions.

"The financial burden has become more than we can carry with everyone threatening to sue," Lucy continued. "We have to either call Talley or shut down the business and sell the trucks and the land."

"I'll call Talley," Marcus insisted. "Cole would put *me* in a coma if he woke up and the business and land was gone."

Marcus called Alicia when he realized he didn't have a direct number for Talley. She was horrified when she heard the news.

"Why the *hell* didn't you call me sooner? You mean to tell me that Cole's been in a coma for more than a month and Talley doesn't know? She'll want to kill you all."

"It's actually been six weeks," Marcus said, awkwardly.

"I could jus' spit! Your whole family is just too damn independent!"

Talley was more understanding.

"We didn't call because we kept expecting him to wake up any day and, well, he'd have been so mad if he knew and..." Lucy stammered to her.

"It doesn't matter," Talley interrupted quietly. "Michael and Narye and I will be on the next flight. I'll call back when I have the schedule."

On the bright late-May morning when Talley finally came home to Atlanta, Marcus, Lucy, Alicia and Joe were all at the airport to meet her. On the flight down, Talley had tried to keep her mind from racing to dark and terrible places. *I'm a different woman now,* she told herself. *I'm stronger than I ever thought I could be. I'm not like my helpless irresolute mother, letting fate buffet me about. For the first time in my life a man I truly love needs me! And I don't care what Cole says or thinks. He's my man and I'm going to take charge of this. I can fix this.*

At the airport, Talley insisted Marcus and Lucy take her straight to the nursing home where they'd moved Cole from the hospital. She sent Narye and Michael with Alicia and Joe to the Coleman house.

She walked onto the ward where Cole was sharing space with seven other men. She gasped at the sight of him, but held her hysteria beneath a surface calm.

Six weeks of intravenous feeding had left Cole's skin hanging off his big-boned structure. His face was sunken and drawn, and he was motionless in his coma.

"Can we take him home?" she asked the doctor.

"Well, yes, if you can afford round-the-clock nursing."

"Cost won't be a problem," she said. "We can get an army of full-time nurses, if need be. I just want him home."

"He'll need a special bed and medical supplies."

"Just tell me what I need and we'll do everything," Talley said crisply. "I want to know the name of the best brain specialist in the city…no…in the country."

"Well, if you can get Dr. George Knight over at Emory to take a look at him…"

"We'll do that. What else can you tell me?"

"His heart is strong, and though he has lost weight because of the intravenous feeding, he should be able to get his muscle tone back fairly quickly. His legs are mending, but he hasn't been on them, so in order to get walking again, he will need to work with a physical therapist. Then if…ah…when he wakes up…"

"Oh, he *will* wake up," Talley said to the doctor, her eyes flashing fire. "He will have to wake up in order to see his child born."

Marcus and Lucy looked at her curiously.

"I'm pregnant," she said to them.

"What?" Lucy nearly choked on the single word.

"Pregnant," Talley repeated.

"Yeah, you're right," Marcus said, swallowing tears. "Cole's gotta wake up for that."

The Colemans found there weren't a lot of other words to be said as Talley went to work. The next day, a bed and medical supplies arrived at the Coleman house. Two nurses were hired to work in shifts and Cole was gently transported to his home and installed in the family room with screens around his bed.

"No wonder they call people like her 'movers and shakers,'" Winston said with an admiring whistle. "She gets it done, don't she?"

Talley called Dr. Knight and used the power and influence of the Pettifore name to get an immediate appointment. She took the X-rays from Grady with her.

"Hmmm," the white-haired, British-born doctor hummed. He was sitting in front of a light wall looking at the X-rays with Talley sitting next to him. He was short and chubby, with a walk like a duck's, but his eyes were shrewd, and he wore an air of complete competence that reassured Talley.

"Brain is swollen. The knocking about, of course," Dr. Knight said crisply in a short, clipped, speaking style Talley quickly adjusted to.

"Is that why he's not waking up?"

"Contributory."

"What else?"

"Bone fragment. Right there." Knight pointed at the X-ray. "Needs to come out."

"Didn't they know that at Grady?"

"Maybe not. Very small. Looks like a shadow. I'm used to seeing these things."

"Will you take it out?"

"In a dangerous place," Knight warned. "Could affect motor skills. Could make him a vegetable. Could snuff him out all together."

"But if all went well, would he wake up?"

"Yes."

"You've done this before, haven't you?

"A few times," the doctor admitted.

"Successfully?"

"Yes."

"How soon could you operate?"

"Swelling needs to come down some more first."

"How soon?" Talley was impatient.

"Two, maybe three weeks. Nurse will schedule it."

The next day, Talley went out to the office trailer at the yard. She stood in front of it with her hands on her hips, shaking her head. Some windows hadn't been repaired after the fight with the Detroit thugs, and they were still boarded up. The paint on the trailer was peeling and cracked.

The inside wasn't much better. Marcus had been fighting a losing battle against daily wear and tear from truckers tromping in and out of the limited space. Vickie was unsuccessfully juggling dispatching with the office work Talley had once done.

"The business has outgrown this trailer," Talley said to Marcus, looking around. "We need more room."

Talley and Marcus walked the yard and he pointed out the spot where Cole had eventually planned to erect a permanent structure.

"Well, we got approval from the Neighborhood Planning Unit to build last year. Let's get that started why don't we?" Talley insisted.

"Cole will be mad as hell if you pay for it, Talley," Marcus worried.

"Cole is lying in bed completely oblivious and you're the acting president. What do *you* say?"

"Hey, I say let's go for it!" Marcus enthused. "But we gotta make you a partner or something."

"I'd like to be a thirty percent owner," Talley said. "Let's have Jerome draw up some papers. You can sign them as acting president."

"Damn straight."

"Did Cole have any blueprints for what he wanted the building to look like?"

"He tore a picture out of a trucking magazine once," Marcus said excitedly. "I think it's still in his office."

"Let's go look," Talley said.

The picture was there, stuck to the wall with a ragged bit of yellowing tape. The clipping had been added to over time, and when Talley pulled it from the wall, she found layers of glued-on details supplemented with inked-in comments. Smoothing her fingers over the careful notes, Talley couldn't help smiling.

"What?" Marcus wanted to know.

"We can do this," Talley nodded, looking into his eyes. "Let's go make this real."

Talley hired an architect to draw up plans and a construction company to begin work right away. They were building a steel-framed structure with offices and a cavernous eight bay repair shop.

Day by day Talley's determination grew. Winston and Marcus reported her progress to Lucy with respect in their voices.

"I know she loves Cole and she's always been real sweet, but now she's…"

"Different," Winston finished for his brother.

Both men squirmed when Lucy grinned. "Little brothers, what you're seeing is 'woman power' in action. And I do believe, you ain't seen nothin' yet!"

Still in motion, Talley sat down with Jerome and went through all the claims against TransportMasters.

"Settle them," she said. "Don't go through the insurance company. Just negotiate with each one and I'll send them a check."

"You want to be able to keep the insurance, huh?" Jerome asked.

"Exactly. If we try to get our insurance company to pay for all this, they'll cancel us, and no one else will take us on. We have to have insurance to operate this business."

"I'll get started," Jerome said.

"And do it fast. Don't worry about the cost. I'm a double-comma kid."

Jerome looked puzzled. She didn't explain.

Later, Marcus asked her, "What you want to do about the truck?"

"Junk it. I'll pay it off and buy a new one. And this time I want a nice big sleeper."

Marcus laughed out loud at that.

"Really, though," she went on, not bothering to blush, "we're going to have to put someone else in it, preferably an experienced driver like yourself or Winston. Dr. Knight said it might take Cole as long as a year to heal completely, and the business will need income in the meantime."

"Winston would love to get in a really big truck," Marcus said. "And he's a good driver."

"What about his school?"

"He graduated this month. But I gotta warn you, he'll probably end up with a girl in every city he goes to."

"That's all right, it'll give him incentive to stay on the road," Talley laughed.

Michael was out of school for summer break. That night as she was tucking him into bed at the Coleman house, he said, "It's good to be home with all my play uncles," as he had begun calling the brothers. "I just wish Mr. Cole could talk to us."

"Me too, sweetie. I wish it too."

"He must be really sleepy. Is he going to get better?"

"Yes. He's going to have an operation in a few weeks and the doctor thinks it will make him better."

"And he'll wake up and play with us?"

"Yes. We hope so."

"Are we going to stay here now? Please?"

"Yes. We're going to stay in Atlanta. Maybe not in this house. In a house of our own."

"But who will live with us?"

"You and me and Narye and a new little brother or sister."

"Where are we going to get this little brother?"

"Or sister," Talley repeated. "I'm growing him or her right now in my tummy. It's the same place that you grew."

"Wow," he said, putting his hand on her tummy. "In here?"

"Yep."

"Wow," he said again, sleepily.

Talley went house hunting. This time she was looking for a permanent home. She also wanted to use strategy. This would be a house big enough for her comfort, but not so big as to intimidate Cole—assuming Cole would live there with her.

It would be near stables where she could board Sunrise, Sultie and Michael's horse, Amber. The pool could be in the backyard, no need for one indoors. But she did need an exercise room and a sauna.

Talley found the house in southwest Atlanta, near I-285. It was perfection, a five-bedroom French country house sitting on two acres of beautifully land-scaped lawns and gardens. The swimming pool in the backyard was a small pond with a waterfall trickling down moss-covered rocks.

Broad beams of sunlight brightened every room through tall windows. The house had everything she wanted, including comfortable quarters for Narye. She stood in the middle of the white-carpeted family room and nodded her satisfaction to the happy real estate agent. Talley could see herself and Cole living in this sun-filled house with their children.

She didn't dwell on the possibility that Cole might not come through the operation. Monsters and dragons abounded there. Nor did she fret about the very real possibility that Cole would wake up and not be happy to see her there.

In all her dreams and imaginings, Cole woke up well and hearty and desperately in love with her. He was ecstatic about the baby and eager to begin their lives together as a family.

Every night she'd sit beside him and talk about what she'd done during the day and what she planned for the next day.

"I need you to know that I'm doing a lot of things with my money that you wouldn't let me do if you were awake," she told him, with a smile. "I'm warning you now, so you won't be able to say I never told you."

It was getting easier to look at him without wanting to sob. She was getting used to the shape of his skull and his hollowed-out cheekbones. She missed seeing his beautiful eyes. Once she parted the lids with a fingertip, but the eyes were empty of his soul.

It was during this period that Talley found comfort in the serenity of the small church the brothers attended. The night before Cole's operation, she sat alone in the dark church and prayed with passionate intensity.

"I've not been perfect, and neither has Cole. But we're good people. We love each other and we love You. Please God, help us now. Make him well."

—ဢ

Though the entire Coleman clan wandered through the waiting room at Grady Hospital's trauma surgery center at one time or another during the eight hours Cole was in the operating room, Talley's ordeal began at eight A.M. and lasted throughout the day.

Uncle Winfrey came and held Talley's hand for a half hour. Both Aunt Jessie and Aunt Maizie came and brought homemade pecan rolls, so sweet they made Talley's teeth hurt. Then Aunt Jessie told Talley the bittersweet family history that made Talley's heart hurt.

"The first Coleman with blue-green eyes was named Ephraim. He was the 'outside son' of Mr. David Kohlman, a wealthy German landowner," she said. "Ephraim took the last name out of deference, but changed the spellin' out of defiance.

"Mr. Kohlman gave twenty acres of land to Ephraim in 1900 as a wedding present," she went on. "And four generations of the family has fought to keep it for 100 years. We've had to sell it back and forth to the Kohlmans to keep it out of the hands of wily developers. And every time we bought it back from them, they pinched a little off. But we hung on to as much of it as we could, even when it nearly caused the lynching of Big Daddy's father by the KKK during the 1930s.

"We was all mad when Big Daddy left the land to Cole," she admitted with a frown at her sister and Uncle Winfrey. "But...well...Big Daddy wanted to keep it all in the family. I guess he knew Cole would never break it up or sell it."

"Yeah, I guess you're right," Uncle Winfrey agreed with a little embarrassed cough. "And, it was Cole who took care of Big Daddy at the end. The boys took turns lookin' out for the old man."

Alicia was with Talley through most of the day, even the period when Talley, full of pent-up frustration from waiting, went into the bathroom and shrieked and sobbed.

"I can't stand this," Talley wailed, pounding the walls. "How long can this go on?"

Alicia kept Talley from hurting herself while she flailed about until she was exhausted and then sat with her on the cold tile floor of the bathroom.

"It's all right, baby," Alicia soothed, stroking Talley's hair. "Let it out. It'll be all right."

At four P.M., Dr. Knight finally came waddling out to the waiting area.

"Went well," he said. "Got the damn thing out. No damage."

Talley looked at him, tears welling. She put her hand out. He took it with a smile. She put his hand to her lips and her cheek. Behind her the family cheered and hugged one another, but for that moment it was just she and Dr. Knight, and he could read the depth of her gratitude in her eyes.

"When can I see him?"

"Right now. But just you."

"Is he awake?"

"Not yet. Tomorrow."

～⌒～

The first thing Cole saw when he opened his eyes was Talley's glowing golden curls. She was sitting beside the bed and had just turned away to speak to the nurse. He reached out his hand, surprised at how much effort it took to lift it, and brushed the spun gold with his fingers.

She turned and smiled at him.

He tried to say her name. His voice sounded strange to him.

"Love you," he croaked.

"I love you, too," she said, tears welling in her eyes in relief and happiness.

He closed his eyes again as memories of the accident came flooding back to him.

"Anyone hurt?" he asked.

"Nobody as badly as you," she said.

"Thought I was going to die," he said, tears starting in his eyes.

He swallowed with difficulty.

"Thought I was never going to see you again," he went on. "Too proud. A coward."

"Yes," she agreed with a smile.

"My truck?"

"We bought you a new one," she said, "with a bigger sleeper."

"So fast?" He was puzzled.

"You were in a coma for nine weeks," she explained. "We thought you'd never wake up. The doctor had to take a bit of your skull out of your brain."

"Ouch," he said, testing a smile. "Do all my parts work?"

"Yes. But you have a lot of work to do to get them back in shape."

"How's Michael?"

"He's here. He wants you to wake up and play with him. He also wants to tell you about the new little brother or sister he's going to have."

Cole was silent for a minute taking this in slowly. "You? Pregnant?"

She nodded. He sighed. Fat tears were running down his gaunt face.

"Want you."

"All you think about is sex," she grinned.

"No, want you to marry me," he said, "now."

"Are you sure you don't want to wait until you can walk down the aisle?"

"No. Get Rev. Brown."

"Nope. Let's get you well, first," Talley said. "I want a church wedding with lots of witnesses."

CHAPTER TWENTY-TWO

Talley took Cole to her house on Eleuthera Island in the Bahamas to recuperate. Narye and Michael stayed behind in Atlanta to supervise the transfer of furniture from Talley's house in Farmington to the new house. They were to join Cole and Talley in a month, bringing a handful of the young Coleman cousins to keep Michael company.

It was Cole's first time outside the United States, and only his second time on an airplane. The big 747 made him think twice.

"If man was supposed to fly, God would have given him some wings," he muttered to Talley as she and Marcus helped him out of his wheelchair and bundled him into his first-class seat.

"Uh oh. You're going to love the flight from Nassau to Gregory Town on the tiny prop plane," Talley teased.

"One of those little things that's always falling out the sky?" Cole's face sagged. "Can't we go by boat?"

"Well, maybe," she grinned, kissing his hollow cheek.

Cole's physical therapist, Vancliff, a big, good-natured Bahamian with dreadlocks and a round face, met their plane in Nassau. He planned to stay with them and get Cole started on his regimen to regain strength in his legs. He needed to learn how to walk again.

Talley's agent in the Bahamas hired a house staff, including a cook to prepare good, healthful food. He made arrangements to have exercise equipment delivered to the secluded five-bedroom villa set on a 40-foot cliff overlooking the Caribbean Sea.

The house had a wrap-around terrace with stone-cut steps leading down to a private crystalline blue-green lagoon. Talley had a ramp built so that Vancliff could get Cole down to the pink-sand beach in the wheelchair. The soothing warm water with multi-colored fish just beneath the surface was an excellent place for Cole to exercise.

"You're taking advantage of my weakness," Cole told Talley one night as they were sitting on the cool terrace, eating fresh fruit and watching a red and gold sun slide into the ocean.

"What do you mean?" she asked.

"You're spending all this money and I can't fight you," he said.

"Good," she said, her oval face strong with determination.

"When I get stronger we're going to have to talk about this," he said sternly.

"Of course," she agreed easily. "Here, have a slice of cool mango."

Cole was committed to marrying Talley, now that he was going to be a father to Michael and a newborn. He was eager to get well and back to the business that would support them. He was particularly eager to see the changes her brothers talked about, to be a "hands-on" participant. The glowing reports that he got daily from Marcus were not enough.

Cole focused on his exercises, pushing himself until he was exhausted, expressing anger and frustration when he failed. Even Vancliff had to tell him to slow down.

"De t'ing, it gonna come, mon," Vancliff told him in his musical accent. "You got to give it the time it take."

At night, in their king-sized canopied bed, Talley put him through her own exercise regimen.

"Just because I'm on top doesn't mean I plan to do all the work," she warned him, easing her body closer. "You have to bend those knees and move your hips."

"You're a regular little Nazi," he told her. "What else do you want me to do?"

"Lift up and kiss my nipples," she demanded. He groaned as he leaned forward to comply. "Careful, they're a little sore," she added.

"Your tummy's getting bigger," he teased, rubbing it. "Won't be long before the only way I can get some will be from the back."

"You'll be able to stand up by then, I hope," she teased back.

One night, Cole called Talley out to the terrace where he'd been sitting and staring out at the ocean, listening to the orchestra of crickets, frogs and egrets. He was walking now. The stiffness was almost completely gone from his legs.

Talley was one of those women who glow with pregnancy. She was six months pregnant and her normally graceful stroll was turning into a waddle. She went regularly to Nassau to see an obstetrician and they had learned she was having a little girl. They had decided to call her Loretta Marie. She was craving orange sherbet and this night she joined Cole on the terrace with a huge bowl of the stuff.

"You're having *more* sherbet?" Cole asked, incredulous.

"I like it," she said defiantly. "And so does the baby."

"Our little girl is going to come out bright orange," he sighed.

"Hrummp," Talley said, her mouth full.

"I've been giving a lot of thought to how we should deal with your money," Cole said solemnly.

Talley rolled her eyes and looked up at the stars.

"You got to understand how I feel," Cole insisted. "It's hard for a man. One of the reasons I got so mad up there in Detroit was because I heard your husband's sisters talking about me like I was some leech." He was surprised at how easily he talked about this now, when the pain had been so deep at the time.

A near death experience has a way of putting things in perspective, he mused.

Talley licked the back of her spoon. "The three witches. They were just jealous."

"No, listen. When I hit that sinkhole, the last thing I thought about was how I would die without ever seeing you again. I just wanted to look at you one more time. Your money didn't mean anything then. Nothing mattered but us and how much I wanted to be with you." Cole stirred in his chair, his eyes moist with the memory.

"But I know what I need in order to be happy and make us work," he continued. "I'm *going to* support my family. I'm *going to* pay the mortgage on that house you bought and everything else. If you want to spend your money buying things for Michael and yourself, fine. But I'm going to pay for anything our little girl needs."

"That's not fair," Talley argued. "Suppose I want to buy Loretta something *I* think she needs. Like a pony."

Cole leaned back in the overstuffed rattan chair. "She's not going to need a pony." But his mouth twitched with a shadow of a smile.

"Yes, she will. She'll want to go riding with Michael and me—and you, too, if you'll come."

"Okay, a pony," he said reluctantly. "But that's it!"

"I can give as much money as I want to that Boys Club you work with, can't I?" she asked nonchalantly.

Cole perked up. "Yeah, we could get them the tools and equipment to set up a nice little garage to train…" He stopped and looked at Talley suspiciously. "Hey!"

Talley ignored him. "What about this villa? Can we keep it?"

Cole looked out over the majestic cliffs at the starlit lagoon and sighed.

"Okay. Since you had it already," he conceded sheepishly.

"And the condo in Paris?"

"Paris? Oh hell, I forgot all about that," he groaned.

"You really must see it before you make a decision about it," Talley said, licking the last bit of sherbet from the bowl. "Maybe we should plan to go there after the baby is born."

"We gotta settle this before we get married." Cole was adamant.

"I don't know why you can't accept the fact that my money comes with me when you marry me," Talley stormed, standing up and pacing. "If you really loved me, you'd overlook that handicap."

"Baby, you know I love you," Cole said.

"No, you don't," she said stiffly, her back to him.

"Yes, I do."

"No, you don't," she insisted, walking away from him.

He frantically struggled to get out of his chair to reach her. "I do, baby, I do!" *How could she think I don't love her? She's everything to me. My whole life!*

She turned and smiled. "How did that feel?" And he remembered all the times he had played the same unpleasant game with her.

"Hmmm," he said. "Didn't feel too good."

"I love you," she said, leaning over to kiss him on his brow.

"Okay. You do. And I love you too," he said, settling back.

"Besides," she went on, "it's not like you're going to be a kept man. We don't have time for such foolish thinking. Your business is growing by leaps and bounds. Your income is getting to be quite substantial, I understand."

"Yeah, it is, isn't it," he said with a proud grin. "I can't wait to get back to work."

"Just a few more weeks," she said. "Michael goes up to school next week. We'll close up and follow shortly after."

"What about Michael? You heard anything more from his Grandfather Pettifore?"

"I've agreed to let him visit for a month every summer. Cedric will have thirty days to do as much indoctrinating as he can."

"And we'll have the rest of the year to let the boy know he has a choice," Cole said.

"I'm not entirely opposed to him going to law school if he shows he has a bent for it," Talley said. "It is in his blood and he does love his Grandfather Cedric."

"On the other hand, he might want to work in my business," Cole suggested brightly.

"Which, by the time Michael finishes school, will be a major national transportation conglomerate with branches all over the U.S.," Talley suggested. "Aside from which, TransportMasters will always need solid legal support. Perhaps Loretta would like to pursue a law degree?"

Cole smiled with great satisfaction. "Yeah, It could happen."

Talley stretched. "I'm going in."

"Wait, just one more thing. I don't want you to put any more of your money in my business," he said with finality. "I guess that's most important."

"Okay. It's a deal. As long as I get to use my money as I see fit in our home life. You can build your business without my help."

"But you can't do anything crazy. Don't go buying airplanes or anything.

"No airplanes."

EPILOGUE

The second Saturday in October seemed a lifetime away, but it finally arrived. Almost a year to the day Cole and Talley had first laid eyes on one another, Rev. Brown stood in the pulpit of the little church Cole had grown up in. Resplendent in a crimson-banded cream-colored robe, he smiled down at those assembled before him.

The perfume of roses, freesia and baby's breath met and mingled with the tender scent of burning candles. *Perfect*, Alicia thought, looking down the long aisle. *This is everything I would have wished for Talley.* She passed a hand over her closely fitted rose satin gown, and her smile broadened when she looked at Cole in his tuxedo. Standing next to his good-looking brother Marcus, the trucker managed to look elegant and stylish. *Who, besides Talley, would have known that the sexy guy would clean up so well?*

He looks almost as good as my Joe, she thought shamelessly. Having married Joe in June, Alicia still hadn't gotten over the wonder of it all. *I just hope it's as good for Talley.*

"Look at my mommy," Michael whispered loud enough to make the entire assemblage turn. From his position as ring bearer, he was in the right place to see his mother and grandfather approach the chapel door. "She looks like an angel," he breathed.

The boy's exactly right, Alicia thought, admiring Talley. Framed by the polished arch of the church doorway in a gorgeous ecru satin empire gown, she was a breathtaking vision. To fully deserve her son's awestruck observation, all Talley needed was delicate wings. *Cole is a lucky man.*

Alicia stood biting her lower lip. Watching Talley walk down the candlelit aisle on her father's arm to stand with Cole before the family and the friends they'd both made, to share her vows to love and honor the man she'd found by accident, brought tears to Alicia's eyes. Hoping that no one noticed, she pressed her lace-gloved fingertips to her eyes and stood straighter—*nobody's going to blame me for making folks cry on this happy occasion!*

Then Alicia noticed the tears streaming down Claudia Quincy's face and relaxed. What was surprising was the tolerant smile on Cedric Pettifore's face. He had astonished everyone by attending the wedding and being exceptionally charming to the entire Coleman clan. *He'll do anything to assure his place in Michael's life,* Alicia noted, *even accept this marriage with good grace.*

At his side, Talley gave Cole her hand and accepted the simple golden band they'd agreed upon. When she smiled up at him, the baby must have kicked in agreement, because Alicia saw the sly movement of Talley and Cole's joined hands as they moved to her rounded belly, and they laughed softly.

Rev. Brown solemnly pronounced them man and wife, and Alicia felt a surge of pride when Joe stepped forward to lay the gilded broom at their feet. Watching Talley and Cole "jump the broom" was the final straw—three tears of joy escaped before she could stop them.

Following the bride and groom back up the aisle, Alicia joined Marcus. "That was the best thing I've ever seen," he whispered. He looked impossibly young and as full of hope as the couple in front of them.

Alicia sniffed and took his hand. "No, you're wrong about that. For Talley and Cole, the best is yet to come."

Hours later, Talley watched Cole shift the new Peterbilt up I-85 on their way to New York. Their first stop was the Flying J just inside the South Carolina border. This time, though, they stopped so that pregnant Talley could use the bathroom.

2009 Reprint Mass Market Titles

January

I'm Gonna Make You Love Me
Gwyneth Bolton
ISBN-13: 978-1-58571-291-5
ISBN-10: 1-58571-291-4
$6.99

Shades of Desire
Monica White
ISBN-13: 978-1-58571-292-2
ISBN-10: 1-58571-292-2
$6.99

February

A Love of Her Own
Cheris Hodges
ISBN-13: 978-1-58571-293-9
ISBN-10: 1-58571-293-0
$6.99

Color of Trouble
Dyanne Davis
ISBN-13: 978-1-58571-294-6
ISBN-10: 1-58571-096-6
$6.99

March

Twist of Fate
Beverly Clark
ISBN-13: 978-1-58571-295-3
ISBN-10: 1-58571-295-7
$6.99

Chances
Pamela Leigh Starr
ISBN-13: 978-1-58571-296-0
ISBN-10: 1-58571-296-5
$6.99

April

Sinful Intentions
Crystal Rhodes
ISBN-13: 978-1-585712-297-7
ISBN-10: 1-58571-297-3
$6.99

Rock Star
Roslyn Hardy Holcomb
ISBN-13: 978-1-58571-298-4
$6.99

May

Path of Fire
T.T. Henderson
ISBN-13: 978-1-58571-343-1
ISBN-10: 1-58571-343-0
$6.99

Caught Up in the Rapture
Lisa Riley
ISBN-13: 978-1-58571-344-8
ISBN-10: 1-58571-344-9
$6.99

June

Reckless Surrender
Rochelle Alers
ISBN-13: 978-1-58571-345-5
ISBN-10: 1-58571-345-7
$6.99

No Ordinary Love
Angela Weaver
ISBN-13: 978-1-58571-346-2
ISBN-10: 1-58571-346-5
$6.99

2009 Reprint Mass Market Titles (continued)

July

Intentional Mistakes
Michele Sudler
ISBN-13: 978-1-58571-347-9
ISBN-10: 1-58571-347-3
$6.99

It's in His Kiss
Reon Laudat
ISBN-13: 978-1-58571-348-6
ISBN-10: 1-58571-348-1
$6.99

August

Unfinished Love Affair
Barbara Keaton
ISBN-13: 978-1-58571-349-3
ISBN-10: 1-58571-349-X
$6.99

A Perfect Place to Pray
I.L Goodwin
ISBN-13: 978-1-58571-299-1
ISBN-10: 1-58571-299-X
$6.99

September

Love in High Gear
Charlotte Roy
ISBN-13: 978-1-58571-355-4
ISBN-10: 1-58571-355-4
$6.99

Ebony Eyes
Kei Swanson
ISBN-13: 978-1-58571-356-1
ISBN-10: 1-58571-356-2
$6.99

October

Midnight Clear, Part I
Leslie Esdale/Carmen Green
ISBN-13: 978-1-58571-357-8
ISBN-10: 1-58571-357-0
$6.99

Midnight Clear, Part II
Gwynne Forster/Monica
  Jackson
ISBN-13: 978-1-58571-358-5
ISBN-10: 1-58571-358-9
$6.99

November

Midnight Peril
Vicki Andrews
ISBN-13: 978-1-58571-359-2
ISBN-10: 1-58571-359-7
$6.99

One Day at a Time
Bella McFarland
ISBN-13: 978-1-58571-360-8
ISBN-10: 1-58571-360-0
$6.99

December

Just an Affair
Eugenia O'Neal
ISBN-13: 978-1-58571-361-5
ISBN-10: 1-58571-361-9
$6.99

Shades of Brown
Denise Becker
ISBN-13: 978-1-58571-362-2
ISBN-10: 1-58571-362-7
$6.99

2009 New Mass Market Titles

January

Singing A Song…
Crystal Rhodes
ISBN-13: 978-1-58571-283-0
$6.99

Look Both Ways
Joan Early
ISBN-13: 978-1-58571-284-7
$6.99

February

Six O'Clock
Katrina Spencer
ISBN-13: 978-1-58571-285-4
$6.99

Red Sky
Renee Alexis
ISBN-13: 978-1-58571-286-1
$6.99

March

Anything But Love
Celya Bowers
ISBN-13: 978-1-58571-287-8
$6.99

Tempting Faith
Crystal Hubbard
ISBN-13: 978-1-58571-288-5
$6.99

April

If I Were Your Woman
LaConnie Taylor-Jones
ISBN-13: 978-1-58571-289-2
$6.99

Best of Luck Elsewhere
Trisha Haddad
ISBN-13: 978-1-58571-290-8
$6.99

May

All I'll Ever Need
Mildred Riley
ISBN-13: 978-1-58571-335-6
$6.99

A Place Like Home
Alicia Wiggins
ISBN-13: 978-1-58571-336-3
$6.99

June

Best Foot Forward
Michele Sudler
ISBN-13: 978-1-58571-337-0
$6.99

It's in the Rhythm
Sammie Ward
ISBN-13: 978-1-58571-338-7
$6.99

2009 New Mass Market Titles (continued)

July

Checks and Balances
Elaine Sims
ISBN-13: 978-1-58571-339-4
$6.99

Save Me
Africa Fine
ISBN-13: 978-1-58571-340-0
$6.99

August

When Lightening Strikes
Michele Cameron
ISBN-13: 978-1-58571-369-1
$6.99

Blindsided
Tammy Williams
ISBN-13: 978-1-58571-342-4
$6.99

September

2 Good
Celya Bowers
ISBN-13: 978-1-58571-350-9
$6.99

Waiting for Mr. Darcy
Chamein Canton
ISBN-13: 978-1-58571-351-6
$6.99

October

Fireflies
Joan Early
ISBN-13: 978-1-58571-352-3
$6.99

Frost On My Window
Angela Weaver
ISBN-13: 978-1-58571-353-0
$6.99

November

Waiting in the Shadows
Michele Sudler
ISBN-13: 978-1-58571-364-6
$6.99

Fixin' Tyrone
Keith Walker
ISBN-13: 978-1-58571-365-3
$6.99

December

Dream Keeper
Gail McFarland
ISBN-13: 978-1-58571-366-0
$6.99

Another Memory
Pamela Ridley
ISBN-13: 978-1-58571-367-7
$6.99

Other Genesis Press, Inc. Titles

A Dangerous Deception	J.M. Jeffries	$8.95
A Dangerous Love	J.M. Jeffries	$8.95
A Dangerous Obsession	J.M. Jeffries	$8.95
A Drummer's Beat to Mend	Kei Swanson	$9.95
A Happy Life	Charlotte Harris	$9.95
A Heart's Awakening	Veronica Parker	$9.95
A Lark on the Wing	Phyliss Hamilton	$9.95
A Love of Her Own	Cheris F. Hodges	$9.95
A Love to Cherish	Beverly Clark	$8.95
A Risk of Rain	Dar Tomlinson	$8.95
A Taste of Temptation	Reneé Alexis	$9.95
A Twist of Fate	Beverly Clark	$8.95
A Voice Behind Thunder	Carrie Elizabeth Greene	$6.99
A Will to Love	Angie Daniels	$9.95
Acquisitions	Kimberley White	$8.95
Across	Carol Payne	$12.95
After the Vows	Leslie Esdaile	$10.95
(Summer Anthology)	T.T. Henderson	
	Jacqueline Thomas	
Again, My Love	Kayla Perrin	$10.95
Against the Wind	Gwynne Forster	$8.95
All I Ask	Barbara Keaton	$8.95
Always You	Crystal Hubbard	$6.99
Ambrosia	T.T. Henderson	$8.95
An Unfinished Love Affair	Barbara Keaton	$8.95
And Then Came You	Dorothy Elizabeth Love	$8.95
Angel's Paradise	Janice Angelique	$9.95
At Last	Lisa G. Riley	$8.95
Best of Friends	Natalie Dunbar	$8.95
Beyond the Rapture	Beverly Clark	$9.95
Blame It on Paradise	Crystal Hubbard	$6.99
Blaze	Barbara Keaton	$9.95
Bliss, Inc.	Chamein Canton	$6.99
Blood Lust	J.M.Jeffries	$9.95
Blood Seduction	J.M. Jeffries	$9.95
Bodyguard	Andrea Jackson	$9.95
Boss of Me	Diana Nyad	$8.95
Bound by Love	Beverly Clark	$8.95
Breeze	Robin Hampton Allen	$10.95

Other Genesis Press, Inc. Titles (continued)

Other Genesis Press, Inc. Titles (continued)

Everything But Love	Natalie Dunbar	$8.95
Falling	Natalie Dunbar	$9.95
Fate	Pamela Leigh Starr	$8.95
Finding Isabella	A.J. Garrotto	$8.95
Forbidden Quest	Dar Tomlinson	$10.95
Forever Love	Wanda Y. Thomas	$8.95
From the Ashes	Kathleen Suzanne	$8.95
	Jeanne Sumerix	
Gentle Yearning	Rochelle Alers	$10.95
Glory of Love	Sinclair LeBeau	$10.95
Go Gentle Into That	Malcom Boyd	$12.95
Good Night		
Goldengroove	Mary Beth Craft	$16.95
Groove, Bang, and Jive	Steve Cannon	$8.99
Hand in Glove	Andrea Jackson	$9.95
Hard to Love	Kimberley White	$9.95
Hart & Soul	Angie Daniels	$8.95
Heart of the Phoenix	A.C. Arthur	$9.95
Heartbeat	Stephanie Bedwell-Grime	$8.95
Hearts Remember	M. Loui Quezada	$8.95
Hidden Memories	Robin Allen	$10.95
Higher Ground	Leah Latimer	$19.95
Hitler, the War, and the Pope	Ronald Rychiak	$26.95
How to Write a Romance	Kathryn Falk	$18.95
I Married a Reclining Chair	Lisa M. Fuhs	$8.95
I'll Be Your Shelter	Giselle Carmichael	$8.95
I'll Paint a Sun	A.J. Garrotto	$9.95
Icie	Pamela Leigh Starr	$8.95
Illusions	Pamela Leigh Starr	$8.95
Indigo After Dark Vol. I	Nia Dixon/Angelique	$10.95
Indigo After Dark Vol. II	Dolores Bundy/	$10.95
	Cole Riley	
Indigo After Dark Vol. III	Montana Blue/	$10.95
	Coco Morena	
Indigo After Dark Vol. IV	Cassandra Colt/	$14.95
Indigo After Dark Vol. V	Delilah Dawson	$14.95
Indiscretions	Donna Hill	$8.95
Intentional Mistakes	Michele Sudler	$9.95
Interlude	Donna Hill	$8.95

Other Genesis Press, Inc. Titles (continued)

Other Genesis Press, Inc. Titles (continued)

No Commitment Required	Seressia Glass	$8.95
No Regrets	Mildred E. Riley	$8.95
Not His Type	Chamein Canton	$6.99
Nowhere to Run	Gay G. Gunn	$10.95
O Bed! O Breakfast!	Rob Kuehnle	$14.95
Object of His Desire	A.C. Arthur	$8.95
Office Policy	A.C. Arthur	$9.95
Once in a Blue Moon	Dorianne Cole	$9.95
One Day at a Time	Bella McFarland	$8.95
One of These Days	Michele Sudler	$9.95
Outside Chance	Louisa Dixon	$24.95
Passion	T.T. Henderson	$10.95
Passion's Blood	Cherif Fortin	$22.95
Passion's Furies	AlTonya Washington	$6.99
Passion's Journey	Wanda Y. Thomas	$8.95
Past Promises	Jahmel West	$8.95
Path of Fire	T.T. Henderson	$8.95
Path of Thorns	Annetta P. Lee	$9.95
Peace Be Still	Colette Haywood	$12.95
Picture Perfect	Reon Carter	$8.95
Playing for Keeps	Stephanie Salinas	$8.95
Pride & Joi	Gay G. Gunn	$8.95
Promises Made	Bernice Layton	$6.99
Promises to Keep	Alicia Wiggins	$8.95
Quiet Storm	Donna Hill	$10.95
Reckless Surrender	Rochelle Alers	$6.95
Red Polka Dot in a World Full of Plaid	Varian Johnson	$12.95
Reluctant Captive	Joyce Jackson	$8.95
Rendezvous With Fate	Jeanne Sumerix	$8.95
Revelations	Cheris F. Hodges	$8.95
Rivers of the Soul	Leslie Esdaile	$8.95
Rocky Mountain Romance	Kathleen Suzanne	$8.95
Rooms of the Heart	Donna Hill	$8.95
Rough on Rats and Tough on Cats	Chris Parker	$12.95
Secret Library Vol. 1	Nina Sheridan	$18.95
Secret Library Vol. 2	Cassandra Colt	$8.95
Secret Thunder	Annetta P. Lee	$9.95

Other Genesis Press, Inc. Titles (continued)

Other Genesis Press, Inc. Titles (continued)

GENESIS MOVIE NETWORK

The Indigo Collection

AUGUST/SEPTEMBER 2009

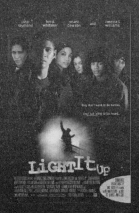

Starring: Usher, Forest Whitaker
When: August 22 - September 6
Time Period: Noon to 2AM

Taps meets The Breakfast Club in the inner city in this late 1990s answer to the Brat Pack flicks of the 1980s (with ex-Brat Packer Judd Nelson in attendance). When an incident with a high school security guard (Forest Whitaker) pushes a decent kid (Usher Raymond) past his breaking point, the boy unites a diverse and troubled student body to take the school hostage until they can make their voices heard.

Allied Media Partners
1629 K St., NW, Suite 300, Washington, DC 20006
202-349-5785

GENESIS MOVIE NETWORK

The Indigo Collection

SEPTEMBER 2009

"TERRIFICALLY ENTERTAINING"

Starring: Robert Townsend, Marla Gibbs, Eddie Griffin
When: September 5 - September 20
Time Period: Noon to 2AM

While being chased by neighborhood thugs, weak-kneed high school teacher Jefferson Reed (Robert Townsend) is struck by a meteor and suddenly develops superhuman strength and abilities: He can fly, talk to dogs and absorb knowledge from any book in 30 seconds! His mom creates a costume, and he begins practicing his newfound skills in secret. But his nightly community improvements soon draw the wrath of the bad guys who terrorize his block.

Allied Media Partners
1629 K St., NW, Suite 300, Washington, DC 20006
202-349-5785

Order Form

Mail to: Genesis Press, Inc.
P.O. Box 101
Columbus, MS 39703

Name _____
Address _____
City/State _____ Zip _____
Telephone _____

Ship to (if different from above)
Name _____
Address _____
City/State _____ Zip _____
Telephone _____

Credit Card Information
Credit Card # _____ ☐ Visa   ☐ Mastercard
Expiration Date (mm/yy) _____ ☐ AmEx   ☐ Discover

Qty.	Author	Title	Price	Total

Use this order form, or call 1-888-INDIGO-1	Total for books	
	Shipping and handling: $5 first two books, $1 each additional book	
	Total S & H	
	Total amount enclosed	

Mississippi residents add 7% sales tax